WHEN WE MET

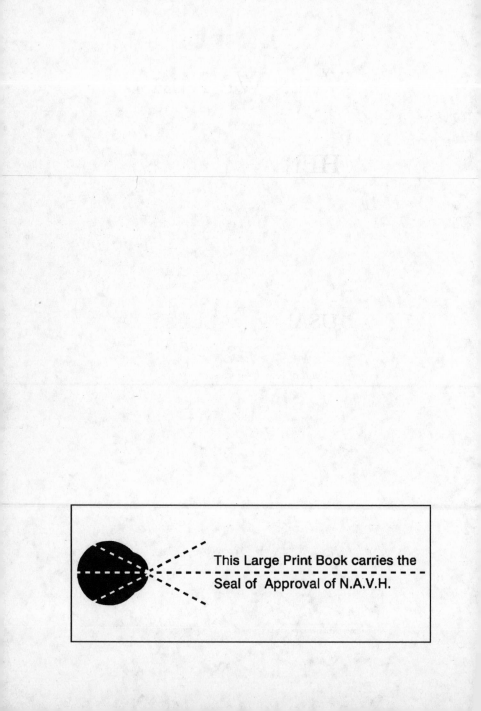

WHEN WE MET

SUSAN MALLERY

WHEELER PUBLISHING
A part of Gale, Cengage Learning

GALE
CENGAGE Learning·

Farmington Hills, Mich • San Francisco • New York • Waterville, Maine
Meriden, Conn • Mason, Ohio • Chicago

LIBRARY OF CONGRESS CATALOGING-IN-PUBLICATION DATA

Mallery, Susan.
  When we met / by Susan Mallery. — Large print edition.
    pages ; cm. — (A fool's gold romance series) (Wheeler publishing group hardcover)
  ISBN 978-1-4104-6915-1 (hardcover) — ISBN 1-4104-6915-8 (hardcover)
  1. Large type books. I. Title.
PS3613.A453W47 2014
813'.6—dc23   2014009419

Published in 2014 by arrangement with Harlequin Books S. A.

Printed in the United States of America
1 2 3 4 5 6 7 18 17 16 15 14

There are few things in this world that are as amazing as my readers. I'll admit there are plenty of wonderful miracles, but on the amazing front, my readers win, hands down. Here's an example.

For five years, Fool's Gold has been "The Land of Happy Endings." For story reasons, I decided to make a change. When you read this book, you'll see why. I hope you think the circumstances are as funny as I do. But I wasn't feeling especially brilliant that week and couldn't seem to come up with anything remotely workable. So I asked for help on Facebook — as I often do — and my amazing readers came through with fabulous suggestions for a new slogan.

The most amazing one came from Crystal B. So this book is dedicated to her. For being brilliant and lovely. Thank you, Crystal. And Mayor Marsha thanks you, too!

CHAPTER ONE

"We both know where this is going."

Taryn Crawford glanced up at the man standing by her table and ignored the rush of anticipation when she saw who he was. He was tall, with broad shoulders and gray eyes. But the most compelling feature — the one she would guess people pretended didn't exist — was the scar on his neck. As if someone had once tried to slit his throat. Taryn idly wondered what had happened to the person who failed.

She supposed there were plenty of women who would be intimidated by the man in front of her. The sheer volume of muscle he had might make someone apprehensive. Not her, of course. When in doubt she put on a power suit and killer heels. If those failed her, she would simply work harder than anyone else. Whatever it took to win. Sure, there was a price, but she was okay with that.

Which was why she was able to stare coolly back and ask, "Do we?"

One corner of his mouth curved slightly in a sort of half smile. "Sure, but if you're more comfortable pretending we don't, I can make that work, too."

"A challenge. Intriguing. You don't expect that to be enough to make me defensive so I start saying more than I had planned, do you?" She made sure she was plenty relaxed in her chair. She would guess the man was paying as much attention to her body language as her words. Maybe more. She hoped he wouldn't make things easy. She was tired of easy.

"I would hate for you to be disappointed," she murmured.

The smile turned genuine. "I'd hate that, too." He pulled out the chair opposite hers. "May I?"

She nodded. He sat.

It was barely after ten on a Tuesday morning. Brew-haha, the local coffee place she'd escaped to for a few minutes of solitude before she returned to the current chaos at her office, was relatively quiet. She'd ordered a latte and had pulled out her tablet to catch up on the latest financial news. Until she'd been interrupted. Nice to know this was going to be a good day.

She studied the man across from her. He was older than the boys, she thought. The three men she worked with — Jack, Sam and Kenny, aka "the boys" — were all in their early to mid-thirties. Her guest was nearer to forty. Just old enough to have the experience to make things intriguing, she thought.

"We've never been introduced," she said.

"You know who I am."

A statement, not a question. "Do I?"

One dark eyebrow rose. "Angel Whittaker. I work at CDS."

Otherwise known as the bodyguard school, she reminded herself. For a small town, Fool's Gold had its share of unusual businesses.

"Taryn Crawford."

She waited, but he didn't make a move.

"We're not shaking hands?" she asked, then picked up her latte with both hers. Just to be difficult, because being difficult would make things more fun.

"I figured we'd save the touching for later. I find it's better when that sort of thing happens in private."

Taryn had opened Score, her PR firm, eight years ago. She'd had to deal with unwelcome passes, assumptions she was an idiot, being asked who the boss was, pats on her butt and people presuming that if she worked with three ex-football players, she must have gotten her job by sleeping with them. She was used to staying calm, keeping her opinions to herself and gaining victory through the unanticipated side run.

This time Angel had been the one to put the first points on the board. He was good, she thought, intrigued and only slightly miffed.

"Are you coming on to me, Mr. Whittaker? Because it's still a little early in the morning for that sort of thing."

"You'll know when I'm making my move," he informed her. "Right now I'm simply telling you how things are."

"Which takes us back to your comment that we both know where this is going. I'll admit to being confused. Perhaps you have me mixed up with someone else."

She uncrossed, then recrossed her long legs. She wasn't trying to be provocative, but if Angel got distracted, it was hardly her fault.

For a second she allowed herself to wonder how she would have been different if she'd been able to grow up in a more traditional home. One with the requisite 2.5 children and somewhat normal parents. She certainly wouldn't be as driven. Or as tough.

Sometimes she wasn't sure if that was a good thing or not.

He leaned toward her. "I hadn't taken you for the type to play games."

"We all play games," she told him.

"Fair enough. Then I'll be blunt."

She sipped her coffee, then swallowed. "Please."

"I saw you last fall."

"How nice," she murmured.

When she'd been scouting locations. Moving a company required time and effort. They'd only truly settled in Fool's Gold a couple of months ago. But she had been in town the previous fall, and yes, she'd seen Angel, as well. Found out who he was and had wondered about . . . possibilities. Not that she was going to admit that to him.

"I watched you," he continued.

"Should I be concerned you're a stalker?"

"Not when you were watching me right back."

He'd noticed? Damn. She'd tried to be subtle. She thought about lying but decided to simply stay silent. After a second, he continued.

"So we've finished sizing each other up," he said. "Now it's time to move on to the next phase of the game."

"There are phases?" Which was an actual

question. No point in mentioning the game. She knew what they were doing. Still, it was entertaining to pretend she didn't.

"Several."

"Do you provide instructions or a score-card?"

His cool gray eyes stayed focused on her face. "You don't play that way."

"Be careful with your assumptions."

"I'm not assuming."

He had an appealing voice. Low with a hint of . . . Not the Deep South, she thought. But there was a cadence. Virginia? West Virginia?

She put down her mug. "If I buy in to your assertion — which I'm not admitting I do."

"Of course not."

She ignored the words and the amusement tugging at his lips. "Where do you see this going?"

He leaned back in his chair. "This is a mating game, Taryn. Or didn't you know?"

Ah, his first mistake. She kept her eyes locked with his and didn't let her triumph show. "You want to marry me?"

A muscle in his jaw twitched. "Not *that* kind of mating."

"If you're not precise, it's difficult to be sure. So you want to sleep with me."

"Yes, but it's about more than that."

She let her gaze drift down his chest, then moved to his arms. Despite the cool late-April temperatures, he wore a T-shirt and no jacket. She could see a tattoo of a rose, along with several scars on his arms. His hands were strong and equally battered.

She returned her attention to the scar on his neck and decided to ask the obvious. "What happened to the other guy?"

He touched the side of his throat, then shrugged. "He had a very bad day."

Taryn lived in the world of business. She could talk finance and sales projections, but her real gift was designing public relationship campaigns that were innovative and successful. At Score the work was divided among the four partners. Kenny and Jack were the rainmakers. They found prospective clients and reeled them in. Sam handled the money. But Taryn was the creative engine that steered the ship.

She was used to executives, graphic artists, bankers and everything in between. In her sphere, she was a power player and no one crossed her. But Angel was from a different sphere altogether. His clout didn't come from a boardroom or the right suit. He carried it in his body. It was part of who he was.

She knew a few odds and ends about him. People she respected and trusted liked him. But the details? They were still a mystery. One she would like to solve.

"What makes you think I'm the least bit interested?" she asked.

"You're still here."

A good point. She didn't want another executive — he would be too much like her. As for sports heroes, she worked with three and they exhausted her. Angel was different. Right now different sounded like exactly what she needed.

"Effort will be required," she told him.

"Ditto."

She laughed at the unexpected statement.

"You didn't think I'd be easy, did you?" he asked.

"Apparently not."

He stood. "Don't worry. I'm good at planning the right op for the right mission and then seeing it through." He crossed to the door, then turned back to her. "And I'm good at waiting."

He walked out, leaving her with her rapidly cooling coffee and an article on consumer confidence that had just gotten a whole lot less interesting than her encounter with an intriguing man named Angel.

■ ■ ■ ■

Smug felt good, Angel thought as he crossed the street and headed for City Hall. He'd been waiting for the right moment to talk to Taryn, and when he'd seen her having coffee by herself, he'd decided to act. She was as intriguing as he'd hoped — intelligent, confident and sexy as hell. A combination he would have trouble resisting under the best of circumstances. But in this town, with her always *around* . . . He'd wanted to make his move the first day.

Waiting had been better, he told himself as he jogged up the stairs to the front of the government building. Now he could put his plan into action. The one that led them down a road of temptation, with an ultimate objective that should satisfy them both.

He took more stairs to the second floor and followed the signs to the mayor's office.

Mayor Marsha Tilson was California's longest-serving mayor. She served the town well and seemed to know everyone's secrets. Angel had yet to figure out where she got her information, but from what he'd seen, she had a network that would put most governments to shame.

He entered her office exactly fifteen sec-

15

onds before the time of his appointment.

Her assistant, an older woman in a black blazer, looked up at him with red and puffy eyes. Angel immediately sensed bubbling emotion and glanced around the room to discover all available exits.

The woman, a full-figured brunette, sniffed. "You must be Mr. Whittaker. Go right in. She's expecting you."

Angel did as instructed, hoping to find a calmer atmosphere in the mayor's office. His cautious optimism was rewarded. Mayor Marsha looked as she always did — perfectly put together. She wore a light green suit and pearls and had her white hair neatly swirled up in a bun. She smiled and stood when she saw him.

"Mr. Whittaker. You made it."

"Angel, please." He crossed the room and shook hands with her, then settled in the seat across from hers.

Her office was large with several windows. Behind her desk were the flags of the United States and the state of California, along with a large seal he would guess represented the city of Fool's Gold.

"Your assistant's upset," he said.

"Marjorie's worked with me for years. But her twin daughters have settled in Portland, Oregon. They're both pregnant. Marjorie's husband retired, so they're going to move closer to family. While she's excited about being nearer to her daughters and future grandchildren, she's sad about leaving all of us here."

More than he wanted to know, he thought, keeping his expression polite.

Mayor Marsha smiled. "Now I'll have to find someone new. Hiring staff is relatively easy, but an assistant is a different matter. There has to be chemistry and trust. One can't let just anyone know the town's secrets." The smile widened. "Not why you came to see me today." She leaned forward and picked up a file from the stack on her large desk.

"All right, Angel, let's see what we have here." She slipped on reading glasses. "You're interested in a project that will involve you with the community."

Angel had been to some of the most dangerous parts of the world in various capacities. He'd taken his sniper training into the private sector and now designed curricula for people training to be professional bodyguards. Not much surprised him. But he would swear he hadn't told anyone his reason for making his appointment with Mayor Marsha, which begged the question: How did the old lady know?

17

She glanced at him over her glasses. "Did I have that correct?"

He decided he had little choice but to simply nod and say, "Yes, ma'am."

The smile returned. "Good. You have a unique background and an unusual skill set. I've given the matter a lot of thought and I think you'd be a perfect Grove Keeper."

Grove what? "Ma'am?"

"Are you familiar with the history of the town?" she asked, then closed the folder. "This is California, so there was the expected exploration by the Spanish in the 1700s, but long before that, Fool's Gold was settled by the Máa-zib Tribe."

Angel had heard something about that. "A branch of Mayans," he murmured. "Matriarchal."

"Yes." The smile returned. "I would guess you'd respect a group of women who only want to use a man for sex."

Angel wasn't sure if he should flinch or pat the old lady on the back. Instead he cleared his throat. "All right," he said slowly. "Interesting."

"It is. We have long celebrated our Máazib culture, and that includes a youth group. Future Warriors of the Máa-zib. Young people start with a two-month introduction to what it's like to be in the FWM. That's

18

followed by four years of membership. We have Acorns, Sprouts, Saplings, Sky-Reachers and Mighty Oaks. Each group or troop is known as a grove, and the person in charge is a Grove Keeper."

She put down her glasses. "We have a grove in need of a keeper, and I think they need you."

Kids, he thought with surprise. He liked kids. His goal had been to get involved with Fool's Gold because he'd decided to stay here and he'd been raised to give back to the community. He'd thought maybe he could volunteer on some advisory committee or teach a continuing ed class — although his skill set didn't exactly fit in the regular world. Still . . . kids.

He hesitated only a second, then realized it had been long enough since he'd lost Marcus. The pain was still there — would always be a part of him, like a scar, or his heart — but it had become manageable. He thought by now he would be able to work with teenaged boys without wanting to argue with the heavens about how unfair it had all been.

"Sure," he said easily. "I can run a grove."

Amusement twinkled in Mayor Marsha's blue eyes. "I'm glad to hear it. I think you'll find the experience fulfilling on several levels. I'll make sure you get your material in the next few days. Then you can meet with the Grove Council."

He grinned. "Seriously? There's a Grove Council?"

She laughed. "Of course. These are Future Warriors of the Máa-zib. What else would there be?"

She rose and he did, as well. "Thank you, Angel. Usually I have to go out and convince new residents to pitch in. I appreciate that you came to me." She studied him. "I assume your interest in giving back is the result of your background. You grew up in a coal mining town, didn't you? West Virginia?"

While the information wasn't secret, it wasn't something he shared very often. "You're a spooky woman," he told her. "You know that, right?"

The smile broadened. "Not many people have the courage to say it to my face, but I do hope that's what they're saying behind my back."

"They are," he assured her.

They shook hands and he left. Marjorie was still in tears, so he hustled out and hit the stairs at a jog. Maybe he would spend the afternoon looking for campsites, he thought cheerfully. He had plenty of survival skills he could pass on to his FWM grove. Ways to help them grow up to be confident men. Yeah — this was going to be good.

"Jack, stop it," Taryn said without looking up from the papers in front of her.

The shifting sound stilled, only to start up again five seconds later. She drew in a breath and glanced across the small conference table.

"Seriously," she told him. "You're worse than a five-year-old."

Jack McGarry, her business partner and ex-husband, rotated his shoulder. "When does Larissa get here?"

"I told you. She gets here tomorrow. In twenty-four hours you'll have her back. Now can you please focus?"

Sam, the only calm, rational partner, leaned back in his chair. "You're trying too hard. You know that never works."

Because it was her job to try hard. She kept "the boys" on a tight leash because if she didn't, they would run all over her.

She'd known Jack the longest. After their quickie marriage and equally speedy divorce, he'd set her up in business. He'd provided the money, she'd brought the PR know-how and Score had been an instant success — helped by Jack throwing a lot of

21

business her way. It had been a great arrangement.

Unfortunately four years later, Kenny had blown out his knee and ended his career. Sam had been thinking of getting out of the NFL, and for reasons Taryn couldn't figure out, Jack had joined them. Her ex had walked away from his starring role as a quarterback with the L.A. Stallions. He claimed he wanted to go out on top, but she suspected his departure had more to do with his friends than anything else. Not that Jack would admit it.

There they were — three ex-jocks — with plenty of cash and fame and no second act in the wings. Oh, wait. Jack was half owner of a PR firm. Before she'd known what was happening, he'd brought Kenny and Sam on board and all four of them were partners.

At first she'd been sure they would crash and burn, but more quickly than she would have guessed possible, they'd become a team and then a family. Jack and Kenny were the salesguys. They brought in the clients and were the public face of the firm. Sam handled the finances, both for the company and for each of them privately. Not only was he smart, but he'd actually gone to his classes in college.

Taryn handled everything else. She ran

the business, bossed around the boys and created the campaigns that had continued to add to their net worth. Theirs was an unconventional arrangement, but it worked for them.

Jack shifted again, the muscle in his cheek tightening. She reminded herself he wasn't trying to be difficult — he was in pain. No one could get through nearly a decade in the NFL and not have the battered body to prove it. Larissa, Jack's personal assistant and the boys' private masseuse, hadn't been able to move to Fool's Gold as quickly as the rest of them. After nearly a month without her healing touch, all three of the former players were suffering.

"Tomorrow," she said again.

"You sure?"

"Yes." She paused. "You could take something."

The statement was made in her most gentle voice, one her partners almost never heard. Because she knew that Jack was going to refuse. With permanent injuries and the discomfort that went with them, painkillers could be a slick road to hell. None of the guys wanted to go there.

"What's next?" he asked, ignoring her words.

"We're up," Kenny told him, then opened

the file in front of him. "Jack and I had a second meeting with the CEO and founder of Living Life at a Run." He reached for the remote in the center of the table and hit a button. The screen at the far end of the room lit up and a logo came into focus.

Taryn studied the angular letters and the quirky acronym. LL@R. She wanted to point out that one of the *a*'s was missing, but she knew there wasn't any point. The company's CEO had a reputation for being eccentric and difficult. But he offered them a shot at traditional retail — one area of the PR market where Score had never had much luck finding clients.

"They're growing fast," Kenny said. "They're trendy and a lot of celebrities are wearing their clothes."

"The clothing is a secondary market for them," Jack added. "Their main focus is sports gear. If we could get them, we could move toward bigger companies. Like REI."

Taryn would love to get her hands on a premium company like REI but the old cliché was true. They would have to learn to walk before they could learn to run.

"What's next?" she asked.

"I have another meeting in a few days," Kenny said.

Taryn waited and sure enough, Jack stared

at his friend. "I? I? Is that where we are? Each out for what we can get? What happened to the team? What happened to us being a family?"

Kenny, all six feet four inches of blond brawn, groaned. "Give me a break. You know what I meant."

"Do I? Sounds to me like this is all about you."

"You need to be specific," Sam said mildly, obviously content to join the mock argument. Taryn knew that any second now he would turn on Jack, because that's what always happened when they were like this.

They were each successful, good-looking and worth at least eight figures. Yet there were times when they were as unruly and mischievous as a litter of puppies. Sam and Jack were both dark-haired. Sam, the former kicker, was lean and just six feet tall. Jack had him by a couple of inches and at least thirty pounds of muscle. Jack's classic quarterback physique — broad shoulders, narrow hips, long legs — had served him well, both on and off the field. Then there was Kenny, the gentle giant of the group.

Her boys, she thought as they bickered. They were responsible for her move to Fool's Gold — something she wasn't sure she was willing to forgive just yet. The town wasn't as bad as she'd first thought, but it sure wasn't L.A. She loved L.A.

"So I'll be in charge?" Jack asked with a grin.

"Your mama," Kenny told him.

"Don't break anything," Taryn said as she collected her papers and started for the door. Because whenever she heard "your mama," body blows were sure to follow.

Sam went with her. "Not going to try to stop them?" he asked cheerfully as they stepped into the hallway.

"That would be your job."

Something hit the wall with a thud. Sam kept walking. "No, thanks."

"The three of you are never going to grow up, are you?" she asked.

"I'm not the one fighting."

She glanced at him. "Not this time."

He gave her a wink, then sauntered away. Taryn continued to her office. In the distance, she heard a crash. She ignored it and checked her schedule for the day. She had a conference call at eleven and Graphics had asked for a few minutes.

"Thanks," Taryn said as she sat at her desk. She glanced at her computer. "Just another day in paradise." And she loved every minute of it.

The boys were her family, and no matter

how many chairs, tables, windows and hearts they broke, she would stand by them. Even if every now and then she fantasized about how much more serene her life would be if she'd gone into business with a couple of pacifist guys who believed in the power of meditation for conflict resolution.

Somewhere in the distance, glass shattered. Taryn continued to look at her computer screen as she kept on typing.

CHAPTER TWO

Taryn stacked dishes on the narrow counter. The kitchen was tiny. A miniature galley-style, with a three-quarter-sized stove and refrigerator. The colors were nice and the appliances updated, but still there wasn't actually room for two people.

"Explain this to me," she said, unwrapping glasses and setting them next to the plates. "I sign the paychecks. I happen to know you could afford a bigger place."

Larissa Owens lifted a pot out of the box she'd put on the table. She'd pulled her long blond hair back into a ponytail and didn't wear a speck of makeup. She was lithe and tan and looked amazing in yoga pants and a T-shirt. If Taryn didn't already adore her, Larissa could be easy to hate.

"I don't need a bigger place," her friend told her. "A small one-bedroom is plenty. The rent is really cheap so I'll have more money for my causes."

Which was exactly what would happen, Taryn thought, picking up scissors and flipping the empty box so she could cut across the tape and then flatten it. Larissa was a giant bleeding heart when it came to causes, especially if there were animals involved. In addition to her full-time job, she volunteered at a couple of shelters, fostered dogs, cats and bunnies and sent money to nearly every organization that asked.

Taryn glanced around at the maybe six-hundred-square-foot apartment. "You won't be getting a pet bigger than a goldfish in here."

"I could get a cat," Larissa told her cheerfully. "I wouldn't want a dog. I'm not home enough. Besides, if I need something bigger —"

"There's always Jack's place," Taryn said, finishing the sentence. "Yes, I know."

Jack, who let Larissa use him to support those organizations near and dear to her. Taryn had never been able to figure out why, but the situation worked for them. As a former NFL quarterback, Jack was expected to throw his weight behind some kind of charity. As he'd lost a twin with a heart condition back when they were both kids, he'd chosen to get involved with kids needing organ transplants. Or rather, Jack wrote the check for housing, transportation, whatever, and Larissa took care of staying in touch.

"He misses you desperately," Taryn told her.

"I've been hearing that in his incessant voice mails." Larissa wrinkled her nose. "He misses my massages. It's not exactly the same thing."

"You're also his assistant. I'm sure he misses you getting him coffee."

Larissa grinned. "That, too." She reached for the scissors and flattened her box. "So, the town. I thought you were kidding when you described it to me."

"Would that I were," Taryn told her. "But, no. It's charming and clean and the people are overly friendly."

"I like it," Larissa said as she handed Taryn another box, then got one for herself. "I feel like I've already made friends. The lady who owns that cute coffee shop paid for my coffee this morning. That was really nice."

"Patience," Taryn grumbled. "Her name is Patience. Yes, she's lovely. They're all lovely. Except for Charlie, who's a firefighter and crabby. I like her a lot."

Actually she liked everyone she'd met, which was kind of annoying. What if all the

30

niceness wore off on her? What if she started smiling at random strangers and saying cheerful things like "Have a nice day"? She shuddered. Being sarcastic and emotionally distant had always served her well. Why mess with success?

"Are the guys settling in?" Larissa asked.

"I guess. You know I try to avoid talking about their personal lives with them whenever possible, so my information may not be totally accurate. But as far as I know, Jack and Kenny seem bimbo-free for the moment, and Sam, well . . ." She grinned. "Poor Sam."

Larissa pressed her lips together. "We shouldn't make fun of him."

"Why not? It's not like he can hear us."

"But it's so sad."

It kind of was, Taryn thought, but it was also really, really funny. Sam Ridge, all-star kicker and multimillionaire, had the worst luck when it came to women. If there was a femme fatale in a fifty-mile radius, Sam found her and fell for her. He'd experienced everything from a stalker to an ex-wife writing a near tell-all to having his girlfriend sleep with his best friends.

"I'm waiting for him to fall for a transvestite," Larissa said with a grin. "Poor Sam."

"I don't get it," Taryn admitted. "He's

31

smart and insightful. But when it comes to women, he can't seem to find anyone normal."

"What about you?" Larissa asked, her tone teasing. "Met anyone tempting?"

The question was meant as a joke. Taryn knew that. She rarely dated. She liked guys, she slept with them, but she didn't get involved. There was no way she was trusting her heart or any part of her psyche to some man. Talk about stupid.

Except when Larissa asked her question, Taryn immediately thought about Angel. And thinking about Angel meant she wasn't thinking about anything else and she couldn't seem to make her mouth move to form the words *What? A guy? With me? No way.*

Larissa put down the frying pan she'd just unwrapped and stared at her friend. "Oh my God. What? You met someone? Who is he? Tell me everything." Her big blue eyes widened. "Is he local? Like a single dad." She sighed. "That would be so romantic. Some sweet guy with a couple of little kids. Like a car mechanic or maybe he owns a little grocery store and they live upstairs. He still misses his wife, but he's ready to move on. Only I don't know how you're going to feel about the kids."

Taryn stared at her. "You don't need me here for this conversation, do you? A widower with two kids and a grocery store? That is not happening."

Larissa's shoulders slumped. "Why don't you like him? He's so nice."

Taryn held in a scream. "There is no grocery store guy. You made him up. What's wrong with you? Jeez. The only guy I'm interested in is a former black ops sniper with a scar like somebody slit his throat."

Larissa handed her the frying pan. "I'd rather date the guy who owns the grocery store."

"The one who isn't real?"

"You always focus on the wrong stuff. So tell me about Sniper Man."

"There's not much to tell."

Taryn starting putting plates and bowls in the cupboards, knowing that wasn't going to be close to enough to distract her friend.

"There's something," Larissa told her. "You're attracted to him."

"Maybe. Yes. A little." She sighed. "At least he's a widower. That should make you happy."

She'd learned that much at least. But it was hard to get information without telling people why she wanted it, and she wasn't ready to tell the world that she thought

Angel was hot.

"It's something. But he won't buy a grocery store?"

"Larissa, I beg you. Stop."

Larissa smiled. "Everyone thinks you're tough, but you're really not."

"I can be, just not with you."

"Okay, this Angel guy. You're dating?"

"Not exactly. We're sizing up each other."

"What does that mean?"

Taryn thought about Angel's announcement that he was good at waiting. A little ripple of anticipation shimmied down her spine as she wondered when he was going to make his move. He was making her wait on purpose, and she respected that. He wanted the game to be intriguing . . . for both of them.

"I have no idea," she admitted. "But I'll let you know when I figure it out."

Angel put the copy of the bridal magazine on the desk. Ford stared at him in disbelief.

"Just like that?" his friend asked. "Did you wake up thinking this would be a good day to die?"

"She's engaged," Angel said, grinning. "She's wearing an engagement ring. I'm celebrating the moment."

Ford held up both hands in a classic move

of surrender, but Angel was feeling adventurous. Lately, he'd had the sense that everything was going his way. The answer to the *Dirty Harry* question of "Do I feel lucky?" was yes. He did. It didn't matter that the movie had come out a year before he was born. He could relate to the character. When in doubt, a bigger gun usually got the job done.

Consuelo, their petite colleague, walked into the office. She looked at the magazine, then at the two of them.

"It was him," Ford said, pointing at Angel. "He did it."

Angel glanced at his friend. "Is that how things are now?"

Ford inched toward the door. "Law of the jungle, bro. While she's feeding on you, I can make my escape. Isabel and I are trying to make a baby. I want to be around to see my kid grow up."

Consuelo, all five feet two inches of muscle and determination, picked up the magazine, flipped through it, then put it back on the desk. She smiled at Angel. "Thanks. That was thoughtful."

He shot Ford a "See?" look, then moved toward her. "I know you and Kent got engaged. I hope you'll be very happy together."

Consuelo stepped into his embrace and hugged him. When he drew back, she casually stepped to the side, grabbed Ford by the arm and flipped him onto his back. He landed on the floor with a thud. When he could breathe again, he sat up.

"Hey, what was that for?" he asked in a tone of outrage.

"For being cynical. You're married and you should know better."

Consuelo turned her back on him, picked up the magazine and headed for the door. "I'll be back after lunch," she called.

"It's not even ten," Ford grumbled as he climbed to his feet. "Why does she get to leave?"

Angel chuckled. "You want to tell her she can't?"

"No."

"Didn't think so. Come on, we'll head out, too."

"Where are we going?" Ford asked, falling into step with him.

"To a nursery."

"Baby or plant?"

"Plant. I ordered an orchid a couple of months ago. It's in and I have to sign the card so it can be delivered."

They went outside.

"Why would an orchid take two months

to get here?" Ford asked.

"It's rare. I wanted a specific one."

From Thailand, Angel thought. An orchid known for its contrasting colors. The outside of the flower was the palest pink, but inside was a dark violet blue. The unusual shade was nearly the exact color of Taryn's eyes.

"Why do you care about flowers?"

Angel glared at his friend. "What's with you today? Stop asking questions. Are you coming with me or not?"

Ford leaned against his Jeep and grinned. "Someone's not getting any. You always get moody when you're not getting laid."

"Shut up."

"Thanks for illustrating my point."

Taryn parked her car and collected her briefcase. She'd gone through paperwork the previous evening, had caught up on emails and then been in bed by ten. As a personal life went, it was beyond sad. She needed to get out more, make some friends. As she'd told Larissa the previous day, people in town were certainly nice enough. The women had all been friendly. It was just . . .

She started across the parking lot and sighed. The town wasn't the problem, she admitted, if only to herself. She was. She had trouble making new friends. She didn't trust easily, so sharing any part of herself was difficult. She'd had more than one man point out that after seeing her for several weeks — and by *seeing,* he meant sleeping with — the guy in question knew absolutely nothing more about her than he had when they'd first met. She never bothered to tell them that was the point. If they were too stupid to figure that out, why should she waste breath telling them?

She hadn't wanted to leave Los Angeles, but she'd been outvoted. Score was now located in Fool's Gold. She had to make the best of the situation. More important, she needed to get her life moving again. There had to be more to her days than work.

She heard the sound of a basketball steadily hitting the sidewalk and ignored it. But Sam was nothing if not persistent and he quickly caught up with her.

"Driving to work?" he asked. "You live a mile away."

She paused and faced him. "Have you seen my shoes?" she asked. "I'm wearing Charlotte Olympia pumps with a five-inch heel. Could you walk to the corner in them? I don't think so. Besides, you can't talk to me today. I'm taller."

Sam sighed. "It's going to be one of those

days, isn't it?"

"You betcha."

She flashed Sam a smile, then disappeared into their building. He walked across the street to the basketball court the guys had insisted be part of the remodeling. Not even a half-court, like at their last office. No, this was regulation size. She didn't know what it had cost and she didn't want to know.

Had any of her business partners been with her, she would have grumbled to them about how annoying they were, but as she was alone, she paused to look out the window. The three of them, Kenny, Jack and Sam, all wore baggy shorts and T-shirts. Sam, six feet tall and muscled, looked small next to the other two, but he was fast and used his brain when he played. Kenny and Jack mostly reacted. Which explained why Sam usually kicked their butts.

They fought for the basketball, and then Sam ripped it away, turned gracefully, jumped and scored. As she watched, Taryn realized that the boys needed more than each other, too. The same three guys playing basketball a few mornings a week couldn't be that much fun.

She started toward her office. When she was at her desk, she picked up her phone but set it back in the cradle. She told herself the guys were well into their thirties and could take care of themselves. That she didn't want anyone — namely Angel — thinking she was angling to find ways to see him. Of course telling him this wasn't about him would only make him think it was. She sighed and picked up the phone again.

"CDS," a man's voice said.

"Justice Garrett, please."

"Speaking."

"Hi, Justice, I'm Taryn Crawford. I know your wife. I'm a partner at Score, here in town."

"Right. Patience has mentioned you. The PR firm with the football players."

"That's us." This was stupid. She felt like a mom trying to set up a playdate for her socially awkward child. Except despite her grumbling about the move, she really did want the guys to be happy. They might annoy her from time to time, but they were all the family she was ever likely to have.

"You have ex-military guys employed there," she began. "They like to work out and stuff?"

There was a pause. Taryn could present a multimillion-dollar PR presentation to the most uptight skeptic with no problem. Why was this so hard?

"Was that a question?" Justice asked.

"No. Okay, so you know about Jack, Kenny and Sam, right? Former football players. They're still competitive and . . ." She told herself to get to the point. "The guys have a new outdoor basketball court. They play a few mornings a week. I thought you and your guys might like to join them."

There was another pause, then Justice chuckled. "My guys and I would like that very much. I hope yours aren't sore losers."

Taryn grinned. "Nice try. Your team is so going down."

"We'll see about that. What time do they start?"

"Six. Day after tomorrow."

"We'll be there."

She hung up, feeling more than a little proud of herself. She logged in to the company's remote data storage and downloaded the work she'd done the previous night, then updated several accounts.

At nine, she met with her graphics and design people. Her team of six was the heart of the organization. All presentations came out of that office, including graphic design, layout and videos for sample commercials and promotional spots.

There was also Sam's staff of two accountants who ran all the numbers; Taryn's assistant who doubled as the office manager;

Larissa, Jack's personal assistant and the boys' private masseuse; along with Kenny and Sam's assistant.

When Kenny, Jack and Sam had first come to her about moving to Fool's Gold, she'd warned them that they would lose valuable staff. One of the few times in her life when she'd been wrong when it came to business, she thought. Everyone had been excited about relocating. Taryn had been the lone holdout.

Who could have guessed that carefully selecting family-oriented, well-adjusted employees would come back to bite her in the butt? she thought with a grin.

Her assistant stepped into her office. "They're ready for you."

Taryn followed her into the smaller conference room. Sam, Jack and Kenny were there, freshly showered after their morning game — because part of the remodeling had included putting in a locker room. Make that two, because while Taryn never planned to bathe at work, she'd insisted on equal facilities for the women. So they, too, had large showers, lockers and a steam room. The difference was she never insisted on holding meetings in the steam room, while the boys had on more than one occasion.

Now she walked to the far end of the table

and opened the laptop there. Then her gaze settled on Jack, who had chosen not to dress after his shower. He sat at the conference table in a white robe and flip-flops.

"Let me guess," she said. "Larissa is here."

"She's warming up the massage table as we speak."

"Tell me you're wearing underwear," she said.

Jack winked.

"My team's been working on several campaigns," she said as she typed on the laptop. Through the company's internal network, she could access her computer files remotely and pull up any necessary information.

"Here's what we came up with for the Klassique Rum campaign. We'll have the sample commercial ready by the end of the week, but in the meantime, here are our thoughts for print ads and the Facebook campaigns."

She touched her computer keyboard, and a slide appeared on the large screen at the opposite end of the room. "We pulled colors from their new labels. Obviously rum means parties and fun."

"Beach parties," Kenny corrected, then grinned at Jack. "That was a hell of a weekend."

The two of them had visited Klassique's headquarters in the Caribbean. While Taryn had been invited, she'd passed. Watching Kenny and Jack in action with dozens of nubile, willing women wasn't her idea of a good time.

The speakerphone in the center of the table buzzed.

"Jack, Larissa's ready," Taryn's assistant said.

Jack was already up and moving. "See you later," he called.

"I really hope he keeps his robe on until he gets into the massage room," Taryn murmured.

"Me, too," Sam told her. "Because he's not wearing any underwear."

Fortunately their employees were good-natured about the idiosyncrasies of working for former jocks, but every now and then Taryn had to field a complaint about too much male nudity.

Usually from the spouse of one of the female employees.

Taryn turned her attention back to the campaign. She went through it slide by slide. Kenny had several insights from the client's perspective, while Sam tallied costs. Two hours later, when they had nearly finished, Jack walked back into the room.

He'd dressed in jeans and a long-sleeved shirt. But more than that, Taryn noticed how much more easily he moved. He sat next to Kenny.

"She says to give her fifteen minutes to relax her hands, and then she'll be ready for you," Jack said.

Kenny nodded.

Taryn glanced at Sam. "You okay waiting?"

"Sure."

As a kicker, Sam had been beat up the least. The other two joked he had the easiest job in the game. Taryn knew differently. While she normally wouldn't have ever bothered learning anything about the sport, her partnership meant she had to know more than the basics when it came to football. The kicker might not take the hits the other players did, but he worked under incredible pressure. Every second on the field meant being at the very center of everyone's attention, often with games hanging in the balance. The NFL was a multibillion-dollar industry, and if you couldn't handle the intense scrutiny, you weren't going to last very long.

"What did I miss?" Jack asked.

"I'll fill you in later," Kenny told him.

Taryn glanced down the list of what she'd

wanted to cover. "I think we're nearly through everything. Sam, are you ready to update us on the party?"

She did her best to ask the question without any annoyance in her voice. Because after moving the entire company to Fool's Gold, the boys had decided to entertain their largest clients with a big weekend party. They'd rented out a part of the Gold Rush Ski Lodge and Resort for a long weekend of the Summer Festival — whatever that was. Now about twenty clients, their spouses and assorted children were going to show up and expect to be entertained.

Sam cleared his throat. "Sure," he began. "We're having the clients in, as we discussed. In July."

"During the Summer Festival, right?" Kenny asked.

Taryn turned to him. "You know about the festivals?"

"Sure. It's one of the reasons we wanted to move here. The town has festivals every month, to celebrate the seasons and different holidays." He nudged Jack. "There's a balloon festival in June. We should get one and go up."

"I'm in," Jack said easily. "I get to drive."

"You don't drive a balloon," Kenny told him.

"Whatever. I'm in charge."

"Great," Taryn said. "So you're sure to crash or burst into flames. Sam, please make sure our key-man insurance policy is paid up."

Jack gave her a lazy smile. "You'd miss me, darlin'."

"That I would and then I'd move on with my life." She turned back to Sam. "About the party," she said again. "Where are we?"

"In the planning stages."

She waited but Sam didn't say any more. "It's just over three months away. You have to get going."

"I am."

This wasn't like Sam, she thought. Normally he was on top of things. "Do you have any details? You know we have to make sure our clients have a good time, right? And they're bringing their families, which ups the pressure. You three are the ones who wanted to move here in the first place. You're the ones who insisted on this party. Don't come to me a week before and say there's a problem, because I'm not going to fix this."

"There she goes," Kenny said conversationally. "Sam, you've riled Taryn, and no good comes of that. Back where I come from —"

Taryn slapped both hands on the conference table. "Do *not* tell me some good-ol'-boy farm story, Kenneth Anderson Scott. You may want the world to think you're just some down-home guy from Iowa, but I know better."

Kenny glanced at his watch. "Look at the time. Larissa should be ready for me now."

He nearly ran from the room. Jack watched him go.

"That wasn't nice, Taryn. You know Kenny hates it when you use his whole name. It reminds him of being yelled at by his mom."

"Yes, and that's why I do it." She returned her attention to Sam. "About the party."

"It's handled," he told her.

Exactly what she wanted to hear. So why didn't she believe him? "You're sure."

"Very."

She nodded and Sam ducked out of the room. Jack stayed in his seat.

"Want to talk about it?" he asked.

"No."

"You're a little crabby."

She pressed her lips together. "It's not like you guys make it easy."

He stood and circled around the table until he was next to her. Then he pulled her close and hugged her. She relaxed in his familiar embrace. His large hands rested on her back and she breathed in the scent of him.

When they'd first met, Jack was the star quarterback of the L.A. Stallions and she was the newly hired PR assistant. She'd never expected their night together to lead to anything more. But one night had turned into two, then a week.

When everything fell apart, they'd stayed friends. She loved Kenny and Sam, but Jack was the one who knew her best. A point he proved when he said, "Still not sure you're going to like it here?"

"It's different. People are nice."

"Damn them."

She smiled into his shoulder, then stepped back. "I'm not like you."

"That's true." His dark eyes crinkled with amusement. "You'd look funny with my penis."

"I'd have it removed."

He winced. "Don't even joke about that." He kissed her forehead. "We're going to be here awhile, Taryn. Relax. Make nice with the ladies in town. Go to lunch and give them a chance to prove they mean what they say."

"They really want me to have a nice day?"

"They do. Let them get to know you while you get to know them. Make friends. It's fun."

"Maybe," she grumbled.

"That's my girl. Always willing to try new things." He put his arm around her and led her from the room. "Come on. I'll buy you some lunch. I'll order the fries."

Because if she didn't order the food, the calories didn't count, she thought, leaning into him. "You're the best," she told him.

"Yeah, I know. My greatness has always been a burden."

CHAPTER THREE

"This came for you."

Taryn glanced up as Larissa walked into her office. She was carrying what looked like a very exotic orchid. One that Taryn had never seen before.

"It's beautiful," she murmured, reaching for the plant.

Larissa grinned. "There's a card."

Taryn touched the soft petals of the flower. The colors were unusual, she thought. Pink and a blue violet. "What does it say?"

"I haven't read it."

Taryn put the plant on her desk, then looked at her friend. "Of course you have."

Larissa laughed. "There's just a place and a time. It's for tonight."

She took the card and studied it. Sure enough, Condor Valley Winery, 7:00 p.m., was written in bold black pen.

An invitation or instructions, she thought,

intrigued by the assumption. What if she couldn't make it?

"Are you going?" Larissa asked.

"I don't know."

Larissa sat in the chair next to the desk. "You have to. You said he's really sexy."

"I don't remember saying that."

"Okay, you thought it. Same thing." She put a small brochure on the desk. "There are instructions that go with your new plant. Apparently it's very rare and delicate."

"You could take it on as a cause," Taryn told her.

"I could, but you got there first." She leaned in. "So, what do you know about Angel? Other than he got you a really unusual flower."

"He's with the bodyguard school, he's a former sniper, he was married."

"That's right. He's the widower. Any kids?"

"I don't know. None in town."

"Why do you like him?"

"I'm not sure I do."

Larissa shook her head. "Fine. Why are you interested in him? I think he's kind of scary."

Taryn thought about all the easy answers. That he was attractive and sexy. That he'd made the first move. That she was pretty sure there was chemistry. That Jack was right and she needed to put herself out there. Although Jack had been talking about making girlfriends rather than taking a lover, but still.

"He doesn't need me to take care of him," she said at last, speaking the absolute truth.

"Unlike the boys." Larissa nodded. "That makes sense. It's just I've always sort of pictured you with a banker."

"Another man in a suit? No, thanks. Been there, done that over and over again."

She didn't want someone like her. She didn't want someone from her world. Angel was different in every way possible. When he looked at her with those cool gray eyes, she had no idea what he was thinking. That was kind of fun. She just hoped it didn't mean he was a serial killer.

"I guess it's okay," Larissa said slowly. "Everybody in town seems to like him, so he must be a nice guy."

"Tell me you haven't been asking about him."

"Just a little."

Taryn held in a groan at the thought of her personal life being discussed.

"I was discreet," Larissa protested.

"Uh-huh. Is there anyone you won't talk to?"

"No, and that's why you love me."

Taryn left work early so she would have time to get ready for her date with Angel. She drove the short distance to her house and parked in the single-car garage.

Usually she preferred condo living — less maintenance for her — but when the company had relocated to Fool's Gold, she'd decided to try a house.

The place was small — only two bedrooms, but they were both a nice size. The house had been remodeled pretty much from the ground up, so she had a new kitchen and a nice walk-in shower in the bathroom. Surprisingly, the feature that most appealed to her was the garden. An old-fashioned stone fence surrounded the backyard. There was a patio and several raised plant beds. She'd never grown anything before in her life, but she'd started doing some research and was thinking of planting some flowers and a few vegetables.

Now Taryn walked through the kitchen. She kicked off her heels and walked barefoot down the hallway and into the master. Although the house had been updated, most of the Craftsman touches had been left in place, including the built-in bookcase by the stone fireplace across from her bed. The fence out back was high enough that she didn't have to pull her drapes for privacy, which allowed a lot of light into the room. She shrugged out of her jacket, then unzipped her skirt and let it fall to the carpet. She removed her blouse, then put on a robe and walked into the bathroom.

She wore her black hair long and loose. Minimal daily products, plenty of conditioner and weekly scalp treatments kept her hair in decent shape. She'd been pleasantly surprised to discover that she could get her favorite hair gloss applied every six weeks here, just as she had done back in L.A.

She pulled her hair back in a cloth headband and washed her face. Then she reapplied her makeup, paying close attention to her eyes. She was going to be wearing black, so she wanted to emphasize her eye shape and color. When she was done with that, she applied a faint shimmering body lotion to her chest, shoulders, arms and legs.

After penciling in a nearly nude lip color, she returned to her bedroom and stepped into the closet. She already knew what she was going to wear — she'd made her decision as soon as she'd seen the invitation. If Angel wanted to play games, she was willing to play them with him. But she was

55

equally determined that she would be the winner.

To that end, she removed her bra and then stepped into the strapless black dress she'd chosen. From the front, it was simple — fitted and nearly to the knee. But in the back it dipped to hip level. Every time she moved, the fabric shifted as if the viewer were going to see something he shouldn't. A killer dress, she thought with a smile. Perfect for a former sniper.

The best part was she would pair the dress with a classic black blazer. With the jacket, the outfit was conservative enough for work. But without . . .

She studied her shoes and chose a pair of Dolce & Gabbana lace pumps with four-inch heels. She wasn't usually a lace-and-bow kind of woman, but these were both sexy and sophisticated. Of course they were D&G, so it wasn't as though she could actually go wrong.

She stepped into the shoes and then studied herself in the mirror. Jewelry should be simple, she thought, and went with diamond studs that Jack had given her when their divorce was final.

She transferred the items she would need for that night to a black silk clutch, then headed out the door.

Condor Valley Winery was set in the foothills, just above the vineyards. Although the sign in the parking lot said they closed at five this time of year, she parked by the main doors and walked up the paved path. She had no doubt that Angel would have made special arrangements. He was a man used to getting his way and he wouldn't let a little thing like regular business hours deter him.

Sure enough a woman in her earlier twenties was waiting inside. She smiled. "Ms. Crawford?"

"Yes."

"If you'll follow me, please."

The woman led Taryn to a small elevator that whisked them to the third floor. From there they went into what looked like a private library — a room filled with built-in bookcases and comfortable, black leather furniture. Double doors stood open and led to a large balcony with a bistro table and two chairs. From where she stood, Taryn could see the whole valley and the sun just beginning to set. Any chill was chased away by the portable heaters set up around the table.

"Let me get your appetizers," the woman said, and excused herself.

A minute or so later she was back with

two plates of small bites. Once she placed them on the table, she returned to the library and collected a bottle of red wine and two glasses. She expertly opened the wine but didn't pour, then smiled at Taryn and left.

Taryn stepped out onto the balcony and breathed in the night air. Anticipation settled low in her belly, but there was also a kind of quiet comfort. It had been a long time since a man had taken care of her this way. Or maybe the fault was hers — maybe it had been too long since she'd *let* someone take care of her.

"Good evening."

She turned and saw Angel standing in the doorway. He looked tall and broad — imposing in a black shirt and black pants.

"Hello," she said, staying where she was, wanting him to come to her.

He didn't disappoint. He closed the space between them and took her hands in his. "You came."

"You're not surprised."

One eyebrow rose. "Maybe I am."

She laughed. "I doubt that. Thank you for my orchid. It's very beautiful."

"It reminded me of you."

His hands were warm, his grip gentle. He didn't try to pull her close or make her feel as if he wouldn't let go. A clever strategy because she found herself wanting to step nearer.

In her four-inch heels, she was nearly his height, so contortions would not be required if they were to kiss. She could just ease forward and find out if the faint heat sweeping through her was all about possibilities or if there was reality to the quivering.

Or not, she thought as she carefully took a single step back.

He released her instantly, then gestured to the chairs by the table. "Shall we?"

When they were seated, Angel poured them each a glass of wine. "This Cab is from their library collection. Aged longer than most of the wine they sell. It's smooth, with a surprising finish."

She hung her bag over the handle of her chair, then reached for the glass. "Why do I get the idea you're talking about more than the wine? Although I'm not comfortable being described as *aged.*"

"Maybe I wasn't talking about you," he said, his gray eyes settling on her face.

"Yourself, then." She tilted her head. "Yes, I can see that. Although I have some concerns about the surprising finish. What does that mean? A little squeak? A fist pump? Should I be worried?"

He chuckled, then touched his glass to hers. "Thank you for joining me tonight."

"Thank you for asking me."

She took a sip. The Cab was smooth, but there was still a hint of tannins at the end. Plenty of berry flavor, without it being overpowering.

"Why did you come to Fool's Gold?" she asked.

"Justice moved the company here."

"Was that a good thing or a bad thing?"

"I like small towns. I grew up in one." He turned his attention to the view. "You're not from a small town."

A statement or a question, she wondered. "No, I'm an L.A. girl at heart. Moving to Fool's Gold has been a transition."

"Then why not keep the company in la-la land?"

"I was outvoted. Jack, Kenny and Sam came here for a Pro-Am golf tournament. I'm still not clear on what happened that weekend, but when they returned to work on the following Monday, they announced we were moving." She sipped her wine again. "Score is a democracy and I was in the minority. Of course they left all the details of moving up to me."

"Naturally."

"Where did you grow up?"

"West Virginia." He glanced at her and smiled. "A place you've never heard of. Coal mining town."

"I've never been in one," she admitted.

"There's good and bad. A lot of poverty with one large employer. The work is hard. My mom died when I was born, so it was my dad and me. I watched him come out of that coal mine day after day and swore I was going to get out."

"Which you did."

"I went into the military. When I left, I got involved with a security company doing about the same kind of work without so many rules."

She wasn't sure what that meant. Black ops stuff? Which, like the coal mining town, was more concept than reality to her.

"I'm sorry about your mom," she said.

"Thanks. I never knew her." His mouth curved up again. "The women on our block decided they were going to take her place. They were always looking out for me. It was like having twelve moms instead of one. Let me tell you, it was tough to be bad."

She laughed. "Which you wanted to be."

His gaze locked with hers. "Nearly all the time. But I learned patience. There were still opportunities, but I had to work for them."

A message? She held in a shiver and reminded herself he was good. Better than she was used to.

"What about you?" he asked. "Suburbs? Two-point-four siblings and a white picket fence?"

An easy question for most, she thought, the need to shiver fading as if it had never happened. Tension crept through her, but she ignored the tightening in her shoulders as she tried to calculate how much to tell. And how to tell it such that he didn't know she was lying.

"It was my dad and me, just like you," she said, confident their situations couldn't have been more different. "My mom left when I was young."

"That's rough."

She shrugged because the truth — that her mother had walked away from her only child, as well as her husband — was bad enough. Worse was the fact that the man had regularly beaten them both and with his wife gone, he'd only had one place to turn.

"It was L.A.," she said lightly. "I had distractions. And now we're both here. The people are very welcoming, if a little too involved in each other's lives."

"The disadvantage of a small town. There

aren't a lot of secrets."

She relaxed as he accepted the change in topic. Every new relationship had to navigate through that rocky space. The exchange of past information. It was done and they would move on.

"How does that work for you?" she asked.

"What do you mean?"

"You're a man of secrets."

He laughed. "Less than you would think. I go to work, hang out with my friends." Humor warmed his eyes. "I do live with a woman."

"So I've heard. Consuelo Ly. She's engaged."

"Damn. And here I thought I was going to rile you."

"It's a little early to play the jealousy card. Besides, you don't cheat." She took a sip of her wine and wished they were sitting closer. The evening would be more interesting without this table between them.

"How do you know that?"

"Am I wrong?"

"No."

She leaned closer. "You're not the type. In my book, with cheating comes shame. You wouldn't allow that emotion." She smiled. "My business partners are guys. We spend a lot of time with each other. Let's just say whatever I didn't know about your gender before we went into business I've since learned."

"Okay," he said slowly. "You're right. I don't cheat."

"How long were you married?" Because she'd heard that he had been. Not that it was easy getting information on Angel without admitting her interest. Something she hadn't been willing to do.

"Sixteen years."

Okay, that was unexpected. "A long time," she admitted. "What happened?"

"She died. A car accident."

Five simple words spoken in a matter-of-fact tone. But Taryn heard the pain behind the sentences. Felt the wound as if it had been inflicted on her.

"I'm sorry," she said automatically, even as she knew the phrase was ridiculous and unhelpful. "How long has it been?"

"Six years."

The way he spoke the words told her there was still emotion there. Still caring. She liked that he hadn't banished his wife to some back part of his memory.

"What about you?" he asked.

"I was married once. Briefly. To Jack."

One eyebrow rose. "Your business partner Jack?"

She nodded. "I left home after high school." A lie, but one she always told. No one had to know she'd run away at sixteen and lived on the streets. It had been tough and scary, and she'd made it through.

"After a year or two of dead-end jobs, I realized if I wanted to make something of myself, I needed to get an education. I worked my way through college and graduated when I was twenty-six."

With a ton of debt and a sense of pride she'd never experienced before.

"Good for you."

"Thanks." She glanced out at the horizon, watching the last of the light fade in the west. Stars had already appeared overhead. The air was cooler, but with the heaters, she stayed warm.

"I was lucky," she continued. "I got a PR job with the L.A. Stallions. I was broke and living in my car, but it was a chance to use my degree."

"Marketing?" he said with a laugh. "You studied marketing."

"I know. Not practical. I kept trying to talk myself into accounting. A solid and stable career. But I loved the creative side of business and I figured I might as well go for it. I waitressed at an all-night diner, went to class, studied and slept about four hours a night. When I got an internship, it was worse, but I didn't care. I knew what I wanted."

She'd thrown herself into her goals and told herself she would get a chance to sleep when she was thirty.

"My third day with the Stallions, Jack caught me eating the leftovers from some catered lunch they'd had." She'd been wrapping sandwiches meant for the garbage in napkins with the idea that they could easily be her meals for the next couple of days.

"He took pity on me and invited me out to dinner." She turned to Angel. "Dinner turned into breakfast. A few days later, I moved in with him."

She waited for the inevitable "Did you love him?" Because the few people who knew the story always asked that. She hadn't known Jack well enough to be sure how much she even liked him, but she'd been homeless and hungry and he was a good guy.

"He was a way out," Angel said quietly, surprising her with his insight. "Better than living in your car."

"He's a great guy. I know that now. But at the time . . ." She shrugged. "Yeah, it was better than living in my car." She paused. "Jack has a kind streak. Once he accepts you, you're in for life. He accepted me. Over the next couple of months, I discovered I really did like him a lot. Then I turned up pregnant."

She drew in a breath, hating how stupid that phrase always made her feel. She'd been careful, but not careful enough. When she'd realized what had happened, she'd been afraid he would think she was trying to trap him.

"So you got married."

"That weekend. We flew to Las Vegas. I tried to talk him out of it. No." She shook her head. "Actually I didn't. Not very hard. Part of me wanted to let him take care of me." Because no one ever had.

She was aware of talking too much, of saying too much, but somehow the words kept on coming.

"Two weeks later, I lost the baby."

It had happened so fast. She hadn't even absorbed the fact that there was a child and then it was gone. She'd gone to see her doctor, who'd confirmed the miscarriage.

"I filed for a divorce the next day," she continued. "Without a baby, there was no reason for us to stay together and I didn't want to take advantage of Jack. Only the Stallions didn't see it that way. All they knew was that their star quarterback was getting a divorce and that having his ex-wife around might make him uncomfortable, so I was fired."

"Hell of a week," Angel murmured.

And not her worst one, she thought. "Jack, being Jack, tried to talk them out of it. When that didn't work, he came to me and offered to be a silent partner in a new PR firm. I agreed and Score was born. A few years later, he brought Sam and Kenny on board and we've been together ever since."

They'd turned a business partnership into a family. No matter what, she and Jack would be there for each other. He hadn't been the great love of her life, but she cared for him more than she'd ever cared about anyone. No matter what, she would be there for Jack and he would there for her. In a way, that was better than romance, because she could depend on it.

Angel smiled at her. "You win. I can't top that story."

"You could tell me about the guy who slit your throat."

"He had a bad week, too. Enough on that. So what's your favorite business in town?"

He was changing the subject — something she was happy to have happen. She'd already said too much and couldn't figure out why. It certainly couldn't be the wine. She was on her first glass.

"I can't pick," she admitted. "I like them all. Favorite season?"

"Summer."

"Girls in bikinis?"

"I like running when it's warm."

"Running as in exercising outdoors on purpose?"

He chuckled. "That would be it, yes."

"My idea of hell."

"You work out in a gym."

"How do you know I work out at all?"

His gaze traveled over her body. "I'm not going to bother answering that."

"I do yoga, too," she murmured.

He chuckled. "Lucky me. Favorite James Bond actor?"

"Pierce Brosnan. James Bond movies should come with a wink. The new guy is too serious. I miss all the gadgets." She looked at him. "You, however, are old-school. Your favorite is Sean Connery."

"He is," Angel admitted, watching the last rays of sun play across Taryn's face. For a second they flashed on her sculpted cheek-bones and then the sun slipped below the horizon.

Lights had already come on around them, but even with them, she was mostly in shadow. Her pale skin gleamed while her dark eyes stayed mysterious.

He held in a chuckle, knowing he was acting like a sixteen-year-old on his first date with the prom queen. Horny and out of his league.

"I'm very much old-school," he said as she rose.

Before he could figure out what she was doing, she slipped off her jacket and hung it over the back of the chair. Whatever he'd been going to say next was lost when he took in her bare back and how the dress dipped low to her hips.

Her skin was smooth, her waist narrow. She settled back in the chair and angled toward him. What had been a tailored dress that hugged her curves had suddenly become so much more than that. His mouth went dry. Hunger boiled and sent blood flooding his groin.

"You're probably the kind of person who enjoys books rather than an e-reader," she said, picking up her wine again.

"I like how they feel in my hands," he said without thinking, his gaze still on her. "The smell of the paper. It's a tactile experience." He raised his gaze to hers. "Nicely played."

"Thank you." She gave him a measured look. "I like that you don't assume I'm easy."

70

"Any man who does that is a fool."

"The world is a foolish place."

"When was the last time you let a man take care of you?"

She paused and something flashed in her eyes. A memory, he would guess. But good or bad? He couldn't say.

"It's been a while. I don't trust easily. Just like you don't give up control."

"I can."

"When was the last time? Nineteen ninety-eight?"

She was teasing. The real answer was 1992. With Marie. But he wasn't going to talk about that.

He rose and walked around the table, then gently drew Taryn to her feet. He liked that they were nearly the same height.

"Love the shoes," he murmured. "Ridiculous but effective."

He put his hands on her shoulders, then lightly drew them down her arms. Every part of her appealed to him. His dick was more than willing, but the rest of him said it would be so much better to wait. Besides, he'd promised. For reasons he couldn't explain, he had a feeling not many men had kept their promises to Taryn. He wanted to make sure he kept his.

She raised her chin, as if challenging him.

He studied her mouth, the perfect shape, the lower lip slightly fuller than the top. He wanted to know how they would fit together when they kissed. How she would taste. He wanted to feel the steady pressure of need building until he had no choice but to guide them toward the inevitable end.

But not tonight.

He stepped to the side and picked up her jacket, then helped her into it. "It's late. Let me walk you to your car."

CHAPTER FOUR

Nothing had happened. Nothing!

The next morning Taryn was still doing her best to grasp that reality. She couldn't decide if Angel deserved extra kudos for leaving her standing there by her car without even a good-night kiss or if she should attack him with one of her high heels the next time she saw him. Yes, he'd told her he was good at waiting, but she hadn't expected him to be *that* good, damn him.

After a restless night, she was forced to use the heavy-duty concealer on the dark circles under her eyes, and it was all his fault. She'd tried to come up with all the things she *should* have said to him, along with imagining ignoring him when he tried to approach her later. Only she didn't want to ignore him, and even if she did, acting that way gave him too much power. She didn't want him thinking he got to her, although he did. Dating guys who were afraid of her was much, much simpler. Although she had to admit despite the lack of sleep, this was way more fun.

She dressed and drove to the office, where her exotic orchid was waiting for her on her desk. She checked the moisture level of the soil, as per the instructions, then turned on her computer and prepared to meet her day. While she waited for her computer to boot up, she checked her voice mail on her work phone. Nothing. And she'd already checked her cell that morning. Twice. The man hadn't called. He hadn't kissed her and now he wasn't phoning. She and Angel were going to have to have a serious conversation about the rules. He was supposed to try and she was supposed to say no. Everybody knew that. His ass-backward plan was really starting to get on her nerves.

Which was probably his strategy all along.

"I don't want to," Larissa said, a distinct whine in her voice.

"Do I look as if I care?" Taryn asked as she parked in front of Jo's Bar. One of the advantages of Fool's Gold during the workweek was that nearly everyone walked everywhere. So there was always convenient parking.

In theory the restaurant was only about a

quarter mile from the Score offices, but in her shoes, it might as well be fifty. Four-inch heels looked amazing but they were a bitch to walk in.

Today she was wearing black-lacquered Gucci pumps with three skinny straps across the top of her foot. Technically they had a five-inch heel, but there was a one-inch platform. They were elegant and simple, not to mention the perfect complement to her Roberto Cavalli reptile-print silk blazer. Underneath she had on a plain sheath dress.

Taryn loved clothes — probably because, until she was thirty, she'd never been able to afford anything that wasn't secondhand. Now she was making up for lost time. And she didn't care if everyone dressed casually in town. She didn't and people would have to get used to that.

Larissa continued to sit in the car. "I'm scared," she admitted. "What if no one likes me?"

Taryn angled toward her friend. "You know you're being silly," she said gently. "Everyone is going to love you. You're sweet and funny and a loyal friend. What's not to like?"

Instead of relaxing, Larissa glared at her. "You're being nice. What's wrong? Am I dying and don't know it?"

Taryn sighed. "You're not dying. I'm being supportive. I can be supportive."

"I know. It's not you. I really like this place and I want to fit in."

"You fit in way more than me, and I've made friends."

Larissa brightened at the thought. "You're right. I'm much nicer than you, too. Okay, let's go."

Taryn collected her Prada bag. "Just give me a second to bask in the warmth of your friendship," she muttered, then climbed out of her car.

When they were both on the sidewalk, Larissa glanced down at her jeans. She'd put a navy blazer over her pink T-shirt. Her blond hair was pulled back in its usual ponytail. "Am I dressed okay? You always look really nice."

"No one dresses up in this town except for me," Taryn assured her. "And the mayor, who is in her sixties. Besides, we're having lunch in a bar."

"I see. What's up with that? You don't like bars."

"That's because it took me two years to break the boys of the habit of having staff meetings in bars." Taryn gave Larissa a little push toward the door. "You'll see. This is different."

Taryn had resisted the first time she was invited to lunch at Jo's Bar. She hadn't understood why the women in town wouldn't want to go to a nice café or tea shop. But once she'd gone into the place, she understood the appeal.

She and Larissa walked into the open space and came to a stop while Larissa looked around. Taryn was already familiar with the mauve walls, flattering light and muted TVs turned to the Style network and HGTV.

There were tables along with booths, a list of specials on a chalkboard and quiet music playing in the background.

Larissa grinned. "Nice. Where do the guys hang out?"

"They have a room in the back. I've heard that at night this is more of a couples place, but during the day, the ladies rule."

She spotted Dellina, Isabel and Noelle sitting at a round table. "Over there," Taryn said, leading the way.

"Are they smiling?"

Taryn rolled her eyes. "You're a freak, you know that."

"Yeah, that's hardly news."

"Hi, all," Taryn said as she approached the table. "This is my friend Larissa. She works for Score. She's Jack's personal assistant and the boys' masseuse. While she's a wonderful person, don't agree to help her with any projects. Larissa was born to rescue the world. Seriously, if you let her, she'll talk you into helping her save some endangered leaf or raid an elementary school to help with a hamster rescue."

"I would never rescue hamsters from schoolkids," Larissa told her. "I trust them to care for their pets."

"So you say now." Taryn pointed to the table. "Dellina is an event planner. Noelle owns The Christmas Attic, an adorable store on Fourth Street. Everything Christmas, of course, but also seasonal gifty things. Shop there for your mother. Trust me, she'll love whatever you buy from Noelle. Isabel owns Paper Moon. It used to be a bridal gown shop. Now she also sells yummy clothes and I'm spending way too much money there."

All three women greeted Taryn and Larissa. Isabel pulled out the seat next to her.

"Taryn, your new suit is back from the tailor," Isabel told her. "Whenever you want to pick it up."

"Thanks." She settled in, then watched as Larissa sat across from her between Noelle and Dellina.

Last fall, when she'd first visited Fool's Gold, she was convinced she would hate living there. Nothing about a small town appealed to her. But now she had to admit, the place had grown on her. She'd made friends and settled into the comfortable rhythm of a life defined by which festival was next.

She'd always thought she preferred Los Angeles, where she could go about her business unnoticed. In Fool's Gold, there were no secrets. Which meant if something bad happened, someone would be there to get her through. While the realization was a little strange, it was also comforting.

"You need a redhead," Jo said, coming up to the table with menus.

Dellina leaned close to Taryn. "She's right. It's you and me against those three blondes."

"We can take them," Taryn told her confidently, then introduced Larissa to the owner of Jo's Bar.

After Jo explained about the specials, she took their drink orders and left.

Noelle put down her menu. "Okay," she said, smiling at Larissa. "We want to know your life story. We'll share ours, too. I'll go first. I moved here last year. I was a lawyer, which turned out to not be my thing. Now I run The Christmas Attic, like Taryn said. I'm married to Gabriel, who is a doctor here in town." She pointed at Dellina.

Dellina drew in a breath. "Me, huh? I'm the oldest in my family. I have younger twin sisters. One of my sisters is a chef. The other has a small business in town. A temp agency. As Taryn said, I plan events. There's no guy and while I wouldn't say no to a long weekend of hot sex, I have no interest in a relationship. I've already raised my two kids." At Taryn's questioning look, she continued. "We lost our folks when I was in high school."

"I'm sorry about your parents," Taryn said. "I hadn't heard that."

"It was a while ago."

"But still." Taryn knew what it was like to be on her own. "I work at Score, where I plan advertising campaigns and try to control my business partners, who are annoying."

"But you love them," Larissa said.

"I do." She held up both hands. "As brothers, I swear. Although I was married to Jack, briefly. Years ago."

Dellina, Isabel and Noelle all stared at her.

"What?" she asked. "It was a couple of months and it didn't work out. We stayed friends and now we work together."

"Did you know this?" Isabel asked Larissa.

"Sure. They're good friends. It's nice that

they still like each other."

"You get more interesting by the day," Isabel murmured. "Okay, me. I was born and raised in town. When I was fourteen, I had a mad crush on my sister's boyfriend. When they broke up, I was thrilled, only he left town to join the navy and I knew I was going to die. When that didn't happen, I started writing him. Flash-forward fourteen years, I came back, he came back and the rest is history." She sighed happily. "Now we're married and I can't believe how lucky I am."

Larissa glanced at them. "I guess that leaves me. I'm one of three girls, also the oldest. I like my job a lot because it gives me the time and resources to focus on helping others. Through Jack, I've gotten involved in organ donor programs and I also work with different animal rescue organizations."

"She's a saint," Taryn said. "I tell myself my genuine affection for her will offset any bad karma I might create on my own."

Isabel turned to Larissa and grinned. "So, you're a masseuse to the football players. What's that like?"

Taryn leaned back in her chair. She'd seen this before. Women were obsessed with the boys. Not only were they actually larger

81

than life, but there was the whole sports hero thing going on. Add to that the fact that they were good-looking and well-off . . . Attention was inevitable. The only question no one seemed to ask was why were they all single.

Taryn knew the answer for each of them, and she wasn't going to say a word. She loved her boys and she would keep their secrets.

Noelle sighed. "Really? Touching them like that."

"Need I remind both of you, you're happily married?" Taryn asked.

"I'm not interested *that* way," Isabel told her with an unrepentant grin. "Just curious. Ford's a former SEAL. I know about guys who work out regularly. Speaking as the woman who sleeps with him, I think being with him is very nice. But this is a whole different level of muscles."

"Exactly," Noelle said. "Our curiosity is purely intellectual."

Larissa laughed. "Sure it is." She thought for a second. "I don't know what to say. They were all professional athletes. They did things their bodies are not designed to do. They were all successful and they all pushed too hard and now there are injuries. I try to make them feel better."

Noelle sighed. "That's so sweet. Are they naked?"

Taryn grinned. "And here we are, to the real question." She looked at her new friends. "Yes, they are naked. They are very comfortable being naked. I can't tell you how many meetings we've had in the company locker room, or worse, the steam room."

She paused as three pairs of eyes widened. "I stay clothed," she added.

"That would be weird," Isabel admitted.

"You get used to it," Taryn told her.

Noelle looked at Larissa. "Yeah, for you, it's no big deal. You're a professional."

Larissa shook her head. "I'm not licensed, if that's what you mean. I took the classes, but I never bothered with the exam. I don't work with the public. I work on Sam, Kenny and Jack and sometimes Taryn."

Jo appeared with their drinks. When she left, Taryn reached for her iced tea. "I notice no one wants to talk about the thrill of seeing me naked."

"I'm sure you look great," Noelle said absently as she continued to talk to Larissa. "Is it weird to see them that way, then around the office?"

Isabel rolled her eyes. "Let's cut to the real question. Who has slept with whom?"

Dellina choked on her drink. "That's direct," she murmured when she could speak.

Noelle looked at her. "A genuine 'it went down the wrong way' or are you keeping secrets?"

Dellina held up a hand. "It went down the wrong way. Although the body talk is fun."

Taryn was less sure. The great bodies were nice, but in her opinion it was what a man could do with that body that was more appealing.

"They're sweet guys," Larissa told her. "But we're like a family. We don't get involved like that. The guys are always bringing around girls."

"Not Sam," Taryn said.

Larissa nodded. "That's right. Sam is more careful. Of course he has the worst luck with women."

Dellina, who had just taken another sip of her soda, started coughing again. "Allergies," she managed, when she could talk. "What are you talking about? What worst luck?"

Larissa sighed. "It's kind of sad, when you think about it."

"And funny," Taryn added.

"Okay, funny. But not in a mean way."

Larissa drew a breath. "Sam seems to find the one woman in the room who's going to be a disaster. His ex-wife wrote a tell-all about their marriage."

Noelle winced. "Seriously?"

"Uh-huh. There have been stalkers and, oh, do you remember the girl who pretended to be pregnant?"

Taryn nodded.

"I feel bad for him," Larissa admitted. "He's a great guy, but he's been burned a bunch of times. Now he refuses to get involved at all. His family doesn't help."

"They're not into boundaries," Taryn said simply, thinking it was time to change the subject. "So, what's new in town? Any hot gossip?"

Jo appeared with chips and salsa, along with a bowl of guacamole. "On the house," she said with a smile. "Because of the new girl."

Larissa blinked at her. "Thank you. That's so nice."

"Yeah, I'm a nice person. Don't let anyone tell you otherwise."

Taryn eyed the chips and felt her stomach growl. Fine. She would add fifteen minutes to her workout that afternoon. Fifteen ugly minutes of gross sweating would be worth it if she could indulge a little.

"Gossip," Isabel said as she grabbed a chip. "Mayor Marsha's assistant is leaving, so she'll be hiring a new one. That is going to be so weird. Marjorie has worked for the mayor for years. Since maybe high school or something."

"I wonder who the new assistant will be," Dellina said, then chuckled. "I'll tell Fayrene. She's the sister with the temp agency. I'm sure she'll offer to fill in during the interview process."

"I need her number," Taryn said. "We sometimes need help with big projects at Score."

"I have a card right here," Dellina told her, and reached into her bag.

"Mayor Marsha is going on vacation," Noelle said, scooping up guacamole. "She was in the other day and bought a couple of things for —"

Both Isabel and Dellina stared at her.

"What?" Noelle asked, visibly shrinking in her seat. "What did I say?"

"The mayor's going on vacation?" Dellina demanded.

"She never goes on vacation," Isabel added. "I mean never."

Taryn didn't get the problem. "Isn't she allowed? From what I've seen, she works pretty hard for the town. Going away might do her good."

Dellina and Isabel exchanged a look. "Maybe," Isabel admitted. "But it's weird. Like she might never come back."

Larissa looked as confused as Taryn felt. "Does she have a husband?"

"She's a widow."

Taryn reached for another chip. "Maybe she has a mysterious, handsome man she travels with," she teased.

Isabel's eyes widened. "Mayor Marsha with a secret lover?"

Noelle shook her head. "Okay, I'm kind of with you on that one. While I want her to be happy, it's kind of strange to think about."

"We should all be so lucky when we're her age," Taryn said firmly. "I vote for the secret lover story. The mayor has earned it."

"Troublemaker," Dellina grumbled.

"You know it."

Taryn was naked. Angel stared at her and felt the breath leave his body. Good thing because that made room for more hot blood to fill his groin. She was tall and leggy and totally naked, with her long hair covering her breasts and hard nipples playing peekaboo with him. And speaking of hard —

"Get up."

87

"I am up," he mumbled only to realize the slightly crabby voice wasn't coming from the vision in front of him but was instead at the periphery of his consciousness. Nor was the voice in question talking about *up* in the sense that he meant it.

He sat up instantly. But even in his newly awake state, he had the sense to make sure the sheets were covering his now painful erection.

Consuelo stood in the doorway of his bedroom. The hall light was on and she was already dressed. He glanced at the clock and saw it was a few minutes to six.

"Why are you awake so early?" he asked.

"We have to be somewhere."

"Where?"

"A basketball game. At Score. It's the PR agency with the football —"

"I know what it is," he said, willing his penis to calm down. There was no way he could stand with Consuelo in the room. She wasn't the type to pretend to ignore it, and he didn't want to take the ribbing.

"You're crabby," she told him. "We're leaving in five minutes. Be ready."

"Yeah, yeah."

He waited until she walked out of the room and closed the door before standing. He pulled on sweats and a T-shirt and then got socks and athletic shoes. Five minutes later, he was presentable in all ways possible and headed out the door.

It was still dark outside, but first rays of light were visible over the mountains. Consuelo stood by her truck, her keys dangling from her fingers. He noticed she'd removed her engagement ring.

"Hey," he said, pausing by the passenger door. "You two set the date yet?"

"Do you want me to start the day by killing you? Because I can."

Her tough talk didn't bother him. He knew the cause. He grabbed her around the shoulders, then twisted her until he had her in a headlock. He wasn't trying that hard and she could have broken free at any second, but she didn't. Instead she leaned into him.

"Don't be scared," he said quickly. "Kent's lucky to have you."

Consuelo shrugged free of his hold and stared at him. "What if I don't know how to be what he wants?"

"Dollface, you're his fantasy."

"Fantasies change."

"He's not going to change his mind. He loves you."

Under any other circumstances he would have added something like "God knows why." But she was vulnerable and he wouldn't tease her when she was down.

"Yeah," she said, not sounding convinced. "I guess."

He pulled her close. She stepped into his embrace. He rested his chin on the top of her head. "Look at it this way. If he does change his mind, you can kill him and I'll help you hide the body."

She chuckled. "Deal."

They drove to Score. On the way, Angel briefly wondered if he would see Taryn, only to realize she wasn't exactly the organized sports type. He'd seen enough of her to know that she had to work out, but in a clean, civilized way. An elliptical, he would guess. Maybe some free weights. Probably pink and with a designer label.

The image made him smile. Yeah, that was Taryn. Not fussy, he thought. Perfect. What he would give to see her with a little mud on her cheeks. Or naked. Naked worked for him.

They pulled up in front of the offices, then Consuelo made a U-turn. Angel saw the full-sized basketball court and the guys waiting.

Ford and Justice were his business partners. He'd met Jack and Kenny around town and knew Sam by sight. Also joining the game were Ryan Patterson, a local engineer, Raoul Moreno and Josh Golden. Which meant they had a full team.

"Hey," he said as he and Consuelo walked onto the court.

They greeted each other and shook hands. He half expected a comment about the *girl*, but her reputation seemed to have preceded her.

Jack stepped into the middle of the group. "Let's divide up into teams and see who gets their asses handed to them. Sam?"

Sam stepped forward with a cloth bag in his hand. "We'll draw chips. Consuelo's team is shirts."

Kenny grinned. "Am I the only one who wanted her on skins?"

Angel prepared to get between them, knowing Consuelo was more than capable of doing permanent damage to the man. It didn't matter that Kenny was more than a foot taller and at least a hundred pounds of muscle heavier. She could have him on the ground and screaming in a heartbeat.

But she only raised an eyebrow and murmured, "In your dreams, rookie."

The guys all laughed, then reached for the bag to pull chips.

Two minutes later, they were sorted into teams. Angel pulled off his shirt and told

Kenny, Raoul and Sam to stay clear of Consuelo. "She'll play to win and she plays dirty."

Justice, also on their team, nodded. "He's not kidding. Don't let her size fool you."

Jack took a basketball out of a bin on the court and tossed it in the air. "Let's play ball."

The game started hard and fast and continued that way. Angel hadn't played in a couple of years and found the stop-start of the game got his heart rate going. Nearly as fun as a run straight up the mountain, he thought, as he stole the ball from Ford and passed it to Sam, who scored.

The sun rose overhead. While the early morning was still cool, they were all soon sweating and swearing. Good thing the court was in a more industrial part of town, Angel thought humorously as Jack let loose a string of curse words that had Consuelo wagging her finger at him.

"You kiss your mama with that mouth?" she asked.

"Funny." He tossed her the ball.

Angel turned, prepared to go after him. Just then Kenny gave a wolf whistle, then yelled, "Looking good, Taryn."

Even as he told himself to focus on the game, he couldn't help looking. Taryn was across the street, walking from the parking lot to the Score building. She wore a pale blue suit that hugged her body the way he wanted to. Her legs were long and bare, and she had on yet another pair of ridiculously high heels. These were beige with a white heel and screamed *Come fuck me.* How was he supposed to resist that?

Her hair hung down her back. She had a purse dangling off her forearm and a brief-case in her other hand. Keys jingled. She looked powerful, sexy and —

Something hard banged into the side of his head. He turned and saw Ford grinning at him as the basketball bounced away.

"Sorry, man," Ford said, obviously not the least bit sorry. "I thought you were paying attention."

Angel gave him the finger, then went after the ball. When he next looked across the street, Taryn was gone and the day seemed just a little less bright.

CHAPTER FIVE

Taryn glanced up at the screen on the wall, then frowned. Normally she had one of her staff work on her PowerPoint slides, but she hadn't been happy with this presentation from the beginning and was determined to get it right. After three tries from the graphic folks, she was tweaking it herself. What she didn't understand was how what looked perfectly fine on her computer suddenly seemed to have less pop on the giant wall screen. Of course if it was a size issue, she should ask one of the boys, she thought with a grin. As men, they would be more sensitive to the topic.

"What's so funny?"

She looked up and saw Sam had walked into the conference room. "Trying to get a presentation right," she told him.

He glanced at the chart on the wall. "I fail to see the humor."

She pressed her lips together rather than

tease him by saying he usually did. In truth Sam had a good sense of humor. But right now he was frowning his "something isn't right" frown.

"What's up?" she asked as she rose and walked toward him.

He glanced down at her bare feet. "Why do you wear those shoes if they're so uncomfortable?"

Because once again she'd kicked off her heels as soon as she'd gotten to her office. "They have a six-inch heel. Even with a one-and-a-half-inch platform, they're hardly something I can wear all day."

"Then why buy them?"

She rested her palm against the side of his face. "Did you see them? They're works of art. Prada bicolor peep-toe pumps. They're suede. Somewhere right now a poem is being written to those shoes."

"But you can't walk in them."

"You can't have sex with Miss April, but that doesn't stop you from buying *Playboy.*"

Sam took her hand in his and lightly kissed her palm. "I haven't bought *Playboy* since I was nineteen. You're a very strange woman and I don't understand your shoe obsession."

She smiled. "But that's not why you want to talk to me."

"No, it's not."

Sam crossed to the glass door of the conference room and looked into the hall. Taryn didn't think he was watching for anything in particular. Obviously whatever he had to say was difficult for him. With Sam, it could be anything. Jack tended to tell her everything, and Kenny shared the normal amount, but Sam often kept things to himself.

"How was the game this morning?" she asked, both to help him relax and also because there was an off chance he might mention Angel, and she would like that.

She'd been so careful not to stare while walking into the building. But once inside, she'd positioned herself so she could see the game. Angel had played well and the man looked good in shorts and nothing else. It was enough to give a girl ideas.

"Good. Intense. Have you met Consuelo?"

Taryn nodded. "Yes. I know who she is."

"Plays a hell of a game." He grinned. "I want her on my team all the time."

Taryn had a feeling that if Sam asked, Consuelo would say yes, even if she *were* engaged. As a rule, women liked Sam. He was quiet but intense. Handsome. For those who found big men intimidating or just too bulky, Sam was the perfect combination of lean and muscled.

Taryn knew the basics of his past. How he'd grown up in a close, athletic family. His father had played professional basketball in the late 1970s and early 1980s. Sam's mother had been an Olympic equestrian. His sisters had excelled at sports, but Sam, the youngest, had been sick as a kid. Sick enough that he never got to do anything.

He hadn't blossomed until college, when he'd discovered he could kick a football better than nearly anyone else. She'd often wondered if the transition from nerdy to hunky had been difficult. With the sudden availability of all kinds of women had come the issue of trusting them. Something Sam had learned the hard way he couldn't always do.

Now she studied him before asking, "Are you seeing anyone?"

He glared at her. "What? No. And I'm not talking about it."

He was nothing if not private, she thought. "Don't bite my head off. I was just asking. It's been a while. Unless you were seeing someone and didn't want us to know."

"Yeah, because that went so well last time," he muttered.

He had a point there. In his previous

relationship Sam had been determined not to let anyone know he had a woman in his life. Unfortunately he'd kept so quiet, not even Kenny and Jack had known. So when the woman in question had come on to them, they'd seen no reason to refuse her invitation. Individually, of course. It was only later they'd discovered they'd inadvertently slept with their best friend's girl.

Sam had dumped her as soon as he found out and had accepted his friends' apologies. But since then, he'd stopped seeing anyone. Taryn understood why but believed Sam needed to get over it. When he wasn't in a relationship, he could get solitary and moody.

"Everything okay with the business?" she asked.

"Fine. We have a good client base and they mostly pay on time." He drew in a breath. "About the client party," he began.

"What? I thought I made my position clear. You three decided to have a big party. I didn't want to. I'll be there, I'll smile and I'll look pretty, but that's it."

Sam held up both hands. "You've said that before. I'm saying I need help. It's a big event to plan. I need some recommendations for someone to help me. And not Dellina."

98

"Why not Dellina? She's great. And suck it up, big guy — she's the only one in town who's qualified. Look, Sam, I don't know what your deal is with her, but she does good work. We have to support the local businesses so we can fit in."

"Since when do you care about fitting in?"

"Since always. PR is our business. Town support is a big deal. Bringing in someone from outside would be a mistake and you know it." She put her hands on her hips. "She's capable — parties like this are exactly what she does. What is your problem with her?"

"It's complicated."

"Then uncomplicate it. If you won't tell me what's wrong, I can't help. Which means this is now your problem and you need to solve it."

His jaw tightened. "This isn't you at your most supportive."

"Do I look like I care?"

He surprised her by smiling. "That's the thing, Taryn. You always care. Unfortunately right now you're being a pain in my ass."

"Then my work here is done."

Angel arrived at City Hall five minutes before the Grove Keepers' meeting. He'd meant to do a little research online beforehand — find out about the organization and who was in charge. But a last-minute redo of an obstacle course had kept him busy for the past couple of days. Still, he knew he would pick up what he needed in plenty of time for his first grove meeting.

For a second he hesitated, thinking about what it would be like to work with the boys. Would they remind him of Marcus? Despite the time that had passed, he thought about his son every day. Missed him every day. Sometimes the memories were easy and sometimes they were hard, but they were always there.

Marcus would approve of this, he reminded himself. He'd liked hanging out with his friends.

Angel took the stairs two at a time and headed for the conference room on the second floor. He walked in and found most of the chairs around the long table were already full. Of women.

Angel paused in the doorway as he worked the problem. It made sense that moms would want to get involved with their sons, he thought. They were the traditional caretakers of the family. But shouldn't there be a few dads in the mix, too?

It wasn't that he didn't like women. They were great. His wife had been a woman. But this was different. Teenaged boys needed a male role model.

A woman in her fifties walked up to him and smiled. "Hello, Angel."

It took him a second to recognize Denise Hendrix — Ford's mother. He'd had dinner at her house a few times since moving to town last year. She was friendly and well loved by her six children.

"Mrs. Hendrix," he said. "Nice to see you."

She shook her head. "Please, don't call me Mrs. Hendrix. That makes me sound older than I already am. I'm Denise."

"Sure." He glanced around the room. "You have an FWM grove?"

"Not exactly. I'm the head of the Grove Council. Thank you so much for volunteering. We're all very excited to have you aboard. Fresh blood and all that. We were afraid we'd lose you to the Boy Scouts, but we didn't and we're thrilled."

She guided him over to one of the empty chairs and started introducing him to everyone. He nodded and put names with faces, then took his seat.

Even as he settled in his chair, he felt a prickling sensation on the back of his neck. Something was wrong. Denise's mention of the Boy Scouts had confused him. Why would there be the FWM to help young men grow up when they could join the Boy Scouts instead? Was Fool's Gold really big enough to support both organizations? Or had he misunderstood what the mayor had been telling him?

Denise took her place at the head of the table and started passing out thick notebooks. As she placed one in front of him, Angel was painfully aware of the fact that not only was it pink but the lettering across the front proclaimed the motto of the FWM.

Growing Our Girls into Capable Young Women.

He swore silently. Girls? He couldn't take care of a grove of girls. He'd never had a daughter, and what he knew about women wasn't exactly helpful to anyone.

Denise walked back to the head of the table and faced the group. "Thank you all for coming today. As you know, Marjorie has run the Grove Council for several years now and has done an excellent job."

Angel saw Mayor Marsha's assistant sitting near the front of the table. She waved when her name was mentioned. While she was still obviously upset, she wasn't currently crying, which Angel appreciated.

"With her moving to Portland, there was

an opening on the council," Denise continued. "All three of my girls were once members of FWM." She smiled. "Although it was a long time ago, I still remember their excitement as they grew from Acorns to Mighty Oaks. FWM was a positive influence on them in so many ways. So when I was asked to take over Marjorie's position on the council, I said yes."

Everyone applauded. Angel joined in. To be honest, it didn't matter who was in charge. Not when he'd just learned he was going to be responsible for *girls.* What happened to the teenaged boys? That he could handle.

"Angel, you're going to be starting with our newest girls," Denise said with a smile. "You can figure it out together. I think that always works best. While your commitment is year to year, I hope we can count on you to stay with your grove until they, too, are Mighty Oaks."

All the women in the room were staring at him, nodding and mostly smiling. A few looked doubtful, which made sense. He was doubtful, too. Or screwed. It kind of depended on how he looked at things.

Denise went through the rest of the "growing season." The other groves had started in September. Only his would have a short season to get them used to the program. She mentioned a few all-grove events, then answered questions.

Angel tuned out the conversation and reached for the notebook. The *pink* notebook. He flipped it open and scanned the table of contents. There were sections on each level of the FWM along with subheadings.

He read the mission statement, then discovered that the Future Warriors of the Máa-zib marked their progress by earning small wooden beads after studying different areas of life. Some lessons were practical like learning knots and reading maps. Some were related to community. His girls were expected to take on a short-term civic project. There were also beads for family and friendship.

He kept turning pages and saw there were girlie activities like face painting. He wondered if there was a bead for style and if he could get Taryn to be a guest speaker.

He could do this, he told himself. Maybe just for the couple of months required for this season. Then he would explain to Denise and the mayor that he wasn't an FWM kind of guy. No way he could take his grove through —

He turned the page and came to a stop.

He swore silently, then began to look for an exit. Holy shit. There was a bead for the feminine cycle. What had the mayor been thinking when she'd suggested this was where he should volunteer? Was the old woman starting to lose her marbles? He couldn't talk to a bunch of — he checked which year that happened in and did the math — ten-year-olds about menstruation.

He carefully closed the notebook and stayed in his seat. When the meeting broke up, he headed directly for Denise. He waited until the other women had left, then faced Ford's mother.

"I can't do this," he said, putting his notebook down in front of her. "I'm not the right person for the job."

She surprised him by smiling. "Done in by the feminine cycle?"

He felt himself flush. "Look, I've faced a lot in my life. There are things I know, things I've done. Camping, sure. Knots and map reading, I'm good. But the rest of it? No way. These are little girls. They need a woman. Or at least a man with a daughter."

Denise's mouth straightened. "Angel, I understand your fear." She paused. "All right, I don't, but I believe it's real to you."

Talk about not being very supportive, he thought grimly.

"Most of the girls who have signed up for FWM this year come from either broken homes or they have suffered some kind of loss. While I want to believe nothing bad ever happens in Fool's Gold, that's not true. Mayor Marsha and I talked about this at length. We believe you're the right man for the job."

She put her hand on his forearm. "You said you'd take this on and I'm going to hold you to your commitment. Not only do I think it will be good for you, but there isn't anyone else I can get at such short notice. Please take the grove through this first short season. If at the end of that you want to be done, you can walk away."

He hesitated, torn by guilt. He *had* given his word, dammit. "Fine. Two months and then I'm done."

"We'll discuss that when the time comes." She pulled an index card out of her handbag. "In the meantime we've come up with what we think will be an excellent civic project for your girls. Max Thurman runs K9Rx Therapy Dog Kennels just outside town. Have you heard of it?"

He nodded slowly. "Dogs that visit sick people. Stuff like that."

"It's slightly more complicated, but that's close enough. Max has a new litter of puppies that need to be socialized. I think seven-year-old girls are perfect for the job. My daughter Montana works for Max. She'll be in touch with you to set up the schedule."

She rattled off a few more bits of information. Angel made note of them on his phone, then, when they were done, grabbed his pink notebook and escaped.

He walked out into the afternoon and told himself it was way too early to get drunk.

Girls. He was going to be responsible for seven-year-old girls. He paused by the curb and stared at his motorcycle. He rode a Harley. What if there were trips with the girls and he was expected to drive? People could die in a car accident. His scarred heart was living proof. He swore again, this time loudly and with emphasis.

He pulled his cell phone out of his pocket and pushed a couple of buttons.

"It's me. What's your afternoon like?"

He waited for Consuelo to tell him she was too busy to bother with him, but she surprised him by pausing and saying, "What's wrong?"

"Nothing. Everything. I'm screwed."

"What do you need?"

He stared at the Harley. He loved riding it. Loved the feel of the wind, the speed.

The sense of freedom.

"I need to buy a car."

"What?"

"I need something safe. That holds a lot of people. Like an SUV." Or a minivan. Only he couldn't even say the word. "One of those three-row ones."

He could feel the walls of life closing in on him.

"Do I want to know why?" Consuelo asked.

"No."

"Okay. See you at home in fifteen minutes."

Taryn stared at the simple dark chocolate truffle that had been delivered to her office, along with a note. There was a restaurant name and a time. No signature, no greeting. Just Henri's and seven o'clock. Either Angel was showing that he was into making an effort or he really didn't like to pick up the phone.

Before she could decide, Kenny and Jack walked in. Kenny dropped a massive backpack onto her desk and grinned.

"You're back," she said, stating the obvious.

"We are back and we're the best," Kenny told her.

Jack sat on the corner of her desk and shrugged. "We can't help it," he said modestly. "We're simply that good."

"Lucky me."

Jack and Kenny had been in Los Angeles for the meeting with the owner of Living Life at a Run.

"So your conversation went well?" she asked.

"You know it. You're going to love Cole," Jack said as he slapped the top of the pack and grinned. "And he's going to love you."

Kenny nodded enthusiastically. "We talked sports, of course. He's a football fan."

"Who isn't?" Taryn asked, trying not to look at the jumbo backpack taking up most of her desk. It was huge and very black. There were poles on one side. If she didn't know better, she would think they went against the body — maybe to distribute the weight more evenly. A horrifying thought.

But the LL@R logo was facing her, so it was unlikely *that* part went against your back. Besides, if it didn't face out, how would you open it? Still, she wasn't sure she was excited about wearing something so heavy that it needed weight-distribution engineering built into its design.

"He skis," Kenny added, sounding impressed. "He knows Kipling Gilmore."

Taryn had learned long ago that it was easier to fit in with her business partners than to fight the inevitable. Besides, there were three of them and only one of her. So she'd learned the language of sports. She could intelligently discuss nearly every game played with a ball or even a puck. She understood which had innings, quarters and periods. Every year she sat with the boys during the NFL draft and listened to them tell what it had been like for them when they'd gone through it. Which meant she knew exactly who Kipling Gilmore was.

Kipling Gilmore was an American skier who had dominated at the Olympics. He'd taken the gold in both the Super-G and the combined events.

"I'm sure they're brushing each other's hair even as we speak," she said.

Kenny shook his head. "Why aren't you impressed by sports celebrities?"

"Because I have you and Sam and Jack already. What could be better?"

"Good answer," Jack told her, and patted the backpack again. "Cole's excited about our meeting. The plan is for us to do an introductory presentation. Then we go camping for the weekend, followed by a more detailed discussion of what we could do for him."

Taryn nodded. This wasn't the first time a client had made that sort of a request. Many of them wanted to be sure the PR firm understood the product. They'd had a great time in Cabo with a client who made tequila. She had a feeling that for her, camping equipment and sports gear wouldn't be as fun. Not that she would get that intimately involved.

She was about to tell them to have a good time when she noticed how Kenny and Jack were looking at everything but each other. And her.

"What?" she demanded. "What aren't you telling me?"

Kenny nudged Jack. "You do it."

"You said you would."

"You were married to her."

Jack sighed. "Chicken."

"I'm good with that," Kenny admitted, then smiled at her. "Jack has something to tell you."

Taryn didn't like the tone of this conversation. "I've guessed that." She looked at Jack and raised her eyebrows. "Yes?"

"Cole wants us to take a weekend trip with him."

She nodded.

"All of us."

"Sure. You, Kenny and Sam." She paused

as his gaze stayed locked on her face, then stood up and stepped behind her chair. Not to mention away from the backpack. "No."

"Taryn, you're a partner in the firm. He said all the partners. It's only for a couple of days."

"It's camping. Outdoors. On purpose. It's one thing if you crash your car and end up in a ravine. That could happen to anyone. Then sleeping outside until you're rescued is no big deal. Because you can't help it. But this is on purpose. In dirt."

"We'd go to a campsite," Kenny added quickly. "With bathrooms."

Jack elbowed him. Kenny winced. "Okay, not the running-water kind."

"That's disgusting. You can pee standing up. That's not an option for me."

She didn't do the outdoors. Didn't like it. When she needed to commune with nature, she dined alfresco. Or bought a plant. Her most athletic project to date was planning how her walled-in garden was going to look. So far it was all on paper. She had yet to touch actual soil.

"Have you seen my shoes? Do I look like a camper to you?"

Jack walked around her desk and approached her. He put his large hands on her shoulders and stared into her eyes.

"Taryn, this is a big account. Not so much in size but in opportunity. We've worked the distribution side of things, but we've never made it in the retail world. This is our way in. It's one weekend of camping. We'll all be there with you. This is important to all of us."

She looked at him and knew he was right. About all of it. She sighed. "I'll do it."

"Really?" Kenny sounded surprised. "That's great. We can help you prepare, if you want."

"No, thanks. I'll take care of that end of things."

No way she wanted the guys watching her struggle to learn whatever it was she needed to know to camp. It was hard enough keeping them all in line without giving them that much ammunition. Besides, she thought, remembering a pair of broad shoulders and cool gray eyes, she had resources.

"You won't regret this," Jack told her with a grin. "It's going to be great. We'll get the account and then there's no stopping us."

He and Kenny headed out of her office. When he was in the doorway, Jack turned back and pointed to the pack. "You can keep that," he said graciously. "It's got everything you're going to need for our weekend."

"Great."

She waited until they left before moving toward her desk. She poked the backpack, then went to pick it up. It didn't budge.

She tried again, this time using two hands, and was barely able to lift it off the desk.

"Very funny," she muttered, unfastening the clasp. No doubt Kenny and Jack had put rocks or bricks inside, just to mess with her.

But when she flipped open the top, all she saw was stuff that looked a lot like camping gear. Not that she'd experienced it in person, but she'd seen pictures.

She tried to lift the pack a third time and not only broke a nail but felt a sharp pain in her shoulders.

"This," she murmured to the empty room, "is going to be a problem."

CHAPTER SIX

Henri's was a five-star restaurant tucked into the grandeur that was the Gold Rush Ski Lodge and Resort. A name that made Taryn wince. Whatever had the owners been thinking? The name was so long that it would always look awkward on signage, and she would guess their business cards were a cluttered mess. When it came to names, less was more. Still, not her rock to carry, she told herself as she stepped out of her car and handed the keys to the valet. Her rock was an oversize backpack still sitting on her desk.

She started toward the building, but before taking a step, she paused. A slight shiver tiptoed up her spine. It wasn't a familiar sensation, but it got her attention. If she didn't know better, she would swear that she was being stalked. Or at the very least, watched. She turned and saw a black SUV had pulled in behind her car.

The windows were tinted, so she couldn't see the driver. Had it been any other vehicle, she would have assumed it was Angel. As much as she would never admit it, he seemed to be the only man who had ever had the power to make her quiver with just a look. Only she'd seen what he drove, and the large, loud, *aggressive* Harley he favored had nothing in common with the Chevy Traverse in front of her.

She was about to head into the hotel when she hesitated a fraction of a second. Then she saw the driver and blinked in surprise. It *was* Angel. Once again dressed in black and looking very man-about-town.

She waited until he joined her, then glanced back at the SUV being driven away.

"Unexpected," she said.

"Long story. I'll tell you over dinner."

"Don't tell me you sold the Harley."

"Never. I still have it."

He took her hand in his and looked her over carefully. She struck a model's pose, then half turned so he could see the back.

She'd bought the dress the previous year, but it was still one of her favorites. A Halston Heritage white knit sheath, with black panels along the side and a black band at the jewel neckline. She'd kept her jewelry simple with gold-and-onyx earrings and a gold link bracelet from Tiffany.

Her shoes were one of her favorites. A Jimmy Choo Vero pump. The front was white, the back was black and there was a gold trim that swept across the top of the shoes before looping around to the back.

"Damn," Angel said. "You don't mess around."

"What?" she asked, glancing down at her dress. "This is casual."

He gave her a slow, knowing smile. "Naked is casual. This is a show."

"Then I hope you're entertained."

"More than you know."

He released her fingers, then placed his palm on the small of her back. "Shall we?"

They walked through the lobby to the rear of the hotel where Henri's was located. It was a restaurant to go to for ambience and food, not the view, Taryn thought as they were shown to a booth in a back corner.

The space was subtly lit with soft music and the kind of waitstaff that prided itself on excellent service.

Once they were seated, a forty-something woman took their drink orders before disappearing as quietly as she'd arrived.

Taryn leaned back in the booth and crossed her legs. The one disadvantage of her dress was that it tended to ride up a little if she wasn't careful. Although tonight that might be a good thing. Angel played the game well. Maybe too well. She had expected to be the one in charge.

Which was the problem, she thought. If she was in charge, she had trouble being interested. She was the boss during the day. She didn't want that same role at night. But giving up control left her feeling vulnerable and uncomfortable, so she avoided relationships where the man wanted control. Probably why she was thirty-four and had never been in love. The emotion required too much of her.

"That's a lot of thinking," Angel said, his cool gray eyes studying her face.

"I'm working things out." She tilted her head. "Explain the SUV."

He surprised her by sighing deeply. "You know that old saying 'no good deed goes unpunished'?"

She nodded.

"A couple of weeks ago I talked to Mayor Marsha about getting involved in town. I wanted a volunteer activity."

And the surprises kept on coming, Taryn thought.

Angel's expression turned sheepish. "It's how I was raised. Small town, people took care of each other. Once I knew I was staying here, I wanted to be helping people. She suggested the Future Warriors of the Máa-zib."

Taryn laughed. "Future what? Are you serious? Is this weapons training for teen-aged boys?"

"I wish. I figured it was a program for young men." He hesitated for a second, making her think there was something he wasn't telling her, but then he continued. "There are stages. Acorns, Sprouts and so on up to Mighty Oaks. The adult is called a Grove Keeper."

Angel was a big, scary guy. He had scars and secrets and he was the last person she could imagine volunteering to work with children. The fact that he had done so made her even more interested in him.

"Good for you. So what's the problem? I can't imagine you being worried about a bunch of unruly boys."

Angel shifted on his seat. "They're not boys. They're girls. Little girls. My Acorns are seven-year-old girls. They earn beads for activities. The keeper handbook is pink." He began to speak faster and the tone of his voice tightened. "They're supposed to learn regular stuff like knots and map reading, but there are also beads for face painting and families and . . ." He paused, then shuddered. "The feminine cycle."

Taryn was relieved their drinks hadn't arrived yet, because if she'd been drinking, she knew she would have started to choke. As it was, laughter spilled out of her. "The feminine cycle?"

He glared at her. "It's not funny."

"Oh yeah. It is."

"We don't talk about the cycle this year."

"Good, because seven seems a touch early. So you're a Grove Keeper."

Their server arrived with a vodka martini for her and a Scotch for him. She asked if they would like more time before ordering. Taryn nodded through bursts of laughter.

"I tried to get out of it," Angel admitted when they were alone. "What the hell was Mayor Marsha thinking? I don't know anything about little girls. I'm in over my head. Denise Hendrix is in charge of the council. The first season is only two months and she wants me to see it through. Then I can quit and they'll find someone else for the girls."

"So it's only for two months. That's something."

He glared at her. "I'm not a bead kind of guy."

She lightly stroked his upper arm, mentally giving herself a moment to enjoy the warm skin over impressive muscle. "You'll be fine. They're just little girls."

"Easy for you to say. You used to be one."

Physically, Taryn thought. She'd been a child. But emotionally, she'd never been young. She hadn't had the chance. In her house, being vulnerable meant dangerous things. She'd grown up fast and had learned the value of remaining invisible as much as possible.

But that wasn't Angel's problem and it wasn't as if she was going to tell him about her past. No one knew about her father — not even Jack.

He reached for his Scotch, then put it down. "That's why I got the SUV. In case I have to drive them somewhere."

"Your Acorns?" she asked, her voice teasing.

"I can't stick one on the back of a Harley. I went online and checked out safety ratings. The Traverse scores high and it seats eight."

"You sound like a soccer mom."

"Go ahead. Kick me when I'm down."

His concern was sweet, she thought. A depth she wouldn't have expected. He was —

A thought popped into her mind. A crazy one that was so unexpected it might work

121

for both of them.

She angled toward him. "Jack and Kenny are wooing a new client," she told him. "Living Life at a Run. They're a smaller version of REI. More equipment than clothes, but a nice get for us. We've never been big in retail."

"Congratulations."

"We don't have them yet, but if we can get them, it would be great. The owner is a big outdoor guy. He's insisting on a camping weekend with the principals of the company before signing on the dotted line."

Angel's gaze locked on her face. "Camping?"

She nodded.

"You?"

"I know. It's not my thing."

He chuckled. "Wait until he gets a look at your shoes."

"I know I won't wear heels camping."

"How much else do you know?"

"Next to nothing. But you're a big outdoor guy."

One of his eyebrows rose. "You want to go camping?"

"No, I want to offer you a deal."

His hand moved from the table to her bare knee with lightning speed. She felt the warmth of his skin on hers, along with a distinct clenching between her thighs. And this was all without him even trying. Imagine how much trouble she would be in if he put a little back into it.

She knew she had to clear her throat before she could speak. Rather than let him know how he affected her, she took a sip of her martini, then gave a little cough.

"I'll help you with the Acorns and you help me get proficient enough with the outdoors so I can fake my way through a camping weekend," she said.

"Done."

She laughed. "You don't want to think about it?"

"Hell, no. You're talking about learning how to hike and maybe kayak. I have two months of weekly sessions with seven-year-old girls. It's not a fair trade for you, but I don't care. You offered and I'm saying yes."

"You're very obsessed with their ages."

"They're babies."

She pretended to look concerned. "You do realize most seven-year-old girls are already dating these days, right?"

His mouth dropped open. "No way."

She laughed again. "Just messing with you because I can."

The palm on her knee moved toward her thigh in a very steady, very purposeful way.

His hand was large, his fingers long. Suddenly nothing was very funny and she found herself wondering if they could get a room upstairs. Just for an hour or two. Or five.

He stopped at the hem of her dress. Just stopped. He didn't move, didn't hint that there was more. Even so, she found herself breathing a little faster. His gaze held hers captive.

"You were saying?" he asked.

"I have no idea."

"Good."

She nodded. "You like that you get to me." Normally she wouldn't have admitted anything like that, but why ignore the obvious?

"It makes things equal between us."

"You're saying I get to you?"

"Why would you think otherwise?"

Because every woman had doubts, she thought. She put her hand on top of his. "Now what?"

"Now we order dinner."

He pulled back his hand, then reached up and tucked her hair behind her ear. He leaned in close enough for her to feel his breath on her cheek, then he spoke very quietly.

"Of course I want you, Taryn. I'm breathing, aren't I? Because it would take being

124

dead to not want you. You told me you wanted me to work for it and I'm more than willing to do that. To wait to feel your skin against mine, your mouth, your breasts, all of you. But when we are together, it's going to be my way. It's going to be slow. There won't be an inch of you I won't touch, won't please. I want to learn everything you like and then figure out how to do it so well I can make you come anytime, anywhere. And I will."

It was both a challenge and a promise, she thought, as a shiver trickled down her back. Her breasts tightened as they seemed to get heavier, and the very center of her began to ache and swell.

She turned her head to face him and found their mouths were inches apart. "That's an ambitious goal."

"Go big or go home."

"I thought it was Semper Fi."

"That's the Marines."

His eyes were made up of a thousand shades of gray. He had a handful of small scars on his cheek and forehead. His mouth was perfectly shaped.

She raised her hand and traced the scar on his neck with her thumb. "He's dead, isn't he?"

"Yes."

He slipped his hand through her long black hair and cupped the back of her head. "I want you," he breathed. "And I'll wait."

Part of her wanted to protest. Not waiting seemed like an excellent idea. But the rest of her wanted to see where this all would lead. When it came to her romantic or sexual relationships, it seemed that all she was doing was going through the motions. Whatever happened with Angel, she would find herself on one hell of a ride. Maybe that was the solution.

But that wasn't to say she was going to make it easy.

She shifted so she was more angled toward him. She drew one leg up, resting her thigh on the seat, parting her legs slightly. Her dress rode up obligingly.

She took the hand that had been on her leg and put it back on her bare skin, then guided it higher until his fingers came in contact with the hot, damp wisp of silk that was her thong.

She'd thought to shock him, to make him squirm. But instead of hesitating, he slid two fingers under the elastic and brushed them unerringly against her swollen, hungry core.

Heat and need shot through her. She had a bad feeling she both flushed and gasped as need threatened to take control. He touched her again, rubbing more firmly once, twice, three more times, then withdrew his hand.

"Think you're playing with a kid?" he asked, his eyes bright with confidence.

She faced front and tugged down her dress. "No. I was making a point."

"Me, too."

And he'd won, damn him. Instead of rattling him, she was the one who wanted to squirm. She had to hold on to her martini with both hands to keep from grabbing his hand and shoving it back under the table so he could keep touching her. She'd never in her life wanted to have sex in a public place, but apparently exceptions could be made.

What was it that he'd just told her? That he would learn how to make her come anytime, anywhere? So much for delusions of grandeur, she thought grimly. From that very brief demonstration it looked as though Angel was going to make good on his word.

"What?" Larissa asked the next morning when she and Taryn met for breakfast. "Didn't you sleep?"

So much for her new "look refreshed" concealer technique, Taryn thought. "No. I had things on my mind."

"Work stuff?" Larissa's voice was sympathetic.

Taryn hesitated. While she didn't like talking about her personal life, she and Larissa were friends.

"It's the guy," she admitted.

Larissa scooted forward on her seat. "Seriously? Wow. You don't usually let them get to you enough to keep you up at night. Start at the beginning. You said hi and he said hi." She paused expectantly.

Taryn laughed. "Okay, then. How we met isn't important."

"It might be to me. I have no love life. I have to live vicariously through yours."

"That is just plain sad." Taryn picked up her coffee and took a sip.

"It's the orchid guy," Larissa said, perking up. "The bodyguard school person. You said he couldn't own a grocery store, which I thought was unfair because he was just so nice that way."

Taryn sighed. "You're insane, you know that, right?"

"I refuse to accept that. So what happened?" Larissa paused. "Or didn't happen?"

"I'm not sure. It's both." Taryn thought about their dinner. There'd been no shortage of conversation or sexual tension. "He confuses me."

"I didn't think that was possible."

"Me, either. Just to make it all interesting, he needs my help with an unexpected project."

She told Larissa about the FWM and Angel being a Grove Keeper. "With Kenny and Jack trying to land the LL@R account, I'm going to have to suck it up and go camping. We're sharing knowledge."

Taryn waited for Larissa to burst out laughing. It wasn't as if Taryn knew much about little girls. Or children of either gender, for that matter.

Instead Larissa sighed. "Those girls are going to adore you."

"Really? Because I'm kind of nervous about it. At the time I thought it would be fine, but then I started thinking that kids aren't exactly my strong suit."

"Don't," her friend told her. "No doubts allowed. You'll be straightforward with them, and they'll love that. Plus, if things get too quiet, show them your shoes and you'll win them over."

"I hope you're right."

Taryn had never thought much about children. Her unexpected and brief pregnancy had terrified her, but before she could figure out how she was going to be a decent parent when she'd never seen one in action, she'd lost the baby.

"Enough about me," she said firmly. "How are you doing?"

"Great. I'm all moved in and getting to know the town. People are friendly here. I like that."

"You would," Taryn told her. "I have to say the boys are better now that you're here."

"I live to serve," Larissa said with a grin. Then her smile faded. "Kenny is going to need surgery on his knee again. When it gets bad, I can barely touch it. I have to admit I don't get the thrill of the game. Sure, it's wonderful while it happens, but then the guys have to deal with the consequences."

There was plenty of pain to go around, Taryn thought. "You know they wouldn't give up what they had for anything."

"Glory days," Larissa said. She glanced around, then lowered her voice. "But don't you think it's strange none of them are married?"

"Sam was and that was a disaster."

Larissa pressed her lips together as if trying not to laugh. "I know," she managed. "It's very sad."

"Stop it," Taryn told her. "Come on. The poor guy can't cut a break when it comes to

130

women. Oh. Speaking of Sam, have you heard anything about him and Dellina?"

Larissa shook her head. "I didn't know they'd been together."

"I don't think they have been. Not romantically. But there's something going on. You know the guys want to have that big weekend party for the clients, right?"

Larissa rolled her eyes. "Of course. Sam asked if I would help pull it together. There's no way I could handle something like that. I'm great at what I do, but an expensive party at a five-star hotel isn't really my thing."

"Now, if it was a hamster rescue," Taryn teased.

"Get off me about hamsters. But yes, that is sort of my point." Larissa frowned. "Dellina's an expert. Sam loves experts."

"Right?" Taryn leaned toward her. "I'm telling you, there's some secret there. Sam isn't going to tell me, so I guess I'll ask Dellina directly."

"I want to know every word."

"I will share because I sense it's going to be delicious."

Their server appeared with their breakfasts. Taryn had gone wild and ordered Applesauce Stuffed French Toast, what with not eating dinner the previous night. Having a man make her feel the way Angel had and then not do anything about it tended to spoil her appetite.

As she picked up her fork, she smiled at her friend. "So, what are you rescuing this month? Obviously not hamsters."

Larissa shook her head. "Not even close. I'm going to be transporting some endangered reptiles."

Taryn shuddered. "On purpose?"

"It's just a few trips down to a facility better able to handle them."

"How do all the causes find you? You must be on every mailing list in the state."

"I like to help," Larissa said calmly. "It's the right thing to do."

"It's frequently horrifying. Reptiles? Can you stick to things with fur?"

"Reptiles need love, too."

"Not from me."

Angel clicked on his mouse. He'd used a basic CAD program to design an obstacle course for a corporate client. The problem was Justice thought it was too difficult for the average desk jockey. While Angel understood the theory of leaving clients alive so they could come back another time, without real danger, where was the fun?

"Wimps," he muttered, and made a few

132

more changes. While he wasn't willing to take out all the good parts, he could put in some places where those not in fighting shape could walk around.

Too bad Justice refused to let him toss live grenades to the side of the course. *That* would add motivation. He knew from personal experience. His personal best time for a quarter-mile run had been in Africa — while being chased by an angry rhino. Imminent death made for a great workout.

He made a few more changes, then saved his work and forwarded a copy to Justice for approval. He'd just logged in to his email program when someone knocked on his door.

He looked up and saw a tall redhead standing in his doorway. He would guess she was in her mid- to late twenties. Her eyes were green and her skin pale with only a faint dusting of freckles.

"Mr. Whittaker?" she asked, her voice soft.

"Angel," he said, rising to his feet and wondering what she was doing here. She didn't look as though she was at CDS to apply for a job. Most of their applicants were lean and muscled. This woman was carrying around an extra twenty-five pounds — although he had to admit, on her, the curves looked good. She also lacked that air

133

of confidence that came from knowing you could kick somebody's ass.

"I'm Bailey Voss. My daughter, Chloe, is going to be in your grove."

He held back the curse words that immediately sprang to mind. He figured the practice was good for him, what with working around little girls.

"Yes, Mrs. Voss. Please come in."

His office was small and windowless. He had a desk and a couple of extra chairs. He'd been offered something larger but hadn't seen the point. He didn't like working in an office, and no windows, plants or fancy decorations were going to make his computer time any better. He was the type who preferred to be doing.

"Thank you." She offered him a shy smile. "Bailey, please."

She took the seat he offered, then waited until he settled across from her.

She clasped and unclasped her hands. "My daughter is very excited about joining the FWM," she began, not quite meeting his eyes. "She's seven. She's really smart and sweet but . . ." She bit her lower lip.

Angel was about to ask what was wrong when he realized she was fighting tears. They flooded her green eyes and one slipped out of the corner of her eye.

134

She cleared her throat. "Sorry. I'm a bit of a mess. The thing is, Chloe hasn't been herself for a while now. Her dad, my husband, was in the army." She flashed him a shaky smile. "He's the reason we moved to town. He had an older uncle here, and Will and I didn't have any family except for each other and Chloe. He was worried about us on our own while he was gone. So he suggested we move here, to be near his uncle. Where we could have a sense of community."

She paused. "It's been great here and Chloe made friends. She was really happy. Then nine months ago, her dad was killed and a few weeks later Will's uncle passed. All that was rough on both of us. Once school started in September, Chloe seemed better, but over the holidays . . ." She swallowed. "We both had a difficult time."

"I'm sorry for your loss," Angel said automatically, glancing toward the door. He wanted to bolt. Barring that, he was hoping someone would walk in and interrupt them. Anyone would be better at this than him.

"Thank you. I thought maybe the FWM would be good for her and when she was enthused about it, I signed her up." She looked at him and more tears filled her eyes. "I'm so worried about Chloe. She's quiet and doesn't spend much time with her friends. She's only seven. I want her to be happy and enjoy her childhood. With the loss of her father, I'm not sure that's possible."

Angel knew he was in over his head. Little girls were bad enough, but now he was expected to deal with one who had lost her dad? No way. No frigging way.

"I didn't want you thinking she was weird," Bailey confessed. "She might need some extra time adjusting. I'm sorry to have to ask for special attention for her, but I don't know what else to do." She brushed away more tears. "When Mayor Marsha mentioned you'd served as well, I wanted to talk to you. Because I was hoping you'd understand."

It took all his considerable strength to stay seated. Because what he really wanted was to run as hard and fast as he could and never look back. But that wasn't an option. Not with Bailey staring at him with her big tear-filled eyes. And Mayor Marsha was an old lady. No way he could tell her what he really thought.

"Don't worry," Angel told her. "Chloe can have all the time she needs. The first season is only two months. I'm new, too. We'll figure it out together."

Bailey smiled at him. While he preferred his women a little older and a lot more difficult, he had to admit, it was a hell of a smile.

"Thank you," she said. "You're very kind."

He wanted to point out he was a lot of things, but kind wasn't one of them. Instead he nodded and stood. "I'll keep an eye out for Chloe and let you know if there are any difficulties. All the girls will be new to the FWM, so they'll all be thinking about fitting in."

"You're right. I hadn't thought about that. Thank you."

He nodded and waited until she'd walked away before looking at the wall and wondering if it would help to bang his head against it.

Consuelo strolled into his office. The raised eyebrows were enough for him to know she'd heard at least part of the conversation.

"They gave me little girls," he grumbled. "Eight of them. I thought I was getting teenage boys."

Consuelo sat on the corner of his desk. "You should be grateful."

"I know how to handle boys."

"Because of Marcus?"

He nodded.

"But you haven't been around them since he died," she said quietly. "I think you're wrong. I think boys his age would have been a lot harder."

He brushed off her words. "What do I know about little girls? They're small and delicate."

She grinned. "They're not breakable, if that's what you're thinking. You'll do fine. You're good with kids."

He glanced at her. "How would you know that? You've never seen me with a kid."

"I've seen you with Ford. It's pretty much the same thing."

"Funny," he grumbled. "Very funny."

CHAPTER SEVEN

"Girls," Jack said. "Children."

Taryn hung her suit jacket, then reached for the button on her skirt. They were in the women's locker room. She wanted to point out the word *women* to Jack but as she was constantly in the men's locker room, she knew he would simply mock her.

"Yes, seven-year-old girls who are, by definition, children."

"And you."

She unzipped her skirt and let it fall to the floor. After she stepped out of it, she picked it up and hung it on a second hanger, next to the jacket. Still wearing her silk blouse, she turned to face Jack.

He stood there, all big-guy tough, leaning against one of the closed lockers. Without her usual heels, she was significantly shorter, which she usually hated. Even so, she walked over to him and put her hands on his chest.

"It wasn't that I didn't want our baby," she began quietly.

His dark gaze locked on her face. "You didn't."

She winced. "I was young and we didn't know each other well and I felt really bad about getting pregnant. There's a difference."

"Not much of one."

She thought about pointing out that he hadn't been all that upset about the loss, either. Having a child would mean getting involved emotionally. Something Jack did his best to avoid. But that wasn't the point.

"I'm helping out Angel, and the girls are a part of that. I think it will be fun."

In a strange way, she was looking forward to being part of FWM, even if only for a couple of months.

"You'll do great," he told her.

She studied him. "Are you okay?"

"The best."

She didn't smile. "Sometimes I worry about you."

"Don't. I always land on my feet."

"It's your heart I worry about," she said without thinking, then shook her head. "Sorry. I meant —"

He pressed his fingers to her mouth. "Don't apologize. I know what you meant."

She leaned into him. He pulled her close and held her. "I'll always love you, big guy," she whispered.

"I'll always love you, too. Even with your bony ass."

"My ass is not bony. I'm trim. I do Pilates."

"You're such a girl."

"Which makes our sexual past easier for you to explain."

He chuckled, then released her. He pointed to the clock on the wall. "You'd better hurry or you'll be late."

She followed his gaze and groaned. "I already am. You know where the FWM hut is?"

"Not a clue."

Okay, Angel thought. He was willing to admit it. Nothing had ever terrified him as much as facing eight seven-year-old girls at his first FWM meeting.

It was Tuesday at three and there were two very, very long hours to fill. He had a handbook, a box of supplies and a large open room in the FWM hut not too far from the Hunan Palace restaurant.

The girls sat in front of him on the carpeted floor. They were wide-eyed and eager, dressed in jeans and T-shirts. They'd been dropped off by the parents and told to have fun. Expectation filled the air and he had no idea what on earth he was supposed to do to fulfill those expectations. Once again he wished Mayor Marsha were forty years younger and a guy, so he could take out his frustrations in a way that made sense to him.

"Hello," he said, conscious of the door only a tantalizing few feet away and the beckoning freedom beyond. "I'm Angel."

They stared at him. He swore silently. Old lady or not, he was going to have to assassinate the mayor.

Just then the door to the hut opened and Taryn walked in. She wore jeans and a silk blouse tucked in to the tight waistband. Instead of athletic shoes, as the girls favored, she had on black boots with four-inch heels.

As she shut the door behind her, she laughed. "I got lost. Can you believe it? Everybody talks about how small Fool's Gold is, but not to me. There I was, down by the park, looking for a hut. This isn't a hut, by the way. It's a building. Why did anyone say it was a hut? And it's sure not by the park."

She walked to the front and sank gracefully to the floor. "Okay, what did I miss? Oh, I'm Taryn, by the way. Did we already do names?"

Angel felt himself start to breathe again. The girls stared at Taryn with amazement. He knew just how they felt. She was larger than life and simply being around her caused a person to feel something good was about to happen.

"We didn't do names yet," one of the girls said.

"Excellent." Taryn smiled at her. "Why don't I start? I'm Taryn. I'm friends with Angel. I'll be helping out for our season. I have never been in the FWM, so I'm really excited to learn all about it."

Each of the girls said her own name. Chloe went last and spoke quietly. Taryn didn't seem to pay any more attention to her, but Angel had called to explain about her special circumstances, so he knew she was keeping track of the girl.

Taryn shifted to her knees and bent over the box of supplies. "I read my handbook last night and I believe we're supposed to have a project today."

"We play get-to-know-you games," a little girl named Allison said. She was blonde with glasses perched on her nose.

"You're right," Taryn said. "Don't you love games?" She looked at him. "We're supposed to divide into two groups," she began.

"Or we could do one big group," he said quickly.

Her mouth twitched. "Is this where I make the clucking sounds?" she asked quietly, before smiling at the girls. "Okay, there should be a ball in here."

She pulled out a big red ball, then motioned for everyone to get in a circle. "I'm going to roll the ball to someone. When she catches the ball, I have to say her name. If I get it right, I get to ask a question. Once she answers the question, she'll roll the ball to someone else, and so on."

She shifted onto her butt and sat cross-legged, then waited while the girls formed a circle around her. She rolled the ball to the girl directly across from her.

"Charlotte, who prefers Char," Taryn said. "Right?"

Char Adelman, a petite brunette, nodded vigorously.

Taryn grinned. "And I get to ask a question. Do you have any twos? Oh, wait. Wrong game."

The girls all laughed. Angel didn't get it. Chloe, who had ended up sitting next to him, leaned close.

"It's Go Fish," she told him. "A card game."

Chloe was tall and thin, with bright red

144

hair and equally vibrant freckles. When he looked at her, she ducked her head.

"Thanks," he said in a whisper.

She nodded without looking up.

"My question," Taryn said slowly. "Do you have any brothers or sisters?"

Char wrinkled her nose. "Two brothers and they're both older. They tease me a lot and try to make me cry. When I get bigger, I'm going to be strong enough to beat them up."

Angel started to say he could help her with that, but before he could speak, Taryn put a hand on his arm, as if urging him to be quiet.

Good idea, he thought. He probably shouldn't offer lessons like that. At least not on the first day.

Char shot the ball across the circle. It headed directly for him and he caught it.

"Hi, Angel," Char said with a shy smile. "Are you and Taryn married?"

"No."

He sent the ball to another girl and asked his question. She returned the ball to him. "Have you and Taryn kissed?"

The other girls laughed.

"I sense a theme," Taryn said, taking the ball from him. Her eyes were bright with amusement. "Angel and I are grown-up friends. We're not married. I wanted to learn more about FWM and he's letting me tag along. Now let's continue with the game, but ask questions of each other, okay?"

There were a few grumbles, but the girls all agreed. At the end of about half an hour, they all knew a lot more about each other. Angel noticed that only one girl had sent the ball to Chloe. He wasn't sure if that had relieved Chloe or hurt her feelings.

Taryn reached into the grove box and pulled out large sheets of paper along with boxes of crayons. There were tables and chairs along the perimeter of the room. Taryn rose gracefully and started putting the paper on the desks. Angel pulled chairs around and then handed out crayons. The girls scrambled to see what was next.

As he got everyone settled, he saw the paper contained lines where they were to list each girl's name and one fact about her. Angel immediately looked at Chloe. The only question to her had been about whether or not she had pets. She'd whispered, "No, but I'd like a dog." Not exactly information someone needed for a lasting friendship.

He waited until the girls were settled, then pulled Taryn to the back of the room.

"What about Chloe?" he asked in a heated

whisper.

"What about her?"

"They don't know anything about her except that she wants a dog. Do you know how bad that's going to look? Char has two brothers and Chloe doesn't have a dog."

Taryn watched the emotion simmering in Angel's usually cool gray eyes. He nearly vibrated with concern, which she found really sweet. The big, bad soldier brought to his knees by a bunch of little girls. It might be a cliché, but it was a good one. Just when she was prepared to go live on Cynics Island, something like this happened and restored her faith in humanity.

She put her hand on his upper arm and squeezed gently. "She's been dealing with things a lot worse than this for a long time," she said quietly. "We're going to help her fit in, but we can't fix the problem in an hour. Stay calm."

"I am calm."

She raised her eyebrows.

He exhaled sharply. "Fine," he grumbled. "I'm not calm. You shouldn't be, either. I've never had a daughter. You don't have kids. We're not qualified."

"Possibly not, but I'm thinking we're not going to do much damage, either. Try to relax. The girls already adore you."

He scowled at her, which was totally cute, she thought happily.

"You can't know that," he grumbled.

"We'll see."

The girls worked on their lists, which were then posted on the walls of the hut. Taryn was pleased to see that girls who knew Chloe from school had added things like "good reader" and "best drawings in class" in addition to a couple of "doesn't have a dog."

Once all the lists were posted, they walked around as a group and talked about them. Taryn noticed that there was a lot more conversation between the girls and everyone, with the possible exception of Angel, was more relaxed.

She walked back to the supply box and lifted out the last two packages. There were plain leather bracelets with adjustable chains by the clasps. She studied the simple leather thong, noting how it was sturdy enough to last through a lot. Good thing, as the girls were expected to wear them for the next five years. There was also a package of small wooden beads. The beads were decorated with a simple carving of two hands clasped. The printed label on the plastic bag said Friend Beads — Acorns.

She sat on the floor and the girls joined her. She waited until Angel had settled next to her before opening the bag of bracelets and passing them out.

"You've earned your first bead," she said with a smile. "For friendship."

Angel shook the small wooden beads into the palm of his hand, and then each girl took one. They strung them onto the leather bracelet, then began helping each other put them on.

"Aren't you going to wear one?" Angel asked with a grin.

She batted her eyes at him. "Only if you are."

"You have to," Char told him. "All the Keepers wear the bracelets."

Suddenly eight little girls were looking at him. Taryn saw the tightness in his jaw and knew there was an internal battle going on. Reluctantly he took the thong she held out and strung a bead into place. The girls cheered as he secured the thong around his wrist.

Taryn noticed it barely fit and there was no way he was going to be able to get more beads on it and keep circulation to his fingers.

"We'll have to talk to someone about getting you a bigger bracelet," she murmured.

"Could we?"

She laughed. "Sarcasm in front of your Acorns?"

She glanced at the clock on the wall. "We still have about fifteen minutes," she said, and reached for her backpack. "Who wants me to braid her hair?" she asked as she pulled out her brush.

"Me!"

"Me, too."

The girls scooted over so they were sitting in a line. Allison sat with her back to Taryn and waited. Taryn gently brushed her hair, then started to braid it.

"I have some ties in that outside pocket," she told Angel as she motioned to her bag. "Would you get them?"

He looked at her as if she'd asked him to stick his head in an alligator's mouth, then collected the ties.

Taryn worked quickly, French-braiding Allison's hair, then securing it with a bright pink tie.

"You could do some," Taryn told him.

Panic flashed on his face. "I don't know how," he said quickly, tucking his hands behind his back as he spoke.

"I'll teach you." She had a feeling there were going to be lots of meetings where there was a bit of time to fill, and this was an easy activity.

Taryn looked at the girls. Her gaze fell on Chloe, who sat more on the edge of the group rather than in it.

She smiled at her. "Chloe, are you feeling like you could be patient while Angel learns on your hair?"

Chloe's eyes widened in surprise. "Okay," she said softly, and moved to sit in front of Angel.

Taryn grabbed a second brush from her bag. She was always losing them, so she made sure she had a spare. After today she would make sure she had two or three and lots of extra ties.

"You know how to braid, right?" she asked Angel.

"Of course."

"Then this will be easy."

As the other girls watched and Chloe sat without moving, Taryn talked him through the process of French-braiding the girls' hair.

Angel's fingers were clumsy, but he kept at it and eventually had a reasonably straight braid.

"Not bad for a rookie," Taryn told him. "What do you think, Chloe?"

The girl touched her braid and offered

Angel a slight smile. "Thank you," she whispered.

The door to the hut opened and the first of the parents arrived. The girls scrambled to their feet and started to talk about their afternoon. The new bracelets and beads were shown off. Taryn rose and introduced herself to some of the parents. Angel did the same. Fifteen minutes later, they were alone.

"We survived," she told him as she collected her brushes and the rest of the ties.

"I need a drink."

She glanced at him and saw he looked shell-shocked. He was kind of pale and there was a glassy expression to his eyes.

"You okay?" she asked.

"I'll never be able to do this."

"You were fine. The girls loved you."

"I French-braided hair."

She couldn't tell if he was proud or horrified.

She grinned. "See? Your first rite of girl passage. Soon you'll grow breasts."

"Funny."

She walked toward the door. "Tell you what. You stop at Hunan Palace and get us Chinese and I'll head by the bakery for cupcakes. We'll have a celebratory dinner at my place."

"What do you have to drink?" he asked.

"Plenty of beer."

When he raised his eyebrows in question, she laughed. "You're forgetting about the guys I work with. I always have beer in the refrigerator and steaks in the freezer. It's in my employment contract."

"I gotta get that in mine."

Getting dinner took a little longer than Angel had planned. There was a line to get takeout at Hunan Palace. Apparently a kids' baseball game had just ended. But he placed his order and waited, then drove over to Taryn's.

He parked in front of her small one-story house and made his way up the front walk. She opened the door before he got there and he nearly dropped the food when he saw her.

She'd traded dark washed jeans and boots for pale, worn jeans and bare feet. Her silk blouse was gone and in its place was an L.A. Stallions jersey with Sam's number on it. Her long hair was loose, her face free of makeup. She looked young enough that if he hadn't known her actual age, he would have told himself to keep moving without stopping.

"A transformation," he said as she approached.

She smiled as her violet eyes brightened with amusement. "The real me."

"I like."

She moved aside to let him into her house. There was a nice-sized living room with a leather sofa and two big chairs. A huge flat-screen TV sat above the fireplace, and to the left was an Andy Warhol–style painting of Jack.

Angel stepped toward the piece of art. The subject was dressed for a game and had taken a knee on the field. His helmet was beside him. Jack looked straight out, as if into the viewer's eyes.

He turned back to Taryn, who was watching him. "Nice," he said.

"It was a gift."

Like her shirt? If he'd had any doubts that the guys she worked with were an important part of her life, seeing all this had made the situation clear. For a second he paused to wonder if he was bothered, and then he remembered what she'd told him about her past with Jack. They'd been married before. They were friends. But they weren't together. He could relate to that — after all, he lived with Consuelo. Although the situation was slightly different — he and Consuelo had never been married, or romantically involved — the principle was the same.

He smiled at Taryn and held up the bag. "Hungry?" he asked.

"Starving."

She pointed through the doorway. He saw the table in the dining room beyond had been set. There were beers in place, along with plates. Music played in the background.

They sat down and started passing containers of food back and forth. Taryn reached for an egg roll.

"You survived your first meeting," she said with a grin. "That has to make you happy."

"It was tough," he admitted. "I'm glad you were there. The hair braiding was brilliant."

"It can become a tradition."

He wasn't sure he was ready for that. "Little girls aren't my area of expertise."

She looked at him. "You would have preferred boys?"

A simple question to which he should have said yes. Because he'd assumed his volunteer position *would* be with boys. Only now, after the fact, he wondered.

She set down her fork. "Angel?"

Her voice was soft, questioning. He had a feeling that if he brushed off the question, she would go with it.

"I had a son," he said slowly, leaning back

155

in his chair. "Marcus."

She continued to study him but didn't speak. As if letting him find his way.

"I went into the army right after high school. My dad died a few weeks before graduation. The coal mines did him in and he made me promise I would get out. I didn't want to leave the town where I'd grown up, but I knew he was right. If I stayed, I would be trapped. So I left."

"That must have been hard."

"It was. I got through boot camp and ended up in Louisiana of all places."

Where he'd met a girl, Taryn thought, sensing where the story was going. She briefly wondered what Angel had been like when he was younger — before he'd met the man who'd tried to slit his throat. Maybe even before he'd begun the kind of work that had put him in that position in the first place.

"What was her name?" she asked.

"Marie. She was beautiful. Tiny and Cajun, with a stubborn streak." He flashed a smile. "She terrified me as much as she intrigued me. Luckily the love-at-first-sight thing happened to both of us. We were married within a couple of months."

Love at first sight? Taryn wasn't a big believer. She'd never seen it in action. She

156

knew that lust could blossom from almost nothing — if the women who showed up in the boys' hotel rooms were anything to go by. But that was different. That was about power by association. The bragging rights.

Love was different. There were —

She reached for her beer, then leaned back in her seat as the pieces all came together. Angel had loved his wife and now he wasn't married. He'd said he'd had a child, but it hadn't been real until now.

"Then you and Marie had Marcus."

He nodded.

She watched the emotions chase across his face and wondered what he was thinking. Love was clear, as was pain and a sense of loss.

She waited, knowing he would answer the most important question when he was ready.

"They died," he said at last. "Marcus was fourteen and Marie was driving him to a baseball game. There was a storm. From what the police could figure out, it was a single-car rollover. The coroner said they went quickly."

Because Angel would have asked. He knew about suffering and wanted to make sure those he cared about didn't. She realized there weren't any words and instead reached across the table and lightly touched his hand.

"I didn't know what to do," he admitted. "I buried them, sold the house, put everything in storage and walked away."

"Did that help?" she asked.

"No." He squeezed her fingers once, then pulled his hand out of reach. "I spent a few months drinking. Quit my job and gave serious thought to ending it all." He shrugged. "But I knew how much Marie would hate that. So I went back to work. But my heart wasn't in it. Then one day, Justice showed up and talked to me about coming here. Once I visited the town, I knew it was the right decision. Fool's Gold reminds me of where I grew up. I can get involved."

And stay disconnected at the same time, she thought.

The idea of tragedy in Angel's past didn't surprise her. She'd been pretty sure he couldn't do what he had done and not be exposed to loss. But the type of loss was unexpected. A wife and a son. A woman he had loved for years. What must it be like to be able to give your heart so completely? She'd never done it. No one close to her had done it successfully. The boys had tried. Well, not Jack, but Sam had, and Kenny . . . Okay, Kenny's situation was unique. But

Sam had been in love when he'd gotten married. And since then, he'd made more than one attempt to find genuine love.

"Then the girls are a good choice," she told him. "Similar and yet different. It might have been difficult to work with teenage boys."

He nodded slowly. "If they reminded me of Marcus. You're probably right."

"And now you know how to French-braid hair."

He relaxed in his seat and smiled at her. "A necessary skill for a Grove Keeper. They should put that in the handbook."

She grinned. "The handbook is pink. I'm thinking they assumed you already knew."

Conversation shifted to the various girls in the grove. How a few had stood out and others would require a bit more time to get to know.

"Chloe was sweet," Taryn said. "I hope the group can help her open up more. I think she wants to participate. I saw flashes of that, but it was almost as if she didn't remember how to make friends."

"She might feel guilty about having fun," Angel told her. "If she laughs, she's not missing her dad." He paused. "It took me a while to recognize that in myself."

"You must miss both Marie and Marcus."

"I do. I think about them every day. I'll never not think about them. But the ache isn't there all the time, even if the guilt is. I should have been there to protect them."

She wondered if that was about the driving or something more. "Because you would have done better navigating in a storm?"

"Because there's no point in saving the world if you can't save the people you love."

An interesting twist, she thought.

She studied the man across from her. The scars, the cold gray eyes. He was dangerous and appealing. Knowing about the sadness in his past only made him more sexy. And yet . . .

To quote him, this wasn't her area of expertise, but if she had to guess she would say that for Angel to heal, he needed to have faith, and she was the last person to help him with that. Trust was an overrated commodity. She'd learned that the hardest way possible.

They were a couple of broken souls, she thought, passing him the spare ribs. A man who had loved and lost and a woman who didn't believe in romantic love at all.

CHAPTER EIGHT

Taryn spent a restless night, which didn't make for a good morning. The night before she'd been worried about her first meeting with the Acorns. Last night she'd been thinking about what Angel had shared with her about his past. She told herself that they all had ghosts to wrestle with, but somehow Angel's seemed more tangible than hers. Or maybe the difference was he'd met his as an adult, while hers were all left over from childhood.

She got into the office, still confused about what had happened or not happened. Their conversation didn't exactly lend itself to a romantic interlude. But somehow learning what she had about Angel had added dimensions to an already intriguing man. The safest and most sensible course of action seemed to be to cut and run. Not exactly an option.

She got to the office and turned on her

161

computer. A few seconds later her calendar appeared with a large red block right in the middle of her day.

"Why didn't I know this before?" she asked out loud, even as she remembered entering the date herself. But it had been a few weeks ago and somehow she had forgotten.

Taryn called over to the graphics department and got one of the guys to set up the main conference room. Then she put a call in to Isabel and explained the crisis.

"I'm going to need food and beer," she said. "Do I call Jo? Does she deliver?"

"Call Ana Raquel," Isabel said. "Dellina's sister. She and her fiancé do catering. They wrote the Fool's Gold cookbook that was out last year. Just tell her what you need and she'll bring it to you."

Taryn took down the number, then made the call. Ana Raquel promised to have the spread there on time. Just as she hung up, Larissa walked in with a couple of DVDs in her hand.

"For later," the blonde said.

"You remembered?" Taryn asked.

"Sure. All the guys have been talking about it for a couple of weeks. You know how it bothers them."

"No one reminded me."

Larissa's eyes widened. "We're not ready? You know how they get."

"I'm very clear on how they get, and it's handled. Sort of. We'll have plenty of food and beer in place when it's time." She looked at the DVDs her friend held. "Let's get those into the player."

They went upstairs to the large viewing room. There were oversize, comfy sofas and chairs, a massive TV and posters of the boys everywhere. There was also plenty of room for food and beer. Larissa loaded the first DVD and pushed Play. After a couple of seconds of blackness, images filled the giant screen.

A very young Jack stood in front of a reporter. Jack's suit looked painfully new and the jacket pulled across his broad shoulders.

The reporter, a seasoned veteran used to rookies, guided Jack through the interview.

"The L.A. Stallions made it clear they wanted you," the reporter said. "That must have helped you get through the process."

Taryn watched as twenty-two-year-old Jack tried not to smile too brightly on camera. But what the hell — he'd just been a first-round draft pick for his dream team. The man deserved to celebrate.

He said all the right things, because

someone had taken the time to give him a few pointers. Back then he'd been seen as a way for the losing team to finally start to win some games. But the older, more experienced quarterback had made a comeback, benching Jack for nearly three years. What the impatient young player hadn't realized was he'd needed the time to refine his game and mature physically. When Jack was given his first shot at starting, he'd already been tested in safe situations and was ready for the responsibility. He'd taken his team to the play-offs six years in a row and had won the Super Bowl.

Taryn had met him the summer between his first and second winning seasons. He'd been hot, in every sense of the word.

Now she looked at the young man he'd been and wondered at the differences.

"He was a baby," Larissa said with a laugh.

"That he was."

The DVD played on. The scene switched to Kenny and then Sam having the same conversation, although Kenny hadn't gone until the second round and Sam had been right after him. Rare for a kicker.

Taryn had seen the interviews dozens of times, but they were still fun to watch. Sam, not wanting to give anything away, and Kenny both excited and concerned. The former because he was going to be a star and the latter because of what was happening at home.

Twenty-two, Taryn thought, doing the math. Kenny was a father-to-be by then. Or so he'd thought.

The door to the TV room opened and the men in question entered. They were older now. All in their mid-thirties. Former players in suits that cost more and fit better. They weren't as muscled, but they were all still fit.

Jack crossed to Taryn. "You remembered."

She thought of the red notice on her computer and held in a need to wince. "I know this day is tough for you."

"A lot of memories."

She handed him the remotes. They would watch the coverage of their own NFL draft before switching over to view today's draft live. They would drink beer and tell stories and get absolutely no work done. Which was okay. They'd earned the break.

Taryn left them and went back to her office. She glanced at her phone and saw she'd received a text from Angel. It showed a picture of a rock-climbing wall. At least she assumed that's what it was. She'd only seen them in the movies or on TV. Next to the picture were a place and time.

She smiled. "You're not one for picking up the phone, are you?"

A second text came through. You helped me. Now I help you.

A man with a sense of fair play, she thought. That was something she could appreciate.

Late Saturday morning Angel arrived at the sports center by the Lucky Lady Casino and Resort. From what he'd heard, the rock-climbing wall was a new addition. There were plenty of cars parked out front. He maneuvered his Harley to the parking lot on the side, then tucked his helmet under his arm as he headed around front. He saw Taryn walking toward the entrance.

She'd dressed appropriately — a loose T-shirt and some kind of fitted workout pants that left virtually nothing to the imagination. His gaze lingered on the length of her legs and the curve of her butt. He barely noticed her athletic shoes or that she'd pulled her hair back into a ponytail. It was only when he realized she'd come to a stop and had put her hands on her hips that he raised his attention to her face.

Both eyebrows were raised. "Really?" she asked. "You can't be more subtle?"

Caught red-handed, so to speak, and he

had no one to blame but himself, he thought with a grin. "I'm unrepentant. You're more temptation than the average man can handle."

"And here I was hoping for better than average."

In flat shoes, she was several inches shorter than him, which he liked. He took her by her wrist and tugged her around the side of the building, then put his helmet on the sidewalk, cupped her face in both her hands and kissed her.

They were in a public place, in the middle of the afternoon. Not exactly conducive to a make-out session, but what the hell? He'd wanted to kiss Taryn from the first second he'd seen her last fall. He'd done his best to play things smart, but how was he supposed to resist her when she looked the way she did and sassed him on a regular basis?

Her mouth was soft and yielding. A bit of a surprise, but maybe she wasn't nearly as tough as she pretended. She put her hands on his sides. The touch was light, as if she wanted connection but didn't need his help to stay standing. Which would be just like her.

He brushed his mouth back and forth, exploring her, getting a feel for how it was going to be between them. Then, when the wanting started to grow, he drew back. He stared into her smoldering violet-blue eyes, pleased to see she'd been as intrigued as he had. He was about to kiss her again when a minivan pulled into a nearby parking space and about sixty kids tumbled out of the vehicle.

Taryn followed his gaze. "I never want that," she said.

"Kids?"

"A minivan." She shuddered.

"Because it would mean surrendering your identity?"

"Because no one needs that many cup holders. My assistant's kids are all grown and she still drives a minivan because she loves it. She brags about the twelve cup holders. Whenever she runs an errand she goes on and on about how much she can hold. It's not natural."

He chuckled and put his arm around her. "The same could be said about your shoe collection. Do you really need that many? And those heels can't be good for you."

She glanced at him. "Angel?"

"Yes."

"Do you have a favorite pair of my heels?"

He thought about how she looked in them and shook his head. "They're all good."

"Imagine what it would be like if I was

wearing them . . . and nothing else."

They'd been walking toward the entrance. He stumbled and had to catch himself as the image she'd planted in his brain blossomed to life size and beckoned him closer. Was it him or was it hot out here? A naked Taryn in five-inch heels. That kind of reality had the power to kill a man.

He swore quietly. She smiled.

"Ever going to mock my shoes again?" she asked sweetly.

"Hell, no."

"Then my work here is done."

"Remind me to congratulate your partners for surviving as long as they have," he grumbled.

She was still laughing when they stepped into the sports center.

Despite the fact that there was a festival going on in town, there were plenty of people wanting to rent racquetball courts or hit baseballs. Angel guided Taryn to the back where they would check in for the rock-climbing wall that dominated the center of the building.

"Ever done this before?" he asked.

"No, and I don't see the point now. The Living Life at a Run guy isn't going to make us climb the side of a mountain."

"You don't know that."

"I'm pretty sure. We don't have those kinds of mountains around here."

She was right, which impressed him. He wouldn't have guessed she paid attention to her environment beyond whether or not it was comfortable.

"Rock climbing helps with coordination and upper body strength," he told her. "Plus, you can talk about it and you'll seem like a jock."

She wrinkled her nose. "Oh, joy. Because my life has been so empty without that."

Fifteen minutes later, they were signed up. Taryn hesitated before signing the waiver, then scribbled her name. She only gulped once when she saw she would be wearing rented climbing shoes.

"Just like bowling," she murmured. "How lovely."

But the joke was on him when she put her keys and cell phone in a small locker, then pulled off the loose T-shirt. Because underneath she had on a formfitting tank top cut low enough to make it hard for him to concentrate. It was going to be a long afternoon, he thought.

Taryn had accepted the rented shoes, the noise coming from the other areas of the facility and the harness that was snug in places that hadn't seen action in a long time. Although after that very brief, very intense kiss earlier, she was hoping to have that chance soon. But what she wouldn't accept was Angel's silent laughter as she clung halfway up the damn fake rock, unable to move up or down.

"Raise your right hand," he said from his position next to her. "Reach out."

Which sounded oh, so easy, she thought grimly. She told herself she was secure. That there was some broad-shouldered college kid holding on to the rope that was clipped to her harness. Should she start to slip, he would catch her. Or at least hold on to her rope and lower her gently to the floor. Only she couldn't do it. She couldn't stretch out to the next hold and she couldn't trust enough to let go.

Angel moved closer and put his hand on top of hers. "Come on," he said, his tone more gentle. "I'll help."

She didn't want his help. She wanted to be somewhere else.

"I can do it," she told him, trying to shake off his touch without releasing her hand. An impossible task.

"It's only a few inches away," he told her.

Her arms and shoulders ached from the unaccustomed movements. Her legs were starting to tremble. Around them monkey children shot up to the top at lightning speed, calling out to each other as they went. She caught sight of an older couple making way more progress than she was.

"I'm going to kill Kenny and Jack," she muttered, stretching out her arm so she could grab on to the next hold. "I'm going to get something heavy and beat them with it until they —"

Gravity was an unforgiving mistress. One second Taryn had a firm hold on the bumpy outcroppings of the fake rock, and the next she was falling toward the earth. She had no idea how far the floor was or how much it was going to hurt when she hit. Well before impact, she suddenly jerked to a stop as the guy holding her line stopped her fall.

The harness cut into her crotch, her hips and her side. She felt burns in places that should never see that much friction. She dangled, arms and legs frantically crawling for purchase, and then she was moving again, more slowly this time until she touched the floor.

The second she was on her feet, her spotter rushed toward her.

"You okay?" he asked. "You didn't scream. When people fall, they always scream."

Taryn felt the adrenaline rush flood her

and knew it was just a matter of time until she was looking for a quiet place to curl up and be sick. Angel expertly lowered himself and hurried toward her.

"You all right?"

She nodded, determined not to let anyone see she was shaken. "I slipped and now I'm fine."

He looked at her for a second, then nodded. "Climbing isn't your sport." He reached for the clip on her harness.

She stepped back. "No. I'm going to do it again."

"Taryn, you fell."

"I know. Now I have to get to the top of the stupid thing. Then I'm never coming back." She glanced at the guy holding her line. "No offense."

"None taken."

Angel remembered the first time he'd seen Taryn. She'd been in one of her suits and ridiculous high heels. She'd been crossing the street, not in a crosswalk. With her confident stride, long dark hair and steady gaze, she'd captured the attention of every man who could see her. He'd half expected one of those movie car crashes because when Taryn was around it was difficult to see anything else.

She ran a successful business, so he knew she had a brain, but until this morning, he hadn't realized she had a spine made of steel. Because despite the fall, she'd gotten back on the rock wall and made her way to the top. It hadn't been fast or elegant, but she'd made it. When she'd reached the floor again, she'd unfastened the harness, stepped out of the straps, walked over to a nearby trash can and promptly thrown up.

She had the heart of a warrior, he thought as he pulled up in front of her house. She did the job and handled the fear later.

He parked his Harley and walked toward her door. They'd agreed to go to the Spring Festival after they'd both gone home and changed clothes.

The front door opened and Taryn stepped out. She'd replaced her skintight workout clothes with skintight jeans. Nice, he thought, wishing she would turn around so he could look at her ass. Studying the curves had a way of anchoring him in a very good place.

She had on some kind of sweater set. The bottom piece was tight enough to be interesting, but not so tight that she couldn't fit in with the families that would be flooding downtown. He glanced down and saw that for once, she'd put on boots with only a two-inch heel.

She followed his gaze and raised her eyebrows. "Making sure I'm able to walk long distances?"

"Didn't know if you expected to be carried."

"I understand the concept of the festivals," she told him, checking to make sure the door was locked then joining him on the walkway. "I've been to several. I bid on casseroles at the Great Casserole Cook-off in February."

"Did you win?"

She tilted her head. "Seriously? You have to ask?"

"Apparently not. How are you feeling?"

"Fine. I had a couple of crackers and sparkling water. I'm better." Her mouth twisted. "Is this the awkward part of the conversation where I point out I brushed my teeth when I got home?" She looked away. "I can't believe I threw up. Or fell. Or any of it."

"You thought you were going to crash into the floor. You reacted. We've all done it."

"Fall off a fake mountainside? I don't think so."

"It's not the mistake," he told her, reaching for her hand. "It's what you do once you realize you've screwed up. You got back

175

on the horse. Or in this case, the mountain."

She started to pull her hand away, then paused and looked at him. He sensed she was about to make a decision. He wanted her to choose him. After what felt like a lifetime, she relaxed and laced her fingers with his.

"I feel like a prize idiot."

"That's the best kind of idiot to be."

They reached the sidewalk and he turned them toward town.

"The first time I met Marie, she was pulled off at the side of the road and changing a flat tire." He paused, remembering the moment and smiling. "I take that back. Two guys had stopped to help or maybe try to pick her up. Either way, they were talking to her and she wasn't looking too happy about it."

"Competition," Taryn murmured. "Let me guess. You ignored them and changed the tire while they attempted to charm her."

"You got it," he said, surprised she had guessed. Although he shouldn't be. Taryn saw things others didn't. "When I was done, Marie told the other two to get lost. She was only interested in a man who took care of things, not ones who just talked about it."

He stopped, startled at the turn of conversation. He never talked about Marie and certainly wouldn't with a woman. Yet here he was, spilling his emotional guts.

Way to get laid, he grumbled silently. Because talking about his late wife was sure to get Taryn hot.

But he'd already plunged into this particular ocean. He was going to have to swim for shore.

"She was tough," he continued. "Confident, but with a soft side. You remind me a lot of her."

She glanced at him. "Thank you. I know how you felt about her, so it's a compliment."

He nodded, pleased that she understood where he was coming from.

They reached the center of town. The parade was over but there were booths set up all over.

"This was my first festival," he told her. "When I got here last year. Shocked the hell out of me."

"I'll bet. And now look at you. An FWM Grove Keeper."

"Yeah, I still haven't figured out how that happened."

"You volunteered."

Taryn smiled at a couple of people she knew and called out a greeting to a third.

She felt ridiculously exposed, walking around with Angel, holding his hand. She wanted to pull away, to put distance between them. But she didn't — mostly because in a weird, twisted way, it felt good to be just like everyone else. Even if it was only for an afternoon.

They stopped by a booth with a display of dried and silk flowers. "You could get a bouquet for your dining room table," he told her.

She rolled her eyes. "Really?"

He grinned. "No. You're not the flower type. You're more edgy. Maybe just the stems in a statement on modern minimalism."

"I'm surprised you know what minimalism is, modern or otherwise."

He flashed her a smile. "I don't. I was faking it."

They walked by the park. Angel bought her some fudge that was delicious enough to be worth the extra time she would have to spend on the elliptical. They browsed the latest bestsellers in Morgan's Books, then headed for Brew-haha.

But before they reached the coffee shop, Angel pulled her across the street toward the park. He circled around kids playing and families sitting on blankets in the late-afternoon sun.

She thought about asking where they were going but decided she didn't care. Not really. Something had happened to her today. She supposed it was the fact that she'd pretty much been at her worst and he hadn't blinked. She wasn't ready to say she would trust him with her life, but she knew things had shifted between them. He knew it, too. Telling her more about Marie proved that.

She wasn't completely surprised when he pulled her to a stop by a large tree that offered privacy from everyone around them. She stepped into his embrace easily, wanting to feel his arms around her. Wanting his mouth on hers and his body providing warmth and support.

He didn't disappoint. The second they were sheltered from staring eyes, he pressed his lips to hers. But this wasn't like the previous kiss. There was no gentleness, no polite introduction. He kissed hard and hot, claiming her with his mouth. She parted and he swept his tongue inside. She wrapped her arms around his neck and leaned into him, wanting to feel his hard body against hers.

He was all muscle — nothing about him yielded. She accepted that just as she accepted the deep, passionate strokes as he kissed her. She accepted and then moved in tandem, needing him to feel what she felt.

Wanting began in her belly and spiraled out in all directions. It heated and melted and made her want to climb inside him. What would he be like in bed? She was tired of polite men who asked too many questions. She didn't want to have to say what she would like this time or rate how good something felt. She wasn't looking to be dominated; she just wanted to be . . . taken.

He drew back and looked into her eyes. "I want you," he breathed. "Naked, wet and screaming my name."

Taryn's throat went dry. "That would be nice."

One eyebrow rose. "But not yet."

"What?" she gasped before she could stop herself. Obviously they wouldn't do it in the park, but . . . what?

He winked. The bastard actually winked. "I told you I was good at waiting."

Then it occurred to her that she had gotten exactly what she'd asked for. A man willing to play by her rules, damn him. Not knowing what else to do, she started to laugh. Angel chuckled with her, and then they walked back to the festival.

"I need a drink," she told him.

"Me, too, dollface. Me, too."

Taryn leaned back in her chair and sipped her coffee. The partner meeting had been scheduled to start right at nine, only Kenny hadn't shown up yet. He'd also missed the basketball game that morning — or so Sam had told her.

Jack glanced at his watch. "Want to go on without him or reschedule?"

Before Taryn could answer, Kenny walked in. He looked rumpled and red-eyed. There was a tension to his shoulders, as if every part of him hurt. And not in an "I used to play football" kind of way.

Sam took one look at him and grinned. Jack slapped him on the back, then loudly said, "Looks like you have a hangover."

Kenny poured himself some coffee and moved toward the table.

"I said —" Jack began, the volume even higher.

Kenny glared at him. "I heard you the first time."

"You should have said something."

"Later, I'll kill you. Just so we're clear."

Sam chuckled. "A blonde or the bottle?"

"Both and I'm never going to let it happen again."

Taryn faked a yawn. "If I had a nickel,"

181

she told him. "You look horrible."

"I *feel* horrible."

"You're too old to party," Jack told him. "The price is too high."

"You think?" Kenny asked as he sank into his seat and closed his eyes. "Why are we having a meeting?"

"We're updating Sam and Taryn on the Living Life at a Run account."

Kenny opened one eye and looked at her. "It's going great," he mumbled, then closed the eye.

"I feel better now," she said. She opened the folder in front of her. All of this could wait, she thought. At least until Kenny rejoined the land of the living. He didn't go for broke often, but when it happened, it wasn't pretty.

She turned to Sam. "What's the update on the party?" she asked.

Sam stiffened. "I'm handling it."

"Does that mean you've done anything? Because I'm not hearing any details. Not to put too fine a point on it, but tick, tick, tick."

"Get off me."

She looked at Jack, who shrugged. "What aren't you telling me?" she asked Sam.

"Nothing about the party."

She studied him as he spoke and noted that he wasn't looking at her. Great, Kenny was a mess and Sam was keeping secrets.

"I swear," she muttered as she got to her feet. "I would get more cooperation from baboons." She pointed at Kenny. "Go home. Hydrate and sleep. I'll send Larissa by later to check on you."

Kenny managed to open his eyes. "Thanks." He staggered to his feet and fled.

She turned to Sam. "I'm going to find out what's going on. You know that, right?"

Sam collected his papers and left without saying anything.

Only Jack was left. "You have something you want to say?" she asked.

He smiled. "Sure. Justice Garrett called. He wants to talk to us about a campaign for CDS."

"The bodyguard school?"

"That's them. Nothing fancy. Not advertising. Just a tweaking of their promotional materials. I thought it would be a fun change for us. We're in a small town now. We need local business."

She waited for him to make a crack about Angel, but he didn't. "Fine. We'll get it on the calendar."

"I made an appointment for you already. It's in an hour."

She sighed heavily. "Of course it is."

CHAPTER NINE

Taryn spent the next hour frantically preparing for her meeting with Justice. Her knowledge of what really happened at CDS — otherwise known as the bodyguard school — was limited to the gossip she'd picked up from her friends and what Angel had told her. She knew the other partners were also former military and that the customers fell into two categories — professional bodyguards and corporate retreats. There were also a few classes offered to the community, but those seemed to be more about building goodwill and not about an actual serious income stream.

By the time her assistant stepped into her office to tell her that Justice was waiting, Taryn had what she hoped was a working knowledge of the industry in general and CDS in particular.

Jack passed her in the hall on her way to

the meeting room. "Want me to sit in?" he asked.

"I think you've done enough damage already today," she said.

He grinned, obviously unrepentant.

Taryn walked into the conference room and smiled at Justice. "Nice to see you," she said, shaking his hand.

"I appreciate you taking the meeting."

He was about six feet, with dark blond hair and deep blue eyes. Handsome, she thought absently, but too refined for her taste. It seemed that these days she was attracted to men who were more overtly dangerous.

Not that Justice was available. He was happily married to Patience, the owner of Brew-haha and Taryn's friend. But it was nice that Taryn could look at him and internally yawn.

They both sat down and Taryn waited while Justice explained what he was looking for.

"When we opened last year, we were more focused on getting up and running," Justice said. "While I like our logo, I'm not happy with any of the other promotional material we have, including our business card design and the website. We have two distinct areas of our business and neither is represented well."

Taryn made notes as he spoke. She'd been over the website and understood what he was talking about. She took the card he offered, along with a sheet of letterhead and an invoice.

"You're looking to give an impression of success and power," she told him. "With a corporate edge for those clients. For the other half of your business, you need less flare. I'm thinking understated without a lot of information. Anyone looking for a company to train bodyguards wants discretion. That isn't the place for testimonials. I'm assuming your bodyguard clients come through word of mouth. If they want to know more, they'll ask."

Justice relaxed in his chair. "Good call."

She smiled. "Jack and Kenny sell what we offer. I'm the one who makes it work for the client. Let me put together some ideas and I'll get back to you. Who are the decision makers at your firm?"

Justice raised one shoulder. "I handle the day-to-day business, but when it comes to something like this, the team will be involved. Ford, Angel and Consuelo."

She nodded without reacting to any of the names. She had no way of knowing if Justice knew about her relationship with Angel, and she wasn't going to be the one to try to explain what was happening. Angel kissed as though he knew what he was doing but then had the self-control to walk away. She didn't know if she should be impressed or find someone to beat the crap out of him.

Neither of which were issues Justice needed to deal with.

"I'll bring an appropriate number of copies," she said.

"I look forward to seeing what you come up with."

Taryn walked into Brew-haha to find Dellina waiting. The pretty brunette had her laptop with her. The computer was open and she was typing furiously. Taryn ordered a latte, then sat down across from Dellina, who looked up in surprise.

"Have you been sitting there long?"

Taryn smiled. "I just got here."

"Good. When I get focused, the rest of the world seems to fade away." She saved her work, then closed the laptop and shoved it into her briefcase. "I'm finishing paperwork for a job I just completed. It's the worst part. Pulling all the invoices together, trying to figure out why I'm not making as much as I'd hoped." She laughed. "The trials of being a small business owner."

"I know that one," Taryn said. "Thanks for meeting me. I'm sorry to take you away from work."

Dellina shook her head. "Don't be. I appreciate the opportunity to get out of my house. I love my home office, but I do need to venture into the world. So, what's up?"

"I have a question," Taryn said. "You know about the party Score wants to hold for its customers in a few months."

"Yes, you dangled the job in front of me," Dellina said.

"I told you we were going to hire you," Taryn corrected, knowing that was still going to happen. "Jack, Kenny and I want someone local. You know the area, you can stay on top of the vendors and you can steer us away from anything that's going to be a problem for the town."

She paused, not sure how to get to what she wanted to know. "But Sam has some kind of problem with all of this and I want to know what it is."

Dellina shrugged out of her blazer and leaned forward. "Is that the holdup? Sam?"

"Yes. He's going to be handling the party. Only he won't get started and he's resisting working with you." Taryn studied the other woman closely as she spoke. "Do you know why?"

She'd thought Dellina might squirm or make an excuse to leave. Both of which would have been warning signs. Instead amusement tugged at the corners of her mouth and brightened her eyes.

"I have a good idea what's going on with him."

Taryn sighed happily. "I want to hear all of it in as much detail as you're willing to tell."

Dellina chuckled. "Okay, but there's a few things you need to know first."

"I'm listening."

Dellina had a mug of tea. She picked it up, then put it down. "I have two younger sisters. Last year Fayrene met this great guy — Ryan. He's an engineer who works in town. Fayrene and Ana Raquel are twins and four years younger than me. They're both driven. Fayrene has a business in town. A temp agency with a pet-sitting business on the side."

"Eclectic."

"You have no idea. Anyway, she has very specific goals, and falling in love wasn't one of them. So when she and Ryan got together last spring, she told him she didn't want to get married for four years."

"That's pretty sensible," Taryn admitted, impressed that someone that young had so much self-control.

"It is, except she's now decided she doesn't want to wait. But she has it in her head that she can't simply tell Ryan she's changed her mind. She needs him to propose on his own. Unfortunately Ryan's a really good guy and wants her to be happy, so he's totally respecting her need to wait."

Taryn saw the problem. "The immovable force meets the irresistible object."

"Exactly. Fayrene has been brainstorming ways to get Ryan to propose. It's kind of a family thing now. I have a dry-erase board in my home office and she has a running list of —" she held up her fingers to make air quotes "— 'ten ways to get him to propose.' "

"Not my style, but sure." Taryn wondered what this had to do with Sam.

"Adding to the excitement at my house," Dellina continued, "is the third bedroom. Right now Isabel is using it to store wedding gowns."

Taryn nodded. Isabel was expanding her store, Paper Moon. In addition to wedding dresses, she would also carry designer clothes. Taryn didn't want to think about how much money she'd already spent at

Paper Moon.

"Last Valentine's Day I went out for drinks with some girlfriends," Dellina said. "I'm chronically single and I figured looking at all the happy couples would either cause me to throw myself back into the dating pool or reaffirm my single state for the next five years."

"Logic I support," Taryn told her.

"Well, I saw this handsome guy sitting across the room."

Taryn straightened. "Sam?"

Dellina nodded. "I would like to say that I'm not the one-night-stand type. Counting last Valentine's Day, I've done it exactly once. But I figured he was cute and he had to know what he was doing, right? I mean based on volume alone. Sam's a famous football player guy. There have been a lot of girls." Dellina paused as she began to blush.

Taryn felt the laughter bubbling up inside her. "You took Sam home?"

Dellina nodded.

"To the house with the wedding dresses and a list on how to get him to propose?" Taryn grinned as she imagined what had happened next. She wished she could have been there.

Dellina sighed heavily. "Yeah. That was me."

191

Taryn's first giggle escaped.

"Don't laugh," Dellina said. "Never mind. I know you can't help it. Yes, we did it and yes, the sex was great. And Sam got up to use the bathroom and on his way back, he went into the wrong bedroom, saw the list and dresses and totally freaked."

Taryn burst out laughing as she pictured the look on Sam's face. He would have been horrified. It was a difficult situation for any guy, but for Sam it would be a total nightmare. "Did he get dressed before he bolted?"

"Not really. He was pretty close to naked as he scampered away across my lawn." Her mouth twitched. "I tried to call him to explain, but he didn't want to talk to me."

Taryn struggled for control. "Of course he didn't. Sam has the worst luck with women. There have been massive disasters. Oh, honey, I'm so sorry if you were hurt."

"I wasn't. It was weird. Like I said, I enjoyed the night, but when he dashed out the door, it was a real mood breaker." Dellina looked at her. "You're going to torture him with this, aren't you?"

"Every day for the rest of my life."

"I'm kind of okay with that." Dellina sighed. "Now you know why he's not thrilled at the idea of working with me."

Taryn drew in a breath. "Of course. He's terrified of you. It's settled. You are so planning that party. If nothing else, I'll be entertained watching him squirm."

"You could explain about the misunderstanding."

Taryn shook her head. "No way. Let him man up and ask you himself. Until then, he deserves to suffer."

"Remind me never to cross you," Dellina said.

"Advice to live by," Taryn told her with a grin.

"Service dogs help people in different ways," an obviously pregnant Montana Bradley said. "Who here has seen a service dog before?"

Angel and his Acorns sat on a wide expanse of lawn. They'd all come to K9Rx Therapy Dog Kennels, outside town, to learn about their community service project. As promised, Denise Hendrix had set up everything. The girls would visit the puppies once a week for the next six weeks. They would play with them, learn how to teach simple commands and generally enjoy being kids having fun with puppies.

Taryn was there, as well. She sat on the grass, surrounded by girls and puppies.

"While all dogs need to be socialized," Montana was saying, "it's even more important for service dogs. Who can tell me why?"

Several of the girls raised their hands. Angel noticed Chloe put hers up by her shoulder, as if she knew the answer, but didn't want to draw attention to herself.

Montana talked more about the dogs and how they worked in the community. She mentioned a reading program and one of the girls said her best friend's brother had been a part of it. Angel waited until they stood to sort out the puppies and divide them among the girls to approach her.

He quietly explained about Chloe, and Montana motioned to one of the puppies that seem to hang back from the rest. Angel scooped up the small blond Lab mix and carried him over to Chloe.

"Hey," Angel said as he sat by the girl. "I need your help with something."

Chloe looked at him with big green eyes that were more sad than confident.

"This is Riley," Angel told her. "He's a little more shy than the other puppies. I wondered if you could make him your special project. He's going to need one-on-one attention to help him become social. Montana thinks he has real potential, but only if he can be a little more outgoing."

Chloe's big eyes widened. "What happens if he doesn't make it in the program?"

"Nothing bad," Angel told her. "He'll be adopted by a family. He's a cute guy — he'll find a home easily."

Chloe took the puppy from him and settled him across one leg. "Hey, Riley. Are you sad because you miss your family?"

The puppy rolled onto his back and wagged his tail. Chloe giggled. "He's funny."

"He's a good guy."

Chloe nodded as she patted him. "I'll help Riley be braver with the other puppies." She stood and patted her leg. "Riley, come on. Let's go walk around."

Angel watched her lead Riley across the grass. The puppy scrambled to keep up at first, then started to run. The other dogs joined in. When Riley stopped, as if not sure what he was supposed to do with all the attention, Chloe got on her hands and knees right next to him. A couple of the girls joined her. Soon there was a giant Acorn-puppy tumbling game going on.

He'd noticed that Chloe's first question to the puppy had been about missing family. Because of her father, he suspected. The loss — Well, he could relate to the pain.

Had it been like that for Marcus? he wondered, having his father leave all the time? Marie had never tried to make him feel guilty when he was deployed and she'd counseled Marcus to be strong, but it had to be hard on a kid when a parent went away.

For a second he thought about trying to say something to Chloe. About being a soldier and serving. But how would words make her feel better?

Angel let his attention drift to where Taryn was helping Montana and the rest of the Acorns teach a couple of puppies to sit. The session seemed to be more about laughing than actual instruction. Taryn grabbed one of the puppies and held her up in the air, then leaned in so the dog could lick her nose.

"Too cute," Taryn said with a sigh.

He had to agree, although his interest had nothing to do with the Acorns or the puppies.

He stood and checked in with each of the groups of girls. They got a big game of tag going with all the Acorns and all the puppies. Soon there was plenty of laughing and yipping. When the puppies started to get tired, the girls helped get them all water, then sprawled on the grass with them.

The two hours sped by quickly. A few minutes before the parents were due to arrive for pickup, Angel got out the bag of beads and passed them out to the girls.

"For service," he said. "There's a second bead when we finish with the puppies."

The girls put the bead on their leather bracelets, then watched as he and Taryn did the same. Once they were done, he walked them all to the waiting area.

When the last of the girls had been delivered to her parents, Taryn turned to him and adjusted the leather thong around his wrist.

"Lucky for you accessories are very hot this year," she told him.

Her touch was light but arousing. She was standing close and he wanted her closer. Soon, he thought, thinking about their last kiss. Anticipation was great, but eventually they would both want more.

She smiled as her fingers lingered. "I'll give you credit, big guy. You're not intimidated by a grove of little girls anymore."

"You think most men would have held out long in fear?"

"I know they would have. And I know there are very few who would be comfortable wearing this." She tapped the leather. "You know I'm coming to CDS, right?"

"Justice mentioned it." Something about branding and how their clients viewed them.

"So you won't mind if I'm in charge?"

He smiled slowly. "Is that what all this is about? No, Taryn, you don't intimidate me, either. I like that you're good at your job. I like that you boss your football players around."

He liked her, but saying that would take them a place neither of them needed to go. They were looking for something fun, not romantic. The challenge, not the fall.

"You're saying I can boss you around, too?" she asked.

"Never going to happen."

"You sound sure of yourself."

"I am."

She leaned against him for a second, then stepped away. "Good."

Taryn had reached the point in her career where she was rarely nervous before a client meeting. But heading to CDS was different. She knew the cause — a certain man with gray eyes and a way of looking at her that made her feel feminine and flirty. She would say uncertain, only that wasn't one of the emotions she allowed herself.

Still, she'd dressed carefully, choosing a Hervé Léger bicolor jacket in black and white and a black pencil skirt. Her shoes were Valentino Rockstud open-toe pumps with a two-inch platform and a five-inch heel. She wanted to be close to the tallest person in the room. With size came power. Kenny had taught her that. She wasn't willing to bulk up, but she could rock a high heel.

She crossed the parking lot to the entrance and stepped into the offices. Justice was waiting by the front desk. He greeted her and shook her hand before leading her back to a conference room.

When they were seated, he offered her coffee, then flipped on a computer that began a PowerPoint presentation.

"As I told you," he began, "our business is divided into two main parts. We provide professional training to people entering the service protection industry."

She looked at him. "You don't really call it that, do you?"

He flashed her a smile. "No." The slide changed from a man in fatigue cargo pants and a T-shirt to a group of men and women in suits. "We also provide corporate events. A chance for a group to experience something outside their comfort zone. It allows them to bond as a unit. We are the shared adversary."

He went over the structure of the company. Justice ran the business, Ford brought in clients, while Angel designed the various exercises, obstacle courses and training programs. Consuelo ran most of the classes directly.

He showed her different ads they'd used and handed her copies of other materials.

She pulled a laptop out of her tote and booted it up. Justice gave her their Wi-Fi code and she logged on to the internet.

"Let's go through your website," she said, moving her finger across the touch pad, then clicking the page. "Here's what I see are the big issues that should be addressed."

Two hours later she and Justice had gone through all their material and every page of the website. She'd made notes about what he said was important and shared her own thoughts on improvements. She'd suggested a secure area for their security-based clients where a log-on would be required. With the right encryption in place, information could be shared without any security risks.

"You've made good points," Justice told her. "Ready for the demonstration?"

"It's what I've been looking forward to most," she said with a grin.

This would be the first time she would see Angel in his work environment. Usually that wasn't something that interested her, but Angel wasn't a guy in an office.

Justice picked up the phone and dialed three numbers. "We're ready," he said into the receiver.

She followed him down the hall and into what looked like a large gym. There were windows up toward the high ceiling. Light spilled in, but no one could see what was happening inside. There were weights and ropes and pads on the floor. Everything seemed to have a hard edge. She noticed there wasn't a single elliptical in sight.

Ford, Consuelo and Angel walked into the room. They were all dressed in green cargo pants and black T-shirts. In Consuelo's case the T-shirt was a tank style. Taryn worked out four or five days a week. She did her thirty minutes of cardio and then a thirty-minute Pilates routine that kept her toned and flexible. She considered herself to be in decent shape. But next to these hard bodies, she felt flabby and weak.

Her boys were guys with muscles, but Angel and Ford were bigger across the chest and . . . harder. Consuelo had definition that Taryn hadn't known was possible in a woman. She suspected it had to do with function. Her boys trained for a game. The CDS folks had trained to stay alive.

"Taryn would like to see a demonstration," Justice said.

Ford nudged Angel, who winked at her. Consuelo glared at them both, then said, "I'll play."

Angel and Ford faced each other. Taryn wasn't sure what to expect, but a round of rock-paper-scissors wasn't it. Ford lost his rock to Angel's paper. Angel walked over to stand next to Taryn, while Ford approached Consuelo.

"Is it that you don't want to fight a woman?" she asked quietly. "Is that why you —"

Consuelo grabbed Ford by the arm. Before Taryn could finish her sentence, the taller, stronger man went flying. Faster than she could believe, Consuelo was standing over him, her booted foot at his neck. Even without military training Taryn could see that with a little pressure, she could easily crush the man's throat and kill him.

Angel grinned. "I don't like to spar with her because she fights dirty and usually wins."

Taryn winced. "I get that. Remind me never to take one of her self-defense classes."

"She goes easy on civilians."

"I suspect we have different definitions of what counts as easy."

He was still chuckling when he joined his friends.

The demonstration lasted about fifteen minutes. They were able to do things with their bodies that left her gasping. The race up the ropes was stunning. She didn't know real people could move that quickly.

When everything was wrapped up, Angel walked her to her car.

"Nice shoes," he said as they paused by her car.

She pivoted on the ball of her foot. "I know. They're pretty fabulous." She put her tote in the backseat and faced him. In the bright sun the scar on his neck seemed more pronounced.

"I'm used to being around physically powerful men," she told him. "But you're different. Kenny, Jack and Sam could snap me like a twig without even trying. You could do that, hide the body and then take a twenty-mile run without breaking a sweat."

"I'd sweat." One corner of his mouth turned up. "Just not a lot."

"Did you like being a soldier?"

He thought for a second. "Yeah, I did. Serving my country made sense to me. War didn't, but I'd been trained not to ask questions. I know I did good."

She took one of his hands in hers and turned it over. He'd been a sniper, she thought. He'd killed because he'd been trained and ordered to do so. There was no way to relate to that. He was also the same man who wore a leather bracelet with beads on it because he was a Grove Keeper for the FWM. A man of contradictions.

She thought about his wife and his son. How he'd loved them and lost them. She would guess much of his heart had died with them.

She stared into his gray eyes. "You don't have to worry. I'm not looking for a happily ever after," she told him.

"Why not?"

"Because I don't believe it's possible."

"Love? Or love that lasts?"

"Both."

He curled his fingers around hers. "You're wrong. They're out there."

Maybe, but they would require a level of trust she didn't have. Everyone carried around lessons from childhood, and that was hers.

"You're not looking to give your heart," she said.

He shook his head. "No. I'm not."

"Then this works out for both of us."

CHAPTER TEN

Jack reached across the conference table and picked up a doughnut. "We about done here?"

Taryn rolled her eyes. "Dear God, can we go one staff meeting without you whining about how long it takes?"

"It's boring."

Taryn returned her attention to her notes. "Somebody hit him."

Chairs moved and there were several scuffling sounds, followed by a thud and a "You'll pay for that, Kenny."

Kenny only laughed. "Just doing what the lady asked."

Taryn looked up as the boys returned to their seats. She waited until they were settled to bring them up to date on the campaign for LL@R.

"You practicing for our weekend with Cole?" Jack asked.

"Yes. I've been rock climbing and this

weekend I'm going kayaking."

Sam raised his eyebrows. "Seriously?"

"Of course." She smiled smugly. "I told you — I can handle whatever the client wants."

Thanks to her deal with Angel and her nightly workout of carrying around the ridiculously heavy backpack, she was feeling more confident about her outdoor abilities.

She hadn't been overly excited about paddling down a river until she'd realized it meant she wouldn't have to hike with the backpack. Instead she could float it. A much easier proposition.

She scanned the rest of her list. "That about does it for me. Do you three have anything to discuss?"

Jack had been leaning back in his chair. Now he brought it down with a thud. "Yes. We have to change the town slogan. It was fine before, but we live here now."

Taryn stared at him. "Excuse me? What are you talking about?"

"The town has a slogan," Sam told her. "You don't know about this?"

"I guess." She thought for a second. "Fool's Gold. The Land of Happy Endings. What's the problem with —" She got the second meaning for "happy endings."

"See?" Kenny said. "It's funny in a way

206

they don't mean it to be funny."

"I'm sure it's just the three of you," she told him. "You're all overgrown teenagers. No one else is thinking what you're thinking."

"You are," Jack said. "Now you won't be able to think of the slogan any other way."

She hated to admit it, but he was right. "Happy ending," in a certain context, could be a euphemism for an orgasm. Usually a male orgasm. "Well, crap. Fine. I'll mention something to the mayor."

"Can I come listen?" Kenny asked eagerly.

"No, you can't. It's going to be difficult enough to explain the double entendre of happy endings to a woman in her sixties as it is. I don't need you giggling in the background."

How on earth was she supposed to start *that* conversation with the mayor?

"Maybe it would help if we brainstormed a few ideas for you," Jack said.

Taryn studied him. "Are you being serious or messing with me? Because I have other things I could be doing."

"There used to be a man shortage," Kenny said helpfully. "Now there isn't."

Sam cleared his throat. "Fool's Gold — Where Men Are Finally Coming."

The three guys all started laughing. Taryn

collected her folders and walked out. Juveniles, she thought fondly. She was working with juveniles.

She started toward her office, only to be stopped by Larissa.

"You have visitors," her friend said. Larissa looked more concerned than pleased. "I didn't know how to stop them."

"That sounds ominous. Who are we talking about?"

Larissa glanced over her shoulder, toward Taryn's office. "They're two old ladies. Eddie and Gladys. I've seen them around town. I want to say they're harmless, but I have a bad feeling about them."

"I'm sure they want the company to sponsor something," Taryn said, moving down the hall. "A race or maybe they bowl." Or maybe they wanted the boys to make a personal appearance. Three former football players as good-looking as Kenny, Sam and Jack had a way of drawing a crowd.

She walked into her office and saw the two older women waiting by her desk. One of them wore a floral print shirt over slacks, while the other had on a bright yellow velour tracksuit.

"Good morning," she said with a smile. "I'm Taryn Crawford. How can I help you?"

"I'm Eddie," the woman in the tracksuit

said. "This is Gladys. We want to talk about the basketball game."

Taryn wasn't sure what she meant. "Which game?"

Gladys and Eddie exchanged a look. If Taryn didn't know better, she would swear they were silently saying they thought she would be brighter than this.

"The one in the morning. With the guys from the bodyguard school. It's not every morning. We want to know which mornings it is."

Taryn sat down behind her desk. "Is the noise bothering you?"

The women exchanged another look. Eddie sighed and spoke more slowly. "We don't live nearby, so no, it's not a bother. We want to know when they're going to play so we can come watch."

"The basketball game the guys have in the morning. For exercise?"

"Yes," Eddie told her, her tone exasperated. "That one. Half of them take their shirts off. It's shirts and skins. We want to watch."

Taryn felt her mouth start to drop open. She carefully closed it, then nodded. "Of course," she said, not sure if elderly women watching seminaked guys play basketball was impressive or creepy. "If you want to

209

give me your email address, I'll send you their schedule."

"That would be very nice," Eddie said as she and Gladys rose.

Taryn escorted them out, then returned to her office. As she sat down she thought about telling the guys what was happening. She shook her head. Better for them to find out on their own.

Angel watched as Taryn pulled in next to his SUV and parked. He'd offered to drive her to the launch spot of their kayaking adventure, but she'd had an unexpected teleconference with a client.

"Sorry," she said as she locked her car and walked toward him. "There's a crisis in the world of sushi restaurants. At least for three of the ones we work for. Sasha Andersson, the actor, claimed a bout of food poisoning, which could be death for a restaurant. Fortunately he was simply sick from too much drinking and has since apologized, but there's still damage control."

Angel nodded as she spoke, more interested in what she wore than what she said. Once again she'd done her research. She had on waterproof running pants and a long-sleeved T-shirt. Her hair was pulled back in a long ponytail and she'd tucked a baseball cap under one arm. She'd already zipped her small wallet into a pocket on the side of her leg and did the same with her car keys.

"Sorry about the sushi crisis," he told her.

"You couldn't care less," she teased.

"I could care a little less, but not much."

She moved close before raising herself on tiptoe and lightly kissing his mouth. "Not into celebrity gossip?"

"Nope."

"There's my macho soldier."

She patted his arm. After that brief kiss, he wanted her touching him in other places, but they had a long day ahead of them. Work first, play later.

He guided her to the two boats tied up by a low dock. "What do you know about kayaking?"

She looked at him. "Really? You don't trust me?"

"I'm getting information for safety reasons."

"That's what they all say. All right — kayaks come in different sizes for different purposes. Some are better on open water and some are better on lakes. There are also larger kayaks for overnight trips, which makes no sense to me. It's way too much like camping."

Angel held in a grin. As he'd suspected, she'd done her homework. He respected that. She told him the basics of maneuvering, moving to and from shore and the best way to get in and out of a kayak.

"It's all about center of gravity," she told him. "What they mean is your butt. Get your butt safely in the boat, and the rest will follow. From what I saw on the videos I watched, getting in seems a whole lot easier than getting out. Want me to demonstrate different paddling techniques?"

"Maybe later," he told her.

He picked up the small cooler he'd brought. There was a light lunch inside. Then they walked over to the dock.

"We're going downriver a few miles," he said. "I walked it yesterday and it's pretty calm. Just remember, this is snowpack runoff. It's cold."

"So I shouldn't fall in." She studied the water for a second. "You know this only flows one way. How do we get back to our cars?"

"We're being met at the other end. I make a call and a guy meets us. We load the kayaks and drive back here."

"We could just drive both ways and admire the view outside the window."

"We could, but we won't."

212

"I didn't think so."

He stored the lunch in his kayak, then handed her a life jacket. She slipped it on. He did the same with his, then put one foot on her boat to steady it.

"Ladies first," he told her.

"Lucky me."

She sidled up to the kayak, then paused. After shaking her head, she sat down on the dock, parallel to the boat, then grabbed the sides of the kayak and swung her butt over until she was nearly in the center. She dropped into place. The boat barely rocked. She pulled her legs in, shifted to get settled and grinned.

"See?"

"Beginner's luck," he said, and handed her the paddle. He untied the line. "Wait for me."

She grinned. "You think I want to be floating down this river by myself? No way." She put the paddle across her knees and hung on to the dock.

Angel got into his boat and untied the line. He pushed off and let the current carry him down until he was next to her. The current was a little rougher than he would have expected but still manageable.

"Ready?" he asked.

She nodded and pushed off, as well.

He stayed with her easily, watching her strokes. She was a little wobbly but not too bad. As she paddled, she got more confident and her boat moved more quickly.

The late morning was bright and clear. They could hear birds around them, and the trees had gotten their leaves. It was mid-May. The only snow left was high up on the mountains.

"This is better than hiking with that stupid backpack," she said.

"Still too heavy?"

"I wear it for half an hour every night. It's getting better. But I swear, once we land this account, I'm going to go find some shoe designers to represent. Or maybe a company that makes fudge. I'd be great at sampling fudge."

He glanced ahead. "There's a bend coming up. We're going to paddle to the outside."

She wrinkled her nose at him. "Because the river will move slower on the outside than the inside? Great. Next you'll make me do fractions."

She'd barely finished speaking when her boat was caught by an underwater current and spun halfway around. Taryn shrieked. Instinctively she stuck the paddle in the water to keep the boat pointing where she wanted to go. The back fishtailed before straightening.

Angel moved toward her. "You okay?"

She sucked in a breath. "I'm fine. I didn't like that."

He thought about the clouds that had piled up against the mountains the previous night. There hadn't been any rain down in town, but he would bet moisture had fallen at higher elevations.

"There could have been some runoff," he said. "The river might be faster today. Stay close."

"Like I said, I don't want to be doing this on my own."

They moved to the outside of the bend and took the corner. As they did, Angel saw that what had been a smooth spot now bubbled with fast water over rocks. He swore under his breath.

"I heard that," she said, looking in front of her rather than at him. "That looks complicated."

They were already going faster. He pointed to the shore. "Paddle over there. We'll walk the boats past this stretch of river."

She nodded and began to paddle. Only she wasn't making any progress. With every stroke she was being drawn toward the small rapids. Angel moved his kayak next to hers, then held out his hand.

"Come on," he said. "Grab me. I'll pull you to safety."

She frowned and shook her head. "I'm okay."

"You're not. You're inexperienced. Take my hand."

She glanced at him. "I'm not doing that, Angel. If I stop paddling I'll —"

Her boat spun away and she screamed. Angel dug in deep, paddling toward her as quickly as he could. But she was caught in some current he couldn't see, and no matter how hard he stroked, she kept slipping farther and farther away.

"Taryn!" he yelled, furious at her for not reaching out to him and at himself for not taking better care of her.

She did her best to keep her kayak pointing downriver and toward the shore. The water flowed faster and faster. Suddenly her boat shifted left, then right. It turned around completely and she nearly lost her paddle. She bumped over rocks and screamed again, only to disappear around a narrow bend.

Angel paddled as quickly as he could, searching as he went, wondering how long it would be before he saw her overturned kayak floating ahead of him or bumping into shore.

He reminded himself she was wearing a life jacket and the water wasn't deep. Sure, it was cold, but she could survive for a few minutes, until he could pull her to safety. Only the tightness in his chest warned him there were a thousand ways she could be injured in seconds on the river. Or worse.

He alternately prayed and swore as he paddled down the river and yelled her name. He saw nothing on either side, nothing in the water. Then he spotted the kayak pulled up onshore and Taryn standing next to it.

He surged forward, willing the boat to go faster. The bow had barely touched land before he was out and running toward her. She stood in place, her face pale, her arms tight across her chest. She was dry, he noted as he grabbed her by the upper arms and shook her.

"What the hell is wrong with you?" he demanded, his voice harsh and loud. "You could have been killed. You don't know what you're doing. Why didn't you grab my hand? Goddammit, that's all you had to do."

Taryn knew in her head that eventually the shaking would stop. The adrenaline would fade and she would be able to breathe and talk and think. But right now there was only trembling and the exhaustion left behind as the fear slowly drained away.

Angel glared at her, his fury tangible. She wasn't afraid of him — she understood she'd scared him. She'd scared herself. When the water had captured her, she'd wondered if she was going to drown on a stupid river in some backwoods wilderness outside Fool's Gold.

She'd fought to stay in control of her kayak. She'd learned that much from the videos she'd watched on YouTube. She'd tried to point the bow in the direction she was going — sort of like coming out of a skid in her car. Only the river had been way more powerful and she'd been swept away.

Once she'd rounded the second bend, the water had slowed and she'd been able to paddle to shore. What had seemed like a lifetime had probably taken thirty seconds. Now she was left with the physical aftermath and the terrified, angry man standing in front of her.

"Dammit, don't you trust me?" he asked.

She pressed her lips together. "I want to," she managed, her voice only trembling a little. "But I can't."

He dropped his hands to his sides and

stared at her. She read confusion and what might have been pain. Because he wouldn't understand. He would think it was personal. That she didn't trust *him,* when in truth, she didn't trust anyone.

"I'm sorry," she said.

He turned away. "No problem. Let me figure out where we are. I'll get the guy to meet us with the trailer and we'll get out of here. You can go home."

He was dismissing her. Dismissing them. Gone was the teasing, sexy man who had intrigued and delighted her. And while she hadn't been looking for a happily ever after, she had wanted to keep seeing Angel. To learn more about him. She'd wanted to make love with him and spend time with him. She'd wanted to laugh and talk, because being with him was both challenging and easy.

She wasn't ready for this to be over.

He pulled out his cell and checked for a signal. After he shook his head, he walked to his kayak and pushed it higher on the shore. He removed the cooler containing their lunch and another small box. Inside was a more complex-looking phone. Probably the kind that worked off a satellite rather than a cell tower, she thought.

He began to dial.

"Stop," she said. "Just stop."

He raised his head.

She hugged herself more tightly. The shaking had faded, but the adrenaline lingered. She felt weak and scared but also empowered. She'd survived. Wasn't that the good news? She'd survived and this wasn't the first time the odds had been against her.

She raised her chin and drew in a breath. "My dad was a mean drunk. When I was little he went on binges every few months. When he did, he beat the crap out of my mom and me, but mostly her. Sometimes he just bruised her and sometimes he put her in the hospital. We lived in Los Angeles. There are a lot of hospitals, so she always saw a different doctor. She didn't tell anyone what had really happened and no one else put the pieces together."

Angel dropped the satellite phone back into the box and watched her. She tried to figure out what he was thinking but couldn't. She knew there was no point in trying. If he didn't want her to know what was in his head, there was no way she could guess. Better to simply get it all out while she could.

"He didn't hit me much," she continued, switching her attention to the ground. That was better, she thought. Safer. Dirt and old leaves, a few branches. "At least not at first. But when I was ten, she left. I came home from school and she was gone."

Taryn remembered the shock of going through their small house and seeing all her mother's things were missing. It was as if she'd never been there at all. She'd been crying when her father had walked in the door. She'd gone to him, expecting comfort.

"That was the first night he beat me," she said quietly. "I was terrified. I knew what he was capable of. I knew what was going to happen next."

"How often?" Angel asked.

She kept her attention on the dirt below. "A couple times a month. Mostly he bruised me, but every now and then it was worse and I had to go to the emergency room. As I got older, it was easier. If the doctor guessed I hadn't fallen down the stairs, I said it was my boyfriend."

She swallowed, remembering the pain, the humiliation. Trying to disguise how much she was hurting.

"I ran away when I was fifteen. He found me in a day and dragged me back home. Then he beat me until I couldn't walk and tied me to my bed for nearly a week. He said if I ran away again, he'd find me and kill me. I believed him."

There were so many other things to say, she thought. How her father was well liked by the neighbors. How he wasn't one of those crazy men who went ballistic over unwashed dishes in the sink. That he'd never sexually abused her and didn't keep track of whether or not she'd done her homework. That when he didn't drink he watched sports and mowed the lawn and went to church. But when he went on a binge, he turned into the devil.

"When I was nearly seventeen, he was up on the roof, repairing some shingles. He asked me to bring him a box of nails." She remembered that she'd felt safe because she didn't think he was drinking. It was still early on a Saturday morning. He had plans with his friends to go to a Dodgers game later. So she knew everything was going to be all right.

She'd climbed the ladder with the nails. But as she'd reached the top, she'd seen the beer bottles next to her father. The fear had been instinctive. She hadn't known what to do and her indecision had made her start to slip.

She remembered screaming. She remembered trying to stay on the ladder, and she remembered reaching out her hand to her father. So he could catch her.

He'd reached out, but instead of grabbing her hand or her wrist, he'd picked up his beer bottle and taken a long drink. Then she'd fallen to the ground and had landed hard on her arm. She'd both felt and heard the break.

Their neighbor across the street had seen the fall and had insisted on taking Taryn to the hospital. The woman, older and a widow, had stayed with her, claiming to be an aunt. Later, when Taryn's arm had been put in a cast, the woman — Lena — had given Taryn five hundred dollars in cash.

This is your chance, Lena had told her. *Disappear, child. Disappear before he kills you.*

Taryn had stared at her. *You know?*

We all know. But we're as afraid of him as you are. Go while you can. Go and never come back.

Taryn returned to the present and gave Angel the bare facts of that final day.

"I did what she said. I disappeared. I hitchhiked to San Francisco and got a series of low-paying jobs that barely supported me. Every week, I went to the library and read the paper. One day there was an article about a man who'd shot himself in the head. He was my father."

The rest of the story was easier to tell.

How she'd returned to Los Angeles and gotten her GED. How she'd worked her way through college. That money had been tight and every couple of semesters she'd had to take off to save up enough to pay for her tuition. How she'd made do with tattered books other students had thrown away.

She finally looked at him and was grateful to see that his expression was just as unreadable as it had been when she'd started.

"No one knows," she admitted. "Not Jack, not anyone. I just say my parents are dead. I don't know if that's true about my mom. I never tried to find her. Why would I? She left me alone with a monster when I was ten. She knew what was going to happen and she left me."

She paused to push down the emotion that threatened. Because she'd learned there were some places she could never go. Not if she wanted to be strong. If she let herself think about the past, ask too many questions, she was never going to make it.

So she'd ignored her past and had only looked forward. She'd gotten tough and learned to survive on her own. Until one day when a handsome football player had found her eating leftover sandwiches as if they were the only food she'd had in three days.

She drew in a breath. "That's why I didn't reach out my hand. I couldn't. Not because of you, but because of him."

Angel stared at her. "I understand," he said at last.

He walked toward her. When he reached her, he put his arms around her and hauled her against him. He held her so tight she couldn't breathe, but that was okay. She wanted to be close. She wanted to be held. And when the tears came, she didn't try to stop them.

CHAPTER ELEVEN

Taryn wasn't sure how long she stood in Angel's strong embrace. The steady beat of his heart comforted her. He was warm and solid and she knew in her gut he would never hit anyone weaker than himself. He wasn't like her dad. Few men were. But the scars ran deep.

Angel straightened enough to wipe her face, and then he lowered his head and kissed her. His mouth was soft against hers. Comforting, she thought. He wanted the kiss to be comforting. But the second she felt his lips on hers, she wanted something else. Something more.

She shifted so she could wrap her arms around his neck and raised herself on tiptoe. She pressed against him and parted her mouth. Heat poured through her and left her hungry. Need followed. She tilted her head and lightly swept her tongue across his bottom lip.

Instantly his entire body changed. She felt the tension of his muscles and the slight hesitation, as if he wasn't sure. Because he didn't want to upset her or take advantage of her, she thought.

She drew back and looked at him. "You pick this moment to act like a gentleman?" she asked as she shrugged out of her life jacket.

A muscle twitched in his jaw. Without speaking, he walked over to the kayak and pulled what looked like a blanket out of the small hold. Probably for their picnic, she thought. How convenient.

As she watched, he let his life jacket drop to the ground. He unlaced his boots and stepped out of them. She felt a whisper of disappointment. So they were going to be civilized about this, she thought. Somehow she'd hoped for something more than each undressing, followed by a pleasant and polite round of sex.

She knew she was still emotional from what had happened on the river and her confession, but jeez, why did it have to be like this? Where was the passion? Why couldn't she find a man who was swept away and —

He stopped in front of her. "You sure?"

She sighed, then nodded.

He reached for her and drew her against him, then he lowered his head and claimed her. Only there was nothing polite about the kiss. It was hot and deep and caught her completely off guard. His tongue plunged into her mouth and circled hers, making her wiggle closer.

His arms came around her, but he wasn't holding on. Instead he was moving his hands up and down her body as if he needed to discover every inch of her that second. As if he couldn't get enough. He was nearly frantic as fingers and palms traced her back, her rear, her hips.

Desire resurrected itself, heating her body and making it easy not to think. She wanted to feel, she thought as she relaxed into his kiss. She wanted to only feel. His hands, his body — all of him and all of her. She wanted to get lost in what they could do to each other.

He tugged on the hem of her T-shirt. She raised her arms so he could pull it off. Seconds later, her bra followed. He cupped her breasts, exploring the soft skin with his fingers before settling on her nipples. He rubbed the tight peaks, rolling the hard points between thumbs and forefingers. Pleasure shot through her, forming a direct line from her breasts to her groin. Muscles tightened as flesh swelled.

She reached for his shirt. He drew back enough to pull it over his head and toss it away. His bare chest was broad with rippling muscles and at least half a dozen scars. Scars she would explore later, she thought, leaning in and kissing the center of his breastbone.

He gave her a quick, wolfish smile before dropping to one knee and unfastening her boots. He pulled them off. Still kneeling, he undid her jeans and pulled them down with a single tug that brought her thong along with them. He steadied her as she stepped out of them.

Taryn had the brief thought that she was now naked in the forest. She didn't know where they were or how close they were to the road. Or even if the guy with the kayak trailer was going to show up any second. Then she decided she didn't care. She wanted whatever was going to happen with Angel and the consequences be damned.

She waited for him to stand up, but he didn't. Instead he put his arm around her and drew her close. He reached for the tender folds of flesh protecting her feminine center and parted them. She barely had time to brace herself before he gave her an openmouthed kiss that had her gasping.

The first stroke of his tongue explored. The second found her clit and the third had her hanging on to his shoulders to keep from falling.

There was no dignified way to stand barefoot while a man sucked and licked her to orgasm, she thought as she parted her legs more and dug her fingers into his shoulders. And she didn't care. She let her eyes close and her head fall back as she gave herself over to the stroking.

He circled her steadily. Every third or fourth time he went a tiny bit faster and harder. He reached for her hands and positioned them so she was holding herself open for him. She could feel his warm breath on her skin and every now and then he ran his tongue across the very tip of her fingers.

Her leg muscles began to tremble. Her breasts ached as every part of her focused on what he was doing to her. Tension grew, pushing her toward the ultimate goal. He cupped her ass with one hand and dug into her skin with kneading fingers. He ran the other up the inside of her thigh and pushed two fingers deep into her.

The invasion was exquisite. She wanted to sink onto him, drawing him in deeper, but she couldn't move. She was already barely standing — her legs spread, her thighs shaking, and still he moved his tongue against her.

She was getting closer. So close, she thought, her breath coming in gasps. A few more strokes.

"Angel," she gasped.

He pushed his fingers into her, then withdrew. Again and again. She was getting there. She could practically see it.

Then he stopped. All of it. His fingers went still, his tongue wasn't moving. There was nothing. She hung there, her body ready, but with no way to —

He pressed his lips to her clit and sucked hard. At the same moment, he pushed into her, curling his fingers toward her front, finding her G-spot and rubbing the swollen middle. She came without warning, trembling and gasping, calling out, afraid she would fall but unable to do anything but let him take her over the edge again and again.

The last shudder had barely rippled through her when he drew back. He grabbed her and then she was being lowered to the blanket on the ground. She was shaky and unfocused. There was movement. She was vaguely aware of Angel tearing off clothes. His jeans landed by her hip. She fingered the soft, worn fabric and wondered when she'd last felt so incredibly satisfied.

Then he was between her thighs. He filled her with one smooth push. She went from hazy to interested in a heartbeat. Her eyes snapped opened. Angel was over her, pushing into her again.

She could see his face, his shoulders, his passion-filled eyes and she smiled. This was going to be good.

He didn't disappoint. The man had control and style. He found a rhythm and depth that touched the very core of her. Just when she was about to relax into the sensations, he shifted slightly and had her chasing to keep up. He pumped slow, then fast, then slow again. She was wet, swollen and surging toward another release.

Just as she was about to wrap her legs around him to draw him in, he somehow flipped them both so he was on his back and she was on top.

She wiggled a little to find a comfortable place on his erection. She unfastened her ponytail and shook her head so her hair hung loose around them. After bracing her hands on either side of his shoulders, she smiled at him and began to move.

"Think you're in control?" he asked as she slowly, so slowly, slid up and down.

"I know I am."

One eyebrow rose. He cupped her breasts, then touched the very tip of her nipples. The light, teasing brush made her insides clench and had her hips pumping a little faster. He massaged her breasts. After her last orgasm every part of her was more sensitive and she found it difficult to remember she was trying to hold back. Because honestly, what was the point? Angel was naked and hard and inside her.

He continued to rub her breasts, his gaze locked with hers.

"Come for me."

The command was unexpected and sexy and dammit all to hell if her body didn't start to tremble as a climax washed through her. She rode him up and down, unable to stop herself from going faster and grinding deeper, pulling every ounce of pleasure from the lovemaking.

Angel dropped his hands to her hips, guiding her as she slid over him. When she was finally surfacing again, he pushed in deep one last time and shuddered his own release.

"What are the odds of you eating lunch naked?" Angel asked when he and Taryn had washed up in the frigid water. He already knew the answer, but figured a man couldn't be judged for inquiring.

He was a guy — he enjoyed looking at the female body. Taryn was tall and lean. He liked her small, perky breasts. Her nipples were slightly oversize and seemed to always be hard. Talk about arousing. Having her long hair play peekaboo with her nipples added to the show. Her legs were long, her pubic area trimmed but not waxed — just the way he preferred.

She looked from the pile of clothes they'd scattered around, to the lunch cooler, then back to him.

"Sure," she said, and dropped to the blanket.

All right!

He got the cooler and passed out sandwiches. There were also bottles of water and cut fruit. Taryn sat cross-legged and reached for one of the sandwiches.

He stared at her. She was totally naked. Her hair partially covered her breasts, but not enough to keep them from being a distraction. Worse, with her legs like that, he could see *all* of her. She was still damp and swollen and he felt himself getting aroused.

She bit into the sandwich, chewed and swallowed. Her mouth twitched. "Is there a problem?"

He swore, grabbed her sandwich and tossed it into the cooler, then bent over her and began kissing his way down her chest.

"You did that on purpose," he accused, just before he licked her nipple.

"I only did what you asked."

"Because you knew what would happen."

"Did I?" she asked with a laugh as she wrapped her arms around him.

Monday morning Taryn walked from her car to the company offices. Across the street the basketball game was in full swing. She paused to watch the action and felt a tiny tug of regret when she saw Angel was on the shirts team. Too bad, because the man looked good without clothes.

They'd managed to make love again, get dressed and eat lunch before their ride found them. Angel had spent the rest of the weekend at her place, mostly in her bed. They'd talked about everything but what had happened and what she'd told him. She had a feeling he would never bring up the topic of her father again.

But it was enough that one other person knew the truth.

She walked into her office and turned on her computer. As she set down her tote, she saw a plain white envelope with her name on the front. She opened it and found a note from Angel.

"Because we never talked about it." The paper underneath was a copy of a blood test from only a few months before.

Taryn sank onto her chair. Other lovers had sent flowers or jewelry after a weekend with her. Some gave her clothes or tickets for island getaways. But this — this was special. Thoughtful, just like the man himself. Angel took care of people.

She was on the pill, so pregnancy wasn't an issue. But they hadn't used a condom until they got to her place. She'd thought they would have to have an awkward conversation, but he'd handled the situation.

She tucked the note and the blood test into a side pocket of her tote, then unloaded the paperwork she'd never gotten to. She had plenty to keep her busy, she reminded herself. There was no time to swoon over a man. Still, Angel seemed very swoon-worthy. And someone she could almost trust. *Almost* being the key word.

Sometime around ten, Larissa walked into her office with two mugs of coffee.

"How's it going?" her friend asked.

Taryn winced. "I have an appointment with Mayor Marsha this afternoon. I get to explain to an old lady why she needs to change the town's slogan. I'm not looking forward to it."

Larissa set one of the coffee mugs on Taryn's desk, then settled in the visitor's chair. "How was your weekend?"

"Good, yours?"

"I went to a conference in Sacramento."

"Greenpeace?"

"No, but it was on animal rescue and preservation." Larissa leaned forward. "What do you know about marmosets?"

Taryn shook her head. "No."

"But they're adorable."

"No. Don't even think about it. No monkeys. Not here and not at your apartment. No."

"But . . ."

"No. I mean it, Larissa. Don't go there. We'll all regret it."

"You should be happy I'm coming with you," Jack said as they drove through town.

"That remains to be seen," Taryn grumbled, not sure how she ended up having to be the one to talk to Mayor Marsha about the town slogan. Although it wasn't as if she could have let Kenny and Jack go by themselves. Heaven only knew what they would have said.

He parked his Mercedes in front of City Hall and walked around to help her out of the car. As he put his hand on the small of her back and guided her up the steps, she had to admit that for all her complaints about the boys, they were basically good men with nice manners. Even better, they respected women, paid their bills on time and in Jack's case, put up with Larissa's craziness.

"By the way," she said. "If Larissa says anything about a marmoset, tell her no."

Jack frowned. "What are they? Monkeys?"

"Yes, and they bite. I checked them out on the internet. They're wild animals and we don't want them anywhere but in their natural habitat. Which is not your house, by the way."

"Okay."

Taryn glanced at him. "Really?"

Jack shrugged. "Sure. I can stand up to her."

Taryn laughed. "Yeah, we've all seen that happen."

"You're saying I can't?"

"I'm saying you won't. There's a difference."

They walked into the old building. Taryn paused to take in the architecture. There were murals and a wide staircase. All very pretty when she wasn't there to deliver bad news and no doubt get sucked into doing something she didn't want to do.

"I blame you for this," she told Jack.

"We're giving back to the community. That's a good thing."

"I'll remind you of that later, when I'm beating you with a stick."

He winked at her and pointed to the stairs. "Mayor's office is that way."

"How do you know?"

"I'm a man of mystery."

"You probably looked it up before we left."

"That, too."

They went up to the second floor. As they approached the mayor's office, a woman came out of another office and walked toward them. Taryn recognized the beautiful, pregnant redhead. Felicia Boylan was in charge of festivals in town. Taryn had met her when she'd first come to check out the town. Felicia was extremely intelligent and more than a little blunt. Taryn admired her for both qualities.

"Good afternoon," Felicia said as she approached. "Mayor Marsha asked me to sit in on the meeting. If the town slogan is changing, we'll have to address that in our advertising for the festivals. Depending on what the change is, we can use it to our advantage. Although I must point out that there are costs involved. Printed material, banners, updating online."

Jack looked startled by the information that accompanied the greeting. Taryn only smiled.

"Nice to see you," she said. "I agree, there will be costs. The question comes down to value."

"I like the slogan," Felicia murmured, leading the way into the waiting area by the mayor's office. "I have my own Fool's Gold happy ending."

Jack made a choking sound. Taryn looked at the other woman's baby bump and knew exactly what he was thinking. She elbowed him to keep him quiet.

As they approached the double doors leading to the mayor's private office, she saw an older woman sitting at a desk.

"Hi, Marjorie," Felicia said, smiling at her. "Should we go in?"

Marjorie nodded and motioned to the half-open door.

Mayor Marsha was waiting for them. She shook their hands, then led them over to a small conference table by the window. The mayor was dressed in a suit, with her hair up in a bun and pearls around her neck.

"How can I help you two?" she asked when they were all seated.

Taryn glanced at Jack, who smiled back. She held in a sigh. Obviously he was going to make her do all the talking.

She wished she'd brought paperwork. Handing out files was always a nice distraction. But what was she supposed to do? Diagram out a "happy ending"?

"We're concerned about the town slogan," Taryn began.

"So you said in your message." The mayor looked pleasant but not overly interested. "Fool's Gold has been the land of happy endings for nearly a hundred years. I'm not sure we want to change now."

Jack started to chuckle. Taryn glared at him.

"I agree with the mayor," Felicia began. "People come here and fall in love. The happy ending is —"

She froze, her mouth still open, as if she were going to continue speaking. Then her jaw dropped and her green eyes widened. "Oh no." She turned to the mayor. "They're right. The land of happy endings. 'Happy ending' is a euphemism for a male orgasm. Like at the end of a massage. When the female masseuse stimulates the man's penis until he —"

"Thank you," Mayor Marsha said forcefully. "I get it." Color stained her cheeks. "None of us ever thought of the name that way, but now that you've pointed it out, it

241

seems like something we should have noticed long before this."

Taryn resisted the urge to squirm in her seat. "Yes, well, Jack, Kenny and Sam noticed it. For obvious reasons."

"They're immature and driven by their need to ejaculate?" Felicia asked.

Taryn grinned. "Yes, that would be it."

"Hey," Jack said, sounded wounded. "There's more to us than that."

Felicia nodded. "Yes, of course. You have emotional depths. It's just the male drive for orgasm is very powerful. It can cause focus problems and poor decision making." She leaned toward him. "I've noticed that falling in love and making a long-term commitment tends to redirect a man's sexual energy. When a man has a partner he truly loves, he is more able to direct his energies in positive ways."

The mayor cleared her throat. "Perhaps we could keep on the topic at hand. The town slogan."

"We're working on several options," Taryn said. "If you want to hear them at a later time. Or you could brainstorm in-house."

"I think I'll leave this to the professionals. Do you have any idea what direction you'll be going in?"

Jack started to speak, but Taryn glared at

him again. No way she wanted him telling the mayor anything like Fool's Gold — Where Men Are Finally Coming.

"It's early yet," Taryn said instead. "Let me put together a presentation."

"That would be helpful," Mayor Marsha told her as she rose. "The work will be pro bono."

The words were a statement, not a question. Taryn nodded. Later she would take up the matter with the boys. But as they'd created the problem by noticing it in the first place, she didn't think they would be in much of a position to complain.

They all shook hands again and the three of them left. Once they were in the hallway, Felicia turned to Jack.

"I have to discuss a matter with Taryn. It's female in nature and will upset you. I suggest you leave now."

Jack glanced between them. "You don't have to tell me twice," he said. "Call when you want me to come get you."

He practically flew down the stairs.

Felicia pointed to a bench in the open hallway. Taryn sat next to her and waited. She couldn't imagine what the other woman would want to talk to her about. Especially under a "female nature" topic.

Felicia angled toward her. "As you know,

I'm pregnant."

Taryn glanced at her baby bump and nodded. "You're past the point of hiding that from anyone."

Felicia smiled. "Gideon and I started trying in December. I believe I got pregnant right away. I took the test the morning of our wedding and it was positive." Her smile faded. "I'm having a girl."

"I don't understand. You wanted a boy?"

"No. I would have been equally happy with a child of either sex. My concern is Gideon has a son. Carter is very helpful and informative. I had thought to draw on his memories of his childhood to help me be a better mother. But he's concerned his experiences as a boy won't give me enough information when it comes to raising a girl."

Taryn didn't know Felicia's whole story. She'd heard bits and pieces — that Felicia had been so intelligent as a young kid that her parents had been afraid of her. As a result, she'd been raised in a university lab. Somehow she'd made her way to the military, where she'd been a logistics expert for a Special Forces team. Now she ran the festivals in town.

While her background was extraordinary, Taryn could see how Felicia would feel unprepared to be a parent. "How can I help? I don't have kids of my own. Or a lot of experience with them."

"That is true. However, you and Angel are working together with a new FWM grove. I've talked a lot to Patience about raising Lillie, but I would like a more robust amount of information. I would like very much to come to a meeting and observe the girls. I thought spending time like that would help me understand them better."

Had the request come from anyone else, Taryn would have told the woman to suck it up and get over it. That having a child would be an on-the-job training experience, as it had been for millions of women. But she knew Felicia was different. Taryn knew all about never quite fitting in. Felicia had experienced it because she was so intelligent. Taryn had been an outsider growing up because no one could be allowed to get close enough to guess the family secrets.

She lightly touched Felicia's arm. "There's going to be a mother-daughter tea. Angel just texted me about it." She smiled. "He's totally freaked, which is pretty fun. If you came to that, you can see the girls and how they are with their moms."

Felicia nodded. "That would be wonderful and very informative. Thank you so much." She paused. "I'd hug you, but I'm not sure our relationship has gotten to that level of intimacy and I don't want to make you uncomfortable."

Taryn laughed, then reached for the other woman. "Let's be wild," she said.

Felicia flung herself at Taryn and held on tight. When they'd both straightened, Felicia was wiping away tears.

"Hormones are very powerful. I find myself crying at the littlest things. It's disconcerting. On the other hand, my sexual desire is significantly increased. Gideon says I'm exhausting him." She smiled. "Which he adores."

"You're really weird," Taryn said. "I like you, but you're strange."

"I know, but I've learned to live with it."

CHAPTER TWELVE

Angel discovered that being a Grove Keeper took a whole lot more time than he had expected. It wasn't the meetings with the girls that were the problem — it was how he was expected to attend biweekly Grove Keeper meetings. This time he'd dragged Taryn along. He'd said it was so he got all the details for the upcoming mother-daughter tea right, but the truth was he wanted the distraction of having her near him.

He liked being around her. Not just looking at her, but breathing the same air. He liked how she moved, how she spoke and how she laughed. Over the past few years, he'd discovered that he liked strong women with attitude. Marie had been like that, in her fiery Cajun way. She could cuss at him in languages he'd never heard.

Consuelo was tough, which was why he enjoyed rooming with her. She had simple rules, and if everybody followed them, life was smooth. If not, the offending party had a fifty-fifty chance of waking up with a scorpion in his bed.

Taryn was just as powerful, but on a completely different plane. She ran a multimillion-dollar business, kept former football players in line and then could spend an afternoon teaching seven-year-olds how to French-braid their hair.

As they walked into the conference room, he leaned close. "You ditched the power suit."

"I wanted to fit in."

He held in a grin. Her idea of fitting in was white capri pants with a black leaf design, a fitted short-sleeve white sweater and black wedge sandals with a bunch of straps. An outfit, he would guess, that cost more than the average car payment. Her handbag had a big bow on it and was made by somebody called Valentino. He didn't know who Valentino was, but Angel would guess he or she had never come to Fool's Gold.

They took their seats at the large table. Taryn leaned toward him. "The ladies like you."

He glanced around at the other participants. They were mostly women, but that was to be expected. "There are a few dads who come to the meetings."

"Yes, but you're getting the special smiles."

He flashed her a smile. "It's the scar. Chicks dig scars."

Her eyebrows rose. "Do they?"

Denise Hendrix walked to the front of the table, took her seat and called the meeting to order.

Each of the Keepers had to report on his or her grove. Angel waited until it was his turn, then stood and said the girls were doing well with their community service project. The puppies were responding well to the attention. He sat down as quickly as he could.

Taryn leaned close and patted his leg. "Well done," she whispered.

When everyone had updated their grove status, Denise shuffled a few papers, then smiled broadly.

"I have some exciting news. As those of you who have been Grove Keepers before know, we try to arrange an all-grove camp-out. For logistical reasons we didn't think we were going to be able to pull it together this year, but the campsite we like best has become available and I say we go for it."

Several of the women cheered. Taryn's

mouth straightened.

"Camping?" she asked quietly. "As in sleeping outdoors on purpose?"

He chuckled. "Think of it as good practice for your Living Life at a Run weekend."

"I'd rather not. You and I are planning to go hiking. Isn't that enough?"

He grinned.

"I'll be emailing each of you the particulars this afternoon," Denise continued. "As we've done in the past, there will be a separate camping area for the parents who wish to stay close." Her brown eyes found him. "Angel, this affects you particularly. You have the youngest grove. For many of the girls, this will be their first camping experiencing. Except for sleepovers, it may be their first night away from their family. That can create emotional reactions."

His pleasure at the thought of a weekend camping out fizzled. "Emotional reactions?"

Several of the women giggled.

"Nothing you can't handle," Denise told him.

Want to bet? But he only thought the question rather than saying it out loud.

"I would suggest you encourage the families to take advantage of the nearby camping area so they can be close if there's any crisis." She paused. "With the girls."

250

Crisis? Why would there be a crisis?

Denise moved the meeting on to other business. Fifteen minutes later, they were done.

The rest of the group quickly left, but Angel stayed in his seat. Taryn sat next to him. Her violet eyes were bright with amusement.

"You're happy," he grumbled.

"I'm amused. There's a difference. Now I'm not the only one worried about the all-grove camping trip."

"I don't want my girls crying." He couldn't handle the tears. "Or being upset. Camping is fun. We'll go on hikes and learn about nature." He had a few simple survival skills he could teach them.

"I'm sure they'll be fine. Denise was simply offering ways to make sure it all goes well. Having the parents nearby is a good idea."

He agreed with that, but still. Crying.

She stood. "If it makes you feel better, we have to get through the mother-daughter tea first. That will be fun."

He rose and put his hand on the small of her back. "That's your idea of helping?"

"You don't like tea? There'll be cookies. Cookies help."

"I'm not five. You can't change my mood

with a cookie."

"Good to know." She paused in the doorway and looked at him. "What would change your mood?"

He thought of what she'd been like by the river. How she'd taken all he had to offer and had left him gasping for air. He thought about their weekend together and no matter how many times he reached for her, she was eager to play the game again.

He thought of her in her damn heels, the way she was both bossy and feminine, how sweet she was with the girls. If he was ever looking to break the rules, it would be with her. But that would never happen.

She leaned in and lightly kissed his mouth. "Good to know," she murmured in his ear.

"Good to know what?"

"How I can change your mood."

He was still chuckling as they went downstairs and out onto the street.

"What's your afternoon like?" he asked.

"I have some work to get done. No meetings."

"You have time for lunch?"

"Sure."

He took her hands in his and guided them toward Fifth. "You been to Margaritaville?" he asked. "Great food."

"Powerful margaritas," she told him. "Not

that I drink at lunch."

"You could make an exception."

"I'd never make it back to the office."

"I know."

She laughed. "Trying to get me to be bad? It wouldn't take much." She pointed to the flower boxes in the storefronts they passed. "They change the flowers constantly. They're always blooming and completely right for the season. When the guys first dragged me here, I thought I'd fallen into some 1950s sitcom form of hell."

"You didn't like the town?" What was there not to like?

"I thought it was small and provincial," she admitted. "The people were way too friendly. No one needs to be saying hi to me every fifteen seconds. I couldn't believe I'd been outvoted and this was where we were going to be."

"And now?"

She looked around. "It's growing on me."

"Like fungus?"

She laughed. "Kind of. But good fungus. It's like truffles. An acquired taste." She squeezed his hand. "You, of course, liked it from the first."

"Sure. Ford grew up here and he talked about it all the time. Justice spent a year here as a teenager. What they said reminded me of where I grew up. By the time Justice asked me to join CDS, I was looking for a place to settle in."

"Roots?" she asked.

"Something like that."

He understood that accepting Fool's Gold as home meant letting a part of what he'd had with Marie and Marcus go. They wouldn't be a part of this. But she would have loved it here. As for his son, well, there was no letting go there. Marcus was with him always.

Taryn drew him to a stop and eased him toward the building so they weren't standing in the way. Then she touched his cheek. "You okay?"

"I'm fine."

Her violet eyes met his. "I meant, can I help? You're getting lost in the past. Thinking about Marie and Marcus?"

He kept his expression neutral, because he could. But inside, he was slack-jawed. How had she guessed?

"It makes sense," she went on. "You were together a long time. You were a family. She'll always be a part of you. Like Marcus." She gave him a soft smile. "I know there are things about the girls that freak you out, but I think it's probably easier on you to be dealing with little girls. Teenage boys might bring back a lot of memories. That could be hard."

He touched her hair. "When did you get so smart?"

"I've always been smart."

He nodded. "I do miss her. I feel guilty."

"For being happy? For moving on? Wouldn't she have wanted that?"

"She would. It's not that. Marie was practical. She wouldn't expect me to stay stuck." He hesitated. "It's my fault they died."

"It was a car accident. You weren't even there."

"And I should have been. I should have kept them safe."

There it was — the truth. Spoken unexpectedly. It was his job to keep people safe, yet he hadn't been able to save the two he loved most. A cliché, he thought, accepting the truth of it.

He waited for Taryn to say he was wrong, or try to talk him into thinking something else. Instead she kissed him, then tugged him along to the restaurant. When they were seated, she talked about her meeting with Mayor Marsha and had him laughing at her description of Felicia Boylan explaining what a happy ending meant.

She might not understand what he'd gone

through, but she accepted his truth and the consequences that went with it. A rare combination. One he'd been lucky to find.

After her lunch with Angel, Taryn was too restless to go back to the office. She strolled through town and found herself in front of Paper Moon. Staring at the familiar logo reminded her of Dellina's story of the stored wedding gowns and Sam's reaction to them. She was still giggling when she stepped inside.

The new entrance was boarded up, which meant she had to step into the refined world of all things wedding. There was a young bride on a raised platform in front of five mirrors. She wore a ball gown confection of white lace and tulle, with what looked like her best friend, mother and grandmother hovering nearby.

Isabel spotted Taryn and hurried over.

"Save me," she murmured. "Everything in that family is precious. She's their precious daughter. They want her to look precious on her wedding day. The groom's family is —"

"Precious?" Taryn asked.

Isabel groaned. "Exactly." She waved at Madeline, her associate. "I'm leaving them in your capable hands."

Madeline grinned. "I'll make the experience as precious as possible."

"You do that."

Isabel made a quick call, then motioned for Taryn to follow her to the back of the store. They parted thick plastic covering a doorway and headed into the space next door. Taryn paused as she took in the changes from the last time she'd visited.

The walls had been painted a pale blue-gray and most of the permanent fixtures were in place. The office space in the rear still needed to be finished and the floor was concrete, but otherwise it looked good.

"You're nearly there," Taryn said.

"I know. They start on the floors next week. We're laying down extra padding so all the walking isn't so hard on our legs. The sound system is finished. Ford and I cranked it up last weekend."

"And partied until dawn?" Taryn asked.

Isabel wiggled her eyebrows. "Something like that." She pointed to a portable clothes rack. "Come on. I have a few things to show you."

Taryn followed eagerly. Isabel had contracted with several new designers for clothes and accessories. The pieces were fresh, the styles appealing. Some were too avant-garde for her, but a surprising number of them were completely wearable.

Isabel held out an emerald-green leather jacket with narrow tucking at the waist. There was a flame-red dress with cutouts at the waist and two tailored suits — one with what looked like snakeskin trim.

"Color me impressed," Taryn said. She stepped onto the towel Isabel tossed on the floor and pulled off her sandals. She stripped out of her shirt and capris, then reached for the red dress.

"Hey, it's me," someone called.

Patience Garrett, Justice's wife and the owner of Brew-haha, came around the corner. She saw Taryn standing in her underwear and came to a stop.

"Oh, sorry," she said, starting to turn her back.

"You're in the right place," Isabel told her. "I pulled out a few things for Taryn and I still have that great little black dress for you." She grinned at Taryn. "Justice and Patience are going out for a romantic evening. He told her there would be a nice dinner out and I'm helping her spruce up her wardrobe."

Taryn moved over to make room on the towel. "Please, join me," she said as she pulled the red dress over her head and shimmied until it settled in place.

When she looked up, Patience was gnawing on her lower lip. Taryn wondered if she
was upset she wasn't getting a private showing of the dress.

"I can come back," she said quickly.

Isabel looked at Patience, who blushed.

"It's not that," Patience assured her. "It's
just you're so comfortable standing there in
your underwear."

Taryn sighed. "Sorry. It's the boys. They've
walked in on me in the locker room a bunch
of times. I used to get upset, but they wore
me down."

Patience nodded. "This is good for me.
Being adventurous. Were you wearing a
thong? Aren't they uncomfortable?"

Isabel laughed. "You're going to have to
give us lessons on being sexy, powerful
women."

"Who wear thongs," Patience added.

She was pretty, with brown hair and
brown eyes. She grabbed the hem of her
Brew-haha T-shirt and pulled it off. Her
jeans followed. Taryn told herself not to
judge the plain cotton bikini briefs and
unadorned white cotton bra. No doubt
Patience was a much better person than she
could ever aspire to be.

Patience took the black dress from Isabel
and pulled it on. It was a simple tank style

— fitted, with princess seaming and a hemline a good six inches above her knee.

"Nice," Taryn said. "It fits you great."

"It's tight." Patience tugged on the hem. "And short."

"Sexy," Taryn corrected. "You need a good push-up bra with that and a matching thong." She grinned. "Only don't let him see you getting dressed or you'll never make it to dinner."

Patience drew in a breath. "You're right. I'm busy with Brew-haha and he's busy with CDS. We have Lillie and everything else that keeps the household running. I need to be more adventurous." She turned to Isabel. "I'll take it!"

"You should," Isabel told her with a grin. "It's Taryn. She inspires us all."

Taryn stepped out of the red dress and put it back on the hanger. "I want this for sure. Now for the snake-trimmed suit."

Isabel sighed. "I won't even ask if you have shoes worthy of this. I've seen what you wear."

"If I don't have the right shoes, I'll buy them. I love clothes and accessories and I don't care who knows it."

"I want to borrow your attitude for a night," Patience told her. "Justice wouldn't know what hit him."

"Neither would Ford," Isabel admitted.

"Your men love you the way you are," Taryn reminded them. "And my attitude comes with a price."

She smiled at them, as if joining in the joke, but she knew she was telling the truth. She copped an attitude because sometimes it was all she had to get her through. She'd learned early not to trust people and that the world could be a cold, unfeeling place. Pretending a strength she didn't always have had gotten her through more than once. Now that she was in a place where maybe she could relax a little, she didn't know how to let down her guard. At least not all the way.

She'd made friends here, and she was grateful. But every now and then she looked at women like Patience and Isabel and envied them. They were loved and could love in return. What would that be like? Not the friendship kind of love, but the romantic kind. Where she was the most important person in someone's life. Where there was commitment and sharing and the promise of always.

For a second she thought about Angel, then shook her head. She knew better. He'd made it clear he wasn't looking and she'd been through too much to ever see the romance of wanting what she couldn't have.

They were good together, the sex was impressive and he didn't get on her nerves. For her, that was plenty and she was going to enjoy it while it lasted.

The invitation had been very clear. Young ladies were to wear dresses to the mother-daughter tea. Taryn took that to mean that older ladies were to do the same.

She appreciated the chance to wear her Naeem Khan print organza cocktail dress. She'd fallen in love with the off-the-shoulder black-and-white-print silk dress a few months ago and hadn't figured out where she could wear it. Okay, sure, it might be a little over-the-top for the event, but she didn't care. The full skirt made her feel like an extra in a 1950s movie. She'd slipped on her Pedro Garcia Candela sandals and twisted her hair up in a bun. Simple pearl studs finished off the look.

All the groves were seated around tables in a smaller ballroom at Ronan's Lodge. The girls were dressed in spring pastels. Some mothers had also gone all out, putting on pretty dresses. A few were in jeans and shirts. Humorously, there was only one man at the event. A dark-haired gentleman with gray eyes and a pained expression.

Taryn walked up to Angel. "Stop looking for the exit," she told him.

He cleared his throat, then fingered the collar of his black shirt as if he wanted to loosen his tie. Only he wasn't wearing one.

"I'm not," he told her.

"You're about thirty seconds away from succumbing to flop sweat."

Those cool gray eyes settled on her. "I've never had flop sweat in my life."

"There's a first time for everyone." She turned and smiled as Regan walked over, her mother in tow.

The pretty seven-year-old beamed at Angel. "This is my mom. Mom, this is Angel, our Grove Keeper. And Taryn. She's helping him."

Regan's mother was probably a couple of years older than Taryn and had on a wide wedding band. But that didn't stop her from batting her eyes at Angel.

"Regan says so much about you," she gushed. "You're doing a wonderful job with all the girls." As she spoke, she put her hand on Angel's forearm. "If you need any extra help, you can give me a call."

If Angel hadn't looked so nervous, Taryn might have been annoyed. Since when had she become invisible? But her irritation was tempered by amusement.

"Oh, look," she said, glancing toward the entrance. "Felicia is here. I'll be right back."

"Don't leave me," Angel said through gritted teeth.

Taryn beamed at him. "Regan, you and your mom will take good care of him, won't you?"

The little girl nodded vigorously.

Angel shot Taryn a look that promised retribution later. She could only hope he would make good on his word. She crossed to where Felicia stood staring at all the girls and their mothers.

"Their clothes are all pastel," Felicia said, then fingered the fabric of her empire-style sleeveless dress. "I wasn't sure what to wear."

"You look great." Taryn linked arms with her and led her toward a table on the side. "The actual tea will start in about forty-five minutes. Until then, the girls are supposed to mingle with each other and the moms. There's a punch station. I thought you'd like to serve the punch. That way you can talk to the girls without being creepy."

Felicia nodded. "Thank you. Having a task is helpful. Standing and staring at the children would cause alarm, and I don't want that." She touched her round belly. "I've been doing a lot of reading, but when

264

it comes to children there are some things that must be experienced rather than taught."

Taryn stopped and stepped in front of Felicia. "I don't know your whole story. I know you're smarter than all of us, and that probably makes you feel like a freak sometimes."

Felicia's mouth twisted. "*Freak* is an excellent word."

Taryn shook her head. "That's not my point. Here's my advice. Love your kid and let her know. That's what children need. The rest of it takes care of itself."

Felicia's expression softened. "Your mother didn't love you?"

"She left me. It wasn't good." In some ways, having her mother leave was worse than her father's abuse. Because her mother had known what would happen to her and she'd walked out anyway.

Felicia nodded. "Thank you. You're right. Carter, my stepson, tells me that, as well. I do love her already. I just want to do the right thing."

"All the time? What are the statistical odds?"

Felicia laughed. "Slim."

They continued walking toward the table with the punch bowl. Felicia pointed to it. "Legend says that British sailors discovered punch in India. The etymology of *punch* comes from the Hindu word for *five,* referring to the five ingredients that made up the liquid. They are supposed to be a sweet flavor, a sour, something bitter, something weak and alcohol. Later versions used tea as a base."

Taryn stared at the pink drink. "I'm hoping there's no alcohol in that, or we're in big trouble."

"I'm sure it's nothing more than a sugar-based drink. The girls will be feeling the effects as the sandwiches are served."

"That will make for an exciting afternoon."

She got Felicia settled, saw that Angel was surrounded by even more mothers and walked in the opposite direction. Let him use his stealthy macho skills to get out of that situation, she thought with a grin.

She spotted Bailey and Chloe chatting in a group. Bailey saw her and said something to Chloe, then walked toward Taryn.

Bailey wore a green dress that was a bit tight. Her long red hair hung over her shoulders and she didn't have on much makeup.

"This is nice," Bailey said as she approached. "I like how the FWM gets the girls together so they all become friends.

When Chloe goes to middle school, she'll already know the older girls." She lowered her voice. "I wanted to thank you and Angel for the extra help you've given Chloe. She's really excited about all the activities. I can see a difference in her already."

"I'm glad," Taryn said. "She's very sweet. When Angel asked her to look out for one of the puppies, she was so gentle with him. She's a great girl."

"Thank you. It's been hard without her dad. I miss him, too, but it's different for me."

Taryn wasn't sure that would make dealing with her loss any easier, but she decided not to say that.

Bailey smiled. "Chloe is always talking about your clothes, and I can see why. That's a beautiful dress."

Taryn twisted back and forth so the skirt swayed. "It's a vice," she said cheerfully. "And I don't care. I love this dress."

"The shoes are great, too."

Taryn noticed that Bailey's flats were scuffed from lots of use. She was suddenly conscious of the fact that her dress had cost nearly a thousand dollars and felt the need to apologize.

"I'm going to have to trade my mom jeans in for something more professional," Bailey admitted.

"Changing jobs?"

"Getting a job." Bailey shrugged. "I've had a few part-time jobs. Mostly so I could be around for Chloe. But she's doing better and we need the money. It's been a while since I was in the regular job market, though. Computer programs change every few years. I need to brush up my skills."

"There are probably classes at the local community college," Taryn offered. "You could get up to speed in a couple of days."

Bailey nodded. "I looked online, but they were really expensive. The community college would be easier and cheaper."

"Plus, you'd meet people in your same situation. You can network. Then go buy a power suit and impress the heck out of your future employer."

Emotions chased across Bailey's face. "That's a great idea." She smiled, but something wasn't right. The warmth was gone. "I don't want to take any more of your time. Thanks again for all your help with Chloe."

Taryn nodded as the other woman walked away. She knew she'd said something wrong but couldn't figure out what. The college idea made sense. How else would Bailey get her skills up to date? So if it wasn't that, was it . . .

"The power suit?" she murmured to herself.

Maybe money was so tight Bailey couldn't afford one. Which made Taryn feel even more upset about her dress. What a ridiculous amount to have spent on a piece of clothing. Sure, she could afford it, but . . .

"You're looking fierce," Angel said, coming up to stand next to her. "What's wrong?"

"Nothing." She twisted her fingers together. "I feel stupid."

"Not possible."

She looked at him. "Am I ridiculous? With the clothes and the shoes?"

"What brought this on?"

"You're not answering the question."

"I don't buy in to the premise. You're a beautiful woman. You dress like you want to dress. Why does that make you stupid?"

"I spend thousands of dollars on my things. Do you know what these shoes cost?"

"No, and I don't care. Do you like them?"

"Yes."

"Can you afford them?"

"Sure."

"Then enjoy them."

She knew he was right, but it also wasn't that simple. She watched Bailey talking with some of the other moms. As Taryn studied

Bailey, she felt an odd clenching in her stomach. A need to help.

"It's this town," she grumbled. "I never wanted to get involved. I'm not like you. I don't connect with people."

Angel gave her a slow, sexy smile. "I hate to be the one to break it to you, Taryn, but it's already happening."

"I want it to stop."

"Too late."

CHAPTER THIRTEEN

Angel was willing to admit he was just as secretly sexist as the next man. Sure, he was all for equal pay and felt there should be more women running Fortune 500 companies. He thought women in combat was a good thing, because the way war had changed, they were there already. They might as well get credit.

But those attitudes were all in his left brain. Conscious. Thoughtful. They had nothing to do with his visceral reaction to watching Taryn present her ideas to the CDS team.

He sat in the back with Ford and Consuelo. Justice was up at the conference table. Taryn sat next to him, touching her computer every few seconds to change the slide on the big screen up front.

She'd provided a detailed explanation about why their logo worked and why the rest of their material didn't. She provided

271

market research, information on corporate trends, even some charts on demographics. Angel wasn't sure, because he wasn't listening. He was watching.

She wore some fitted black suit with what he would swear had snakeskin trim. Only Taryn, he thought in admiration. Her shoes had a heel so thin and high they could be classified as a weapon. Her long black hair hung straight down her back. She looked both powerful and unbelievably sexy. It wasn't hard to picture her with a whip . . . or handcuffs. Not that he was into either, but if she wanted to play he didn't think he had it in him to refuse her anything.

Which made sitting there, listening to her talk, physically uncomfortable. While he kept trying to control himself, he'd spent the past hour with a hell of a hard-on. He was careful not to shift in his chair too much. The last thing he needed was for Ford to notice and start ribbing him. While he wasn't keeping his relationship with Taryn a secret, there was no way he wanted to undermine her.

The slide changed again, showing letterhead and business cards. There were several different designs — all variations on a theme. Taryn talked more about what she liked and why. Justice asked a few questions.

Angel let the conversation drift out of focus as he wondered what Taryn would have been like if she'd gone into the military. She would have been tapped for OCS, he thought. She would have liked the discipline and challenges. She would have hated the uniforms.

When the meeting ended, Taryn shook hands with everyone. Justice said they would discuss her ideas and get back to her by the end of the week. Angel knew his friend had liked what he'd seen but didn't want to say so without team feedback.

"Your girl's got some brains," Ford said.

Angel grinned. "Tell me about it. I'll meet you back at CDS."

Ford nodded and left with Consuelo. When Angel was alone with Taryn, she picked up her computer and started down the hall.

"So, what did you think?" she asked.

"Good presentation. It was clear and you'd obviously done your homework."

They walked into her office. He closed the door and adjusted the blinds on the windows so that no one could see in. Then he moved toward her.

"CDS is an interesting case," she was saying as she put her laptop back into its docking station. She didn't notice him approaching. She shrugged out of her jacket and tossed it over a chair. "There are two distinct branches of the company. That's not generally a successful business model, but in this case —"

He grabbed her by her upper arms and turned her toward him. In her damn heels, she was about his height, so they were at eye level. But that was okay as it made it easier for him to kiss her. Which he did.

Taryn leaned into Angel and wrapped her arms around him. His mouth was hot and hungry against her own.

"Here I was hoping for a little more feedback on the presentation," she said, her voice teasing. "But I guess I can accept this instead."

He moved close and rubbed himself against her. She felt his rock-hard erection. "You're sexy when you talk business. Or talk about anything. Or walk. Or breathe."

Feeling his arousal caused her body to respond in kind. Her belly clenched and she was instantly annoyed by all the unnecessary layers of clothing between her and the magic that was his hands on her bare skin. She glanced toward the closed door and saw he'd thoughtfully locked it.

"I'm not generally a sex-at-the-office kind

of girl," she murmured, pressing her lips to his jaw as he reached behind her for the zipper to her skirt.

"Me, either."

She smiled as she breathed in the scent of him. "You're thinking on the desk?"

"I am."

A shiver rippled through her. Tacky, she thought. But equally wonderful.

He lowered the zipper of her skirt. It fell to the floor. She was already pulling off her blouse. He took care of her bra and thong, although he left her high heels in place. Kinky, she thought with a grin.

He reached for her, but she shook her head, then waved her index finger up and down. "You're dressed. That doesn't work for me."

She pushed her computer aside, then sat on her desk and spread her legs. "I'm waiting."

She had to give Angel credit. He took about five seconds to look her over, lingering at her breasts and between her legs. His eyes dilated, his jaw clenched, as if he were holding himself back. But once he started taking off his clothes, he moved so quickly he was a blur. Then he was naked and gathering her in his arms.

His mouth found hers and he pushed his

tongue inside. At the same time he slid his erection deep into her. He filled her all the way, igniting nerve endings as he moved. She clenched around him, tightening as he withdrew. They both whimpered.

She wrapped her legs around his hips and pulled him close. He continued to kiss her, moving his tongue against hers. At the same time he cupped her breasts with his hands and rubbed her tight, aching nipples. He pulled out and pushed in again, driving her closer. He dropped one hand between them. His palm was flat against her belly as he slipped his thumb down to her center and began to rub her clit.

It was too much, she thought frantically. Their kiss, his hands, how he knew exactly how hard and fast to fill her. She drew back slightly so she could stare into his eyes. Heat burning as his muscles tightened.

She felt him getting closer, even as she climbed toward her release. But she wanted to hold back — just for a second. Just to enjoy the trembling anticipation as she hung on the verge of —

Her orgasm claimed her. Every part of her shuddered and she drew in a breath to scream out her pleasure. Even as her brain warned her that was a very bad idea, considering their location, her body lost itself in release and her control slipped to the point where she just didn't care.

But as she opened her mouth, Angel silenced her with a kiss. The sound died as she rubbed her tongue against him, wanting him to feel how good it was. Then he was coming and they were straining together in mutual climax.

Angel was glad he'd gone on his run by himself. He didn't want to have to explain his ever-present grin. He felt relaxed, yet strong as he made his way up the mountain. Damn, he had a good time with Taryn.

He'd clocked their session in her office, and from the time he'd closed the door until they were both dressing and giggling like teenagers, all of four minutes had passed. Under other circumstances he might have been embarrassed by his lack of control, but she'd come just as quickly. She was eager and responsive — a difficult combination to resist.

He jogged past a stop sign and the road that led to the highway and was about to head east along a trail when he spotted a car at the side of the road. It was a ten-year-old import with a dent in the fender and a woman standing beside it.

Angel slowed, then came to a stop. It took

him a second to place the woman. She was blonde and dressed in yoga pants and a T-shirt with tiny flowers all over it. Laura? Leslie? He frowned. Larissa. She worked with Taryn. Something touchy-feely, maybe?

But even though he knew who she was, he couldn't be sure she had the same information about him. He slowed to a walk and kept his arms loose in an attempt to look as nonthreatening as possible.

"Hi," he said. "I'm Angel. I work for CDS in town. Car trouble?"

Larissa smiled at him. "So you're the mysterious Angel. I've heard all about you. Nice to finally meet you."

They shook hands. He glanced at the car. "What's the problem?"

Larissa sighed. "I'm transporting a couple of endangered snakes to a reptile refuge in the desert. I was going to take the interstate through the mountains. I thought it would be a pretty drive."

She mentioned several wildflowers that were in bloom and how important wildflowers were to the ecosystem. Angel waited patiently.

When she paused for breath, he motioned to her car. "Why did you stop?"

"Oh, right. I'm not exactly a snake person. I know they're people, too, but I prefer things with fur. So when I happened to glance over and realized the lid wasn't completely secure on the container, I sort of freaked out. I think one of them is loose in the car." She held out her cell phone. "I was just about to call Jack."

For a second he thought about letting her do just that. Taryn had warned him Larissa was a do-gooder who loved to drag everyone into her projects. Here was a living demonstration. But in truth he had no problem with snakes, and how long could it take to capture one in a car?

"I'll take care of it," he said. "Did you secure the lid before you got out?"

Larissa shook her head. "I kind of screamed and stopped the car. The keys are still in the ignition."

He held in a smile. "If you're afraid of snakes, why did you agree to drive them anywhere?"

"Someone had to. They need a home."

Yup, a do-gooder. Taryn was right — Larissa was trouble. But once he got the snake or snakes back in their container, not his problem.

He moved toward the car. "Do you know if they bite?" He opened the door and moved into the vehicle.

"I'm not sure. Oh, and someone mentioned they might be venomous."

"I told you," Taryn said firmly. "I was extremely clear. But did you listen?"

If Angel hadn't been feeling as if something had clubbed him with the side of a mountain, he would have enjoyed the fussing. But right now he was having trouble focusing and his body ached, as if he was getting the worst flu ever.

"Yeah, you said," he admitted.

He was in a bed, which meant he wasn't still on the side of the road. But he didn't remember much about the trip. He saw the IV connected to his arm and knew the bed he was in wasn't his.

"Hospital, right?" he asked.

"Yes, you're in the hospital. You were bitten by a venomous snake, which is totally ridiculous."

"I feel like crap," he told her. "How about some sympathy?"

"I'm not sure you deserve it." But she sat next to him on his bed as she spoke and she put a cool cloth on his forehead.

"I thought Larissa was kidding," he admitted, the events from earlier that day coming back to him. The snake, the bite, Larissa calling for an ambulance. "I did get the snake back in the container."

"Yes, you did. Larissa is very appreciative and she feels guilty."

He looked at Taryn. "You're going to yell at her, aren't you?"

"Over and over again."

"It's not her fault."

She stroked the side of his face. "You're defending her? She was transporting venomous snakes without proper precautions and she could have died. *You* could have died. If she's crossing state lines, I'm sure there must be a permit, but did she bother? No. She loves her causes and sometimes she doesn't think."

"I'm okay." He put his hand on top of hers. "You can be intimidating. Go easy on her."

Taryn glared at him. "I can't believe you're acting like this. You could have died."

"But I didn't."

Her fierceness was kind of nice, he thought as he did his best to ignore the throbbing throughout his body. Her touch helped. The gentleness of her hands. He wasn't surprised that Taryn had a caring side — he knew that while she complained about "the boys" she would do anything to protect them. However, he hadn't expected that he would find himself the subject of her concern.

Consuelo appeared in the doorway. "You

have a couple of visitors," she said.

He stared at his roommate. "What are you doing here?"

She shrugged. "I heard what happened. I couldn't believe you were that stupid. I came to make fun of you."

Defiant words, but he saw the concern in her eyes. "I'm touched."

"Later you're going to be hit," she grumbled, and turned away.

Taryn stood and shifted to the chair by the bed as Bailey and Chloe walked into the hospital room. Chloe was all big eyes. She'd gone pale and her freckles stood out. As she saw him in the hospital bed, her eyes filled with tears. Not knowing what else to do, he held out his arms.

"Hey, kiddo."

She rushed at him. He wrapped his arms around her, amazed at how small she felt. But fierce. She hung on as if she would never let go.

"I was scared," she whispered against his chest. "I thought you were going to die."

Bailey smiled apologetically. "I told her you were going to be fine, but she needed to see for herself. I'm sorry we're intruding."

"You're not," Angel told her. "It's okay."

"It's just . . ." Bailey paused. "Because of

her dad."

Angel touched Chloe's chin until she looked at him. "Chloe, your dad was a hero. I'm just a guy who got bit by a snake. It was dumb on my part. But the doctors took care of me and I'm going to be okay."

Chloe sniffed. "Did it hurt?"

"A lot."

"Is the snake okay?"

"Yes. It wasn't his fault. He was being a snake. That's why we have to learn to respect nature. I was trying to help the snake, but he didn't know." He paused. "I'm not going to die."

She pressed her lips together and nodded, then started to cry again. He hugged her close. Taryn surprised him by moving to Bailey and holding on to the other woman. Consuelo shook her head and walked toward the doorway.

"No one is hugging me," she said firmly before ducking out into the corridor.

Taryn glared at Jack, who sat in one of her visitor chairs. He showed no sign of budging, which meant he was planning to stay through her meeting with Larissa.

"This has nothing to do with you," she told him.

"Sure it does. You're going to get mad.

You don't get mad often, so people forget what you're like. But I know what's going to happen. You'll get verbal and eviscerate Larissa, who already feels bad enough. Then she'll cry and run off."

"You're protecting her?" Taryn asked, putting her hands on her hips. "You know what happened."

"I do. She was wrong. It's okay to say she's wrong. It's not okay to make her feel worse than she does. I don't want her quitting."

"Which is really what this is about. How you'd be put out if she were gone."

"You'd miss her, too."

Something Taryn could grudgingly admit. "I'm not going to fire her or try to get her to quit. But she has to stop, Jack. At least this part of it."

"I know." The words came from the doorway.

Taryn glanced up and saw Larissa walking into the office. She looked as pale as Chloe had the day before, but without the freckles. She'd pulled her long blond hair back into a ponytail and had on jeans and a T-shirt. There were shadows under her eyes, and her mouth was down-turned.

She walked into Taryn's office and sat next to Jack. She swallowed before speaking.

"I'm so sorry," she whispered. "I never wanted anyone to get hurt. You have to know that."

"I do," Taryn said, finding it difficult to stay angry now that she saw how upset Larissa was. "But you can't keep doing this."

Larissa nodded. "You're right. It's one thing to rescue butterflies, but dangerous or venomous animals are different. I don't have the training." Tears filled her eyes. "It's just when they called, they made the situation sound desperate."

"They always do," Taryn grumbled.

Jack shot her a look, then rubbed Larissa's back. "You were trying to help. It's your thing."

"She didn't help Angel," Taryn snapped. "And it's not the first time. Remember those fighting dogs she kept at your place? You had to move to a hotel. This is more of the same."

Jack started to speak, but Larissa shook her head. "She's right. I put Angel in the hospital. If we'd been farther away from a doctor, he might have died and it's my fault." She swallowed again, then straightened. "I have to look at what I'm doing and be more responsible. I'm sorry."

"Apology accepted," Taryn said, not wanting to torture her friend. "Please tell me you get it."

"I do. I promise. I can't say I'll stop helping, but I'll be more careful in the future."

Jack shot Taryn a warning glance, as if to say they'd gone far enough. Taryn nodded.

"That's what I needed to hear," she said, then stood. "I'm not mad."

"You were," Larissa told her, rising to her feet.

"Just a little."

The two women hugged.

"I really am sorry," Larissa told her.

"I know."

Jack led Larissa from the room.

Taryn crossed to the window in her office and stared out. She was pretty sure she looked normal on the outside, but she was still shaking on the inside. Being mad at Larissa had helped her keep her worries at bay, but now she didn't have a distraction. She'd been reveling in the afterglow of her unexpected morning encounter with Angel when she'd gotten the call that he was in the hospital, suffering from a snakebite. Talk about a random event.

She hadn't liked knowing he was in danger and she'd been shocked by the intensity of her concern. Her relationship with Angel was supposed to be fun. A couple of adults having a good time together. No strings, no promises. She didn't want it to be different. There was no win there. Because neither of them wanted a happily ever after. He'd already had his and there was no way she was trusting anyone with her heart.

CHAPTER FOURTEEN

Taryn's assistant walked into her office. Taryn glanced up and saw the worry on the other woman's face.

"What?" she asked, instantly coming to her feet. "What happened?"

She knew Angel was okay. He'd been released from the hospital a good three days ago and was better every time she saw him. He'd been cleared to resume normal activities and had planned to go to work today. Which left the boys. Knowing them, there was no way to guess what disaster one of them had gotten into.

"You have a visitor," Jude said. "She doesn't have an appointment." She gave a little shrug. "To be honest, I'm a little nervous about telling her she has to make one."

Taryn relaxed. "I have to see who has flapped the usually unflappable you."

She followed her assistant out into the

waiting area and saw Consuelo pacing there. The petite brunette wore her usual tank top and cargo pants. She looked like a caged animal waiting to pounce.

Taryn grinned. "Don't worry. I can handle this. Come on, Consuelo. You're frightening the staff."

Consuelo walked with her to her office, then stood in front of Taryn's desk. She crossed her arms over her chest and stuck out her chin.

"You have to make it stop," she announced.

"Okay." Taryn sat down and motioned for Consuelo to do the same. The other woman remained standing. "Make what stop?"

"The people. The food. Do you know that we have over twelve casseroles in the refrigerator right now? And even more in the freezer. Women and children stop by without phoning. They want to know that Angel's okay, and then they want to talk to me."

Taryn didn't bother to hide her amusement. "How horrible. They're all bitches."

Consuelo's eyes narrowed. "Are you mocking me? Do you think that's safe?"

"I'm feeling brave and tough."

"Then you're a fool."

"Very possibly." Taryn crossed her legs. "What do you want me to do about it?

Angel is a member of the community. People care about him." She decided the moment was too good to pass up. "You do realize they would do the same for you, if you were sick or injured, right?"

Consuelo took a step back and glanced around, as if expecting the walls of a trap to close in on her. "Shit. You're right. That would be awful. They're so nice and normal."

"Disgusting," Taryn agreed.

Consuelo's angry stare returned. "You are clear that I could kill you where you sit, right?"

"Or pretty much anywhere else. But you won't. Enjoy the food. I'm sure it all tastes good."

"There is that," she admitted grudgingly. "But they're in my house."

"Stay with Kent for the next couple of days."

Consuelo's eyebrows rose. "At *his* place? He has a child."

"He has a teenage son who has probably guessed the two of you have had sex at least once."

"Oh my God. You didn't just say that."

Taryn loved that the normally taciturn and tough Consuelo was living so close to the emotional edge. Oddly, it made her feel closer to her.

Taryn leaned forward and lowered her voice. "We've all guessed."

Consuelo sank into one of the chairs and groaned. "I hate it here."

"No, you don't."

"I don't," she admitted with a sigh. "It's just hard, you know. To fit in."

Something Taryn could relate to. "The niceness can be grinding."

"Right? Having to say hi to everyone. Asking about family members. And they're all breeding. Everyone is pregnant or getting pregnant or has just had a baby. Kent and I aren't having kids."

"I didn't know you'd decided that."

"We haven't talked about it, but there's no way." Consuelo's mouth twisted and her tone became wistful. "Unless he would like us to have a baby."

"You'd be a great mother. You wouldn't take crap and you'd love fiercely. That's nice."

Consuelo's gaze snapped back to her. "Do not say that word when you're talking about me."

Taryn wasn't sure if she meant *mother* or *nice,* but either way, she was willing to comply. "Yes, ma'am."

"I should kill Larissa. This is all her fault."

"It is and she's apologized to Angel more than once. She's learned her lesson. Leave her alone."

Consuelo studied her. "Defending one of your own?"

"Yes." It was one thing for Taryn to snap at Larissa, but very different for someone outside the family.

"Fine." Consuelo stood. "You know I hate this, right?"

Taryn wasn't sure if she meant the invasion by the town, the "niceness" of it all or the expectations she wasn't sure she could handle. Regardless, she nodded.

"I do know. And you're going to get through it."

"I hope so. Because if I don't, I'm not going down alone."

Taryn laughed. "That's the spirit."

A week after the snakebite, Angel was feeling back to normal. Larissa had apologized so many times he was officially avoiding her — which was tough. Fool's Gold was a small town.

Now, as he crossed the street to head to a meeting, he looked both ways. Not for cars, but for a specific blonde who still blamed herself for the snakebite.

He managed to make it to the building he

wanted without an encounter. Something he considered a win. He went inside and gave the receptionist his name. A couple of minutes later, he was shown back to Raoul Moreno's office.

Raoul had moved to Fool's Gold a few years before. He was a former football player who now spent much of his life helping disadvantaged inner-city kids with his summer camp — End Zone for Kids — along with scholarships. Most of the latter were funded through his Pro-Am golf tournaments.

When Raoul had scheduled the meeting, he'd refused to say what it was about. Angel had read up on him. His training had taught him that a thorough background investigation could make the difference in any situation. But he hadn't found anything that would indicate why Raoul wanted a meeting. His company was too small to benefit from a corporate bonding experience at CDS. Even if that was his point, he would have contacted Ford, who was in charge of sales. If he was looking to connect with more of his kind, Angel thought with a grin, he should have gone to Score.

He walked into the building and found Raoul sitting alone in an open space. There were plenty of desks but no private offices.

He could see a glassed-in conference area in the back.

Raoul rose from his desk and walked toward Angel. The other man was tall, with dark hair and eyes. He had the easy walk of a man comfortable with himself. Raoul was in decent shape and could probably handle himself on the streets, but in a real fight, he'd go down like the civilian he was.

"Thanks for coming," Raoul said.

"You made it sound important."

"It is."

The two men shook hands. Raoul led the way to the conference room and motioned for Angel to take a seat. Raoul did the same and turned on a small laptop. A permanent screen was on the opposite wall.

Raoul leaned toward him, his forearms resting on the desk. "You know about my program? End Zone for Kids?"

Angel nodded. "Inner-city kids come here for a couple of weeks in the summer. They get to be away from the stress at home and live in nature. Kids from Fool's Gold go to a day camp. They get to know each other, see life from others' perspectives. They all sing 'Kumbaya' at the end."

Raoul grinned. "Something like that. Without the singing. This is our fourth year. We're expanding the program all the time. I had the idea that eventually we'd turn it into a year-round school. Maybe offer science classes or something. That plan was derailed when one of the local elementary schools burned down."

Angel thought about his encounters with Mayor Marsha. "Let me guess. They took over the facility until the new school was rebuilt."

"Yeah. So we focused on the summer camp. Now there's a new school and I have my camp back. I'm still not sure what to do with it in the winter months. Kids today face a lot of problems we never did."

Angel nodded. "Sure. When we went home, we could escape. With social media, that's not possible. There's constant contact. Nothing gets forgotten."

"Bullying doesn't end at three." Raoul studied him. "That's what I want to focus on first. An antibullying campaign. There are a lot of studies that talk about why kids become bullies. If we could break the cycle, even at one school, it would be a start."

"Interesting idea." Not that Angel knew what it had to do with him.

"I thought so." Raoul leaned back. "I have a trained psychologist on my staff. Dakota has been studying this for nearly two years. She has some theories I want to put to the test. If we find a method that works, we can come up with a program. After we test that, we can take it out to schools around the country."

"Ambitious."

Raoul shrugged. "I've been blessed. I had a successful career that left me a wealthy man. Someone close to me taught me the importance of giving back. This is how I've chosen to do it."

Angel knew that most people would think the summer camp itself was enough.

"I want you to sign on as one of my volunteers," Raoul told him.

Angel wasn't used to being surprised. "Why me?"

Raoul grinned. "I've heard good things."

"The guys at Score speak football. I don't."

"They're good men and I thought about them, but I think you have the skill set I'm looking for." He chuckled. "For one thing, you're going to scare the crap out of the average teenage boy. That means he'll be listening."

Angel lightly touched the scar on his neck. He knew he looked intimidating. Or at least he had. Between his time in Fool's Gold and the way his Acorns swarmed around him, he was able to forget from time to time.

"It's not a big-time commitment," Raoul told him. "Two or three hours a week. We'll be figuring it out as we go. Once we have some idea of what's working and what isn't, we'll bring in other volunteers and expand the program."

Angel thought about how he'd first planned on working with teenage boys. Because of Marcus. He hadn't been there for his son — he hadn't been able to keep him safe. Maybe giving back would lessen the gnawing sense of having failed at the one thing that mattered — protecting those he loved.

"Sure," he said. "I'll do it."

"Great." Raoul stood. "Let's go."

Angel rose. "Go where?"

"The high school. Several of the boys have a study period in about fifteen minutes. We can pull them out and talk to them." He flashed another smile. "I cleared it with their counselor a couple of days ago."

"You were that sure of me?"

"I asked around. You seemed like the type to agree."

Angel didn't bother asking what type that was — mostly because he didn't want to know.

Just about fifteen minutes later he and Raoul were walking into Fool's Gold High

School. They signed in at the front desk and were then shown to an empty classroom. They'd barely walked inside when five guys joined them.

The students were younger than Angel had expected. They were still small and skinny. Awkward in their bodies, with too-long legs and arms. Later they would fill out, but right now they were trapped between childhood and manhood. Sophomores, he thought, taking in their curious expressions.

He would guess they were about the same age Marcus had been. Marcus, who had loved baseball and comic books and "Halo 2." Who'd been good at math, loved to read but hated writing essays in English. Marcus, who had been bugging his parents to get him a dog and who'd helped his mom make breakfast every Sunday morning.

Time seemed to bend and shift. The classroom disappeared. Angel had been on a job, protecting some rich banker who'd pissed off the wrong South American drug runners. He and his boss at the time, Tanner Keane, had been holed up with the family at an out-of-the-way cabin near Asheville. Because who would look for the banker and his family in North Carolina?

Angel had been in town buying groceries

when the call came in. A state trooper had broken the news about the rainstorm and the single-car rollover. He'd said that both the driver and passenger had died instantly. They hadn't suffered.

Angel remembered listening to the information but not believing it. Not understanding Marie and Marcus were gone. Later, he'd been grateful for the knowledge that they'd gone quickly, but at the time he'd told the officer he was wrong. He had to be wrong. Because Angel had spoken to Marie not an hour before. She'd never said it was raining.

Tanner had sent Angel home on the company jet. Their family doctor, also a close friend, had identified the bodies, but Angel had insisted on seeing them. He'd ignored the blood, the broken bones and held each of them. But he'd been too late. They were cold and whatever had made them the people he loved had been gone.

Tanner's wife, Madison, had made all the arrangements for the funeral. Angel had started drinking and he hadn't stopped for nearly six months. In that time he'd thought about putting a gun to his head. The only thing that had stopped him was the knowledge that Marie would be so disappointed if he did.

He'd tried to work through the stages of grief — but he kept coming back to anger. And the person he couldn't forgive was himself. Because if he'd been there — if *he'd* been driving — they would both still be alive.

"Angel?"

Angel felt more than heard Raoul speaking his name. He was pulled back to the present with a gut-clenching jerk. The past faded and he was left standing in a classroom with five teenage boys staring at him.

He forced himself to remain in this moment, to introduce himself and shake hands with the kids. He learned their names and their stories. But all the while, all he could think about was his son. The son he would never see again. The son he hadn't been able to save.

Taryn studied the graphics for the preliminary presentation for Cole and the LL@R team. She wasn't sure they'd captured the spirit of the company yet. But as she studied the pictures and lettering, she had the thought that maybe she and Angel could brainstorm some kind of art project using computer graphics. The Acorns would love it. There had to be an FWM bead for being creative. There seemed to be a bead for everything else.

But not art for the sake of it, she thought. There would have to be a practical use. Posters for a festival, maybe. Or an awareness campaign. It seemed that every month celebrated something. They could pick a cause and design posters. The girls would love that.

She went online and started searching for lists of what was celebrated when. There was national ice cream month — something she could seriously support. Maybe a day was better, she thought. Something about community service might be nice. National something . . .

She continued to search online. Her phone rang and she picked it up. "This is Taryn."

There was a pause before the caller spoke. "It's Justice."

Taryn stopped typing. There was a problem. She could hear it in his voice. "What is it?"

"I don't know," he admitted. "Angel had a meeting this morning with Raoul Moreno. He's a local former football player."

"I know who he is," she told Justice. Raoul was the one who had invited the boys to Fool's Gold in the first place. They'd played in his Pro-Am golf tournament and subsequently changed her life forever. Although she was less annoyed about that than she had been.

"He got back and went into the workout room. He's on a punching bag."

"Okay," she said slowly, not sure what to do with the information.

"You should get here as soon as you can," Justice told her.

The statement wasn't a request.

"Give me five minutes," she said, and hung up.

Which was about how long it took her to grab her bag, head to her car and drive the few blocks to CDS. When she arrived, she parked, then hurried inside. Justice was waiting by the door.

"Sorry to bother you," he said with a shrug. "He won't talk to me or Ford. I can't find Consuelo, so . . ."

"I'm glad you called."

They were walking down the hallway. She was aware of a thunking noise that got louder with each step. They walked into the big workout room and she saw Angel hitting the punching bags over and over. Even from across the large space, she could see he'd taped his hands and yet blood seeped through the tape and dripped onto the floor.

But what really scared her was the look

on his face and the expression in his eyes. It was as if he'd seen a monster. No, she thought. Not a monster. Something much bigger and more frightening. He'd seen into the pit of hell, and whatever was there was coming after him.

She took a step toward him. Her high heels made her sway on the mat. She bent down and took them off, then walked barefoot to where he continued to punish the bag. Or maybe just himself.

She stopped next to him. "Angel."

He looked at her. She could tell he wasn't seeing her. Not at first, then his eyes cleared.

"Taryn? What are you doing here?"

"I came to get you. Come on. We're going to my place."

"What? Why?"

He was pale. Sweat drenched his T-shirt. When she touched his upper arm, his skin was clammy. She pulled gently.

"Come on. Let's go."

She'd thought he might fight. Instead he nodded and moved toward her. She led him across the mats. After stepping into her shoes, she headed for the front of the building. Justice met them in the hall. He handed Taryn a small black duffel bag.

"A change of clothes," he said.

She took them. "I'll call you later."

She and Angel walked out of the building and toward her car. When she'd unlocked the passenger door, he got in without being asked.

She watched him fumble with the seat belt. But his hands were taped and swollen and he couldn't move his fingers. She bent down and fastened it for him, then kissed his cheek.

He turned toward her. For a second, she would have sworn she saw tears in his eyes. Then he blinked and it was as if they'd never been there at all.

CHAPTER FIFTEEN

Angel didn't speak on the short drive to Taryn's house. She kept glancing at him, trying to see if he was okay, but she couldn't tell much from his profile. When they got to her place, she guided him inside. She checked the duffel and saw that Justice had given her a full set of clothing, so she led Angel to the bathroom off the master and started the shower.

After kicking off her shoes and shrugging out of her jacket, she pulled off his T-shirt. He toed out of his sneakers and pulled off his socks, then stood immobile while she carefully unwrapped the tape on his hands.

She went as slowly and carefully as she could, but she knew she had to be hurting him. His skin was cut, raw and bruised. Blood seeped from open wounds. He looked as if he'd been in a hell of a fight and she supposed he had been. She wondered who the opponent had been and suspected it had been himself. But why?

When she was done with the tape, she opened the shower door. "Finish undressing," she told him. "Take a shower. I'll be back in five minutes."

He nodded. She went out and closed the bathroom door behind him. She exhaled slowly when she heard him close the shower door.

She changed her clothes quickly and then dug out an old first aid kit. By the time she returned to the bathroom, Angel was toweling off. His blood left stains on her towel, but she didn't care.

After he was dressed, she took him to the dining room, where she'd set out her supplies. At least now his hands were clean. She used an antiseptic spray and the largest bandages she owned to patch him.

"Is this going to be okay?" she asked. "Should you go to a doctor or the hospital?"

"Just a few scratches," he told her.

His voice was low and rough. As if he hadn't spoken in days. Or had been screaming until he was hoarse. She knew neither was true. She kept her hands lightly on top of his, careful not to put any weight on his wounds. She studied him.

His hair was mussed — damp and sticking up in places. He was pale. Still broad through the shoulders. Powerful, yet not fully with her.

"Angel? What happened?"

He looked at her. There was something in his eyes, she thought. A vacancy. For a second she wondered if he even knew she was in the room.

He swallowed. "We were both so damn young, Marie and I. Kids, really. I was a new recruit and she worked in her uncle's store. Her family wasn't happy about us dating. Not at first. But I was like that stray dog you can't shake. No matter what, I wouldn't go away. So they accepted the inevitable and we got married. Two months later, I shipped out."

He was still staring at something she couldn't see. Telling the story to her or to someone else? Maybe himself? She knew it didn't matter. That in the telling came whatever healing he would have today.

He swore. "I missed her and I loved what I was doing about the same. Which made for a difficult time. When I got home a year later, she held out a baby boy. She'd been pregnant and hadn't told me. She'd said she didn't want to worry me. That I was doing dangerous things and needed to concentrate. She'd named him Marcus, after my dad."

"That must have made you feel good," she said quietly. "Happy."

"I was. We were. We were a family and I loved them both."

She moved her hands to his forearms and squeezed. She didn't know why he was dealing with this today, but she could feel his pain. "It's not your fault. It was an accident."

"If I had been there . . . If I had been driving . . ."

"It's not possible for one person to protect another from life."

"I know." His voice filled the room as he roared the words and stood. "I know that I couldn't shield them from accidents and pain. But I should have tried. I should have been there. I loved them and I didn't keep them safe."

He crossed to the window and stared out at her small yard. She watched him, not sure what to do. She could intellectually understand his pain but couldn't know what it felt like in her heart. Because she'd never allowed herself to love that much. Not even Jack, who had squeezed his way in more than anyone else.

She'd never been in love, had never wanted to be. Faced with his tangible grief, she wondered if it was ever worth it.

"What happened today?" she asked.

"I talked to Raoul Moreno. He wants my help with an antibullying program he's starting. I said I would and he took me to the high school. I talked with some teenagers there. Boys."

He turned slowly and faced her. His jaw tightened, as if he was holding in as much as he could.

"You know the irony?" he asked. "When I went to see Mayor Marsha about volunteering and she told me about the FWM, I thought I'd be working with boys. I figured I knew what that was like because of Marcus. Then, when I found out about the girls, I freaked."

She smiled. "Yes, I was there."

His mouth curved up slightly, then twisted again. "I was wrong. Being with those kids nearly did me in. All I could think about was Marcus. What he was like, how he died. I could barely talk. Raoul covered for me. I'm going to have to tell him what happened."

And get over it, she thought. Because there was no way Angel was going to back away from the challenge.

"I didn't know what to do," he admitted. "The bag's a safe place."

By "bag" he must mean the punching bag,

she thought. Hitting that was safer than driving too fast, or getting drunk and then driving. Her gaze dropped to his bandaged hands. Not that it was an easy way to deal with emotion.

"I'm sorry to put you through this," he told her.

"Why?" She stood and crossed to him. "You're feeling what you feel. You had a wife and a child. You lost them both in a horrible way and every now and then you're in a bad place."

He looked into her eyes. "That's it?"

"What else would there be?"

"You could tell me to get over it. That it's time to move on."

"Not my job or my style," she said.

His love for his family had nothing to do with her, except maybe to point out that nearly everyone was capable of that kind of commitment except her. Love required trust, and there was no way she would go there. She'd made a choice a long time ago and saw no reason to change her mind.

He reached for her and pulled her close. His strong arms held her tight.

"Thank you," he whispered.

"Anytime."

He didn't speak, which was okay with her. Because if he did, if he'd said he would take her up on that, it would send them to a place that neither of them wanted to go. Marie would be the love of his life for as long as he lived. Taryn knew she would never be able to trust anyone with her heart. It made them perfect for each other. Neither of them would allow things to get serious.

While the realization should have been comforting, instead she felt an odd sense of sadness. As if she'd lost something important. Something she'd almost been able to grasp, until it had somehow slipped away.

"If you wore flats, this wouldn't be a problem," Larissa said as Taryn parked in front of Jo's Bar.

Taryn looked at her friend. "You're wearing flats. You could have walked."

Larissa grinned. "I was being supportive."

"By driving with me and then complaining about my shoes. It's an unusual way to show support."

"I'm an unusual person."

When Taryn had come in to work this morning and seen the lunch date on her calendar, she nearly canceled. Since picking up Angel the previous afternoon, she hadn't been able to shake the sense of her world being out of whack. Then she'd reminded herself that life had to go on and hanging

out with girlfriends was about the most af-
firming activity she knew.

Taryn collected her tote and got out of
the car. The crocodile-and-glittered-python
satchel bag had been delivered that morning. She'd seen it online the day after
Angel's snakebite and had bought it in a
gesture of solidarity. So far Larissa hadn't
noticed, which was good. Larissa didn't
believe in using animals or reptiles for bags
or shoes. Although, as Taryn liked to point
out, Larissa did occasionally wear leather.

They walked into Jo's Bar and saw that
Isabel, Felicia and Dellina had already
claimed a table. The three women waved
them over. Taryn smiled as she approached,
not wanting anyone to know she wasn't feeling her perky best.

She couldn't shake what had happened
yesterday with Angel. After the incident with
the punching bag, he'd stayed with her.
They'd slept together and in the morning
he'd made love to her — swollen hands and
all. She could say that, yes, he was back to
who he had been . . . but *she* wasn't. She
was still wrestling with all the emotion he'd
been dealing with. The pain and suffering.

She wasn't sure what she was feeling, so
she didn't know how to make it better — or
make it go away. Either would be a help.

But instead she was left wallowing in something she didn't understand and the growing sense that she might well be in over her head.

She and Larissa had just taken their seats when Consuelo joined them. Jo walked over with menus and mentioned she had a new pulled pork nacho plate, if they wanted to try those.

Isabel groaned. "I'm trying to lose ten pounds."

Dellina smiled at her. "Don't take this wrong, but you're always trying to lose ten pounds. The pulled pork nachos sound great."

Consuelo studied Isabel. "I could work up an exercise program," she offered. "Get you into fighting shape."

Isabel shook her head. "I don't want to fight anyone. To be honest, I think I'd rather complain about the extra pounds than do something about them. No offense."

"None taken." Consuelo turned to Taryn. "You should do less cardio and more weight training. You have good core strength, but another five pounds of muscle would make a big difference in your metabolism."

Taryn thought about the weight room at Score and knew that any of the boys would be delighted to take her through a workout.

"I'd rather have a root canal," she murmured. "And now I want the nachos, too."

Larissa leaned toward Consuelo. "So you're secretly working for Jo's nacho vendor?"

"I guess," Consuelo muttered. "Now I want a margarita."

Dellina grinned. "That sounds great. But I feel compelled to point out it's only lunch. Alcohol means a very slow afternoon."

Isabel tossed her menu on the table. "I'm walking."

"I'm gestating," Felicia said. "Jo has agreed to make me a nutritious smoothie that will aid fetal development."

"We drove," Larissa said, glancing at Taryn. "It's her shoes."

Taryn reached for her bag and dug out a pair of flats she kept tucked away for emergencies. "I can stagger back to the office if you can."

Larissa's eyes lit up. "I say we go for margaritas."

Consuelo rested her head on her hand. "Me, too. Getting drunk sounds like fun."

Isabel waved at Jo. "A pitcher of margaritas for the table. And nachos."

Jo studied them. "You girls are getting wild. Everyone walking?"

They all nodded.

"Margaritas it is. And a smoothie for Felicia."

Less than five minutes later Taryn was sipping the cold sweet-tart drink and waiting for the tequila to work its magic. She couldn't remember the last time she'd sat around with girlfriends over drinks and just had a good time. Probably because she'd never been very good at finding girlfriends. After her mom had left, she'd emotionally shut down. She'd been too scared of her dad to invite anyone over. What if he'd shown up drunk?

After running away, she'd spent all her time trying to keep herself fed and safe. She hadn't had time for wasted afternoons. Eventually whatever small girl-talk skills she'd managed to acquire had atrophied. Until she'd moved here.

Not that she was going to tell the boys she was really settling in to life in Fool's Gold.

"I am very close to the unveiling of the newly remodeled Paper Moon," Isabel said, reaching for her drink. "I'm really happy with how everything has turned out." She looked at Taryn. "Madeline is working out well. She's come into her own with the bridal half of the business."

"Better for you." Taryn knew that Isabel preferred working with the designers and buying inventory than dealing with the emotional ups and downs of brides-to-be.

"It is. She's really patient with them. She can handle the mothers and mothers-in-law, which is an art." She paused. "I really want to keep her in the store. Right now a monetary bonus isn't going to happen, but I was thinking maybe a small percentage of ownership."

Dellina glanced between them. "That sounded like a question, not a statement. Are you looking for advice?" She turned to Taryn. "I didn't know you'd been in retail."

Taryn could already feel the tequila going to work — probably because she was starving. No doubt Isabel was reacting to the same. Otherwise, this was a conversation they would have had in private.

"I haven't," Taryn said, deciding there was no point in hiding the truth. Not that it had ever been a secret. More like something she hadn't shared with a bunch of people. "I'm an investor in Isabel's business."

"More than that," Isabel told them. "She basically paid for the remodeling. I used my savings to put a large down payment on buying the business."

Consuelo raised her eyebrows. "Buying local?"

Larissa stared at her. "That's so nice. I'm

surprised."

Dellina chuckled. "You're saying she's not nice?"

"What?" Larissa shook her head. "No. Of course she's nice. It's just not always obvious. Like this." She clapped her hands together. "You have to let Madeline be a part owner. It's so perfect."

Which was just like Larissa, Taryn thought affectionately. Leaping in without knowing all the facts but with the idea the world should be saved.

Taryn could have mentioned the venomous snake incident, but Larissa had finally stopped apologizing. She didn't want to start that up again.

Jo arrived with two plates of nachos. Taryn stared at the steaming meat, the melted cheese and the piles of guacamole on top, and knew she was in for an extra session on the elliptical tomorrow. Still, she had a feeling it was going to be worth it.

She took her first bite and nearly groaned as she tasted the spices on the tender pork, along with the subtle heat of the salsa.

Felicia turned to Consuelo. "What's wrong?" she asked.

"Nothing. Why do you ask? Why does something have to be wrong?"

That sounded tense even for the petite

firecracker, Taryn thought. She saw everyone was staring at Consuelo, who glared at them.

Felicia poured her friend a second margarita. "You're extremely tense. You keep shifting in your seat and you're twisting your engagement ring so quickly I'm concerned you'll injure yourself. You're showing classic psychological signs of tension and anxiety."

Taryn found herself grateful she was sitting across from the other two because Consuelo wasn't the type to take that kind of criticism well. Taryn half expected to see her go on the attack. But Consuelo only slumped down in her seat and sighed heavily.

"It's Kent," she mumbled. "He wants us to set a date for the wedding."

Larissa frowned. "I don't get it. Aren't you engaged?"

Consuelo stared at the diamond ring on her finger. "Yes, we're engaged."

"A wedding seems like the next logical step," Dellina murmured. "From a professional's perspective, at least."

Consuelo crunched on a chip. She chewed and swallowed, then gulped from her glass. "I'm not ready," she said when she'd put it back on the table. "He's pressuring me. Why does he have to pressure me?"

Felicia smiled. "You're afraid. This is fear. You're not feeling pressured about planning the wedding. It's the actual marriage that concerns you. You don't think you can be in that kind of stable situation. You're going to be moving in with Kent and Reese. Be a part of a family. You haven't had that in many years and you've forgotten what it's like."

Once again Taryn waited for the attack, but Consuelo only nodded as her brown eyes filled with tears. "I know. It's horrible. I'm so emotional and moody and yes, scared. I hate it!"

"Kent's a great guy," Isabel said. "He's crazy about you. If you're worried about expectations, you don't have to be. He's not looking for you to take over things at his house. He can handle all of that himself. He's done that for years."

"I know," Consuelo said. "But what if I can't do it?"

"Do you love him?" Taryn found herself asking.

Consuelo sniffed. "Uh-huh. More than anything. At first my feelings were frightening, but now I'm used to them. To us. I need him and I can't stop needing him. It's the being normal part I don't know how to deal with."

Something Taryn could relate to. Normal wasn't part of her world, either. That and being vulnerable. Neither made her comfortable.

"Kent chose you," Felicia told her friend. "He knew you weren't normal when you first met."

Consuelo smiled. "That makes me feel a little better. But I still don't want a big wedding. Or a small one. I don't want to *get* married, I just want to *be* married. If I was sure he wasn't expecting me to be normal, I think I could handle that."

Felicia nodded slowly. "But you're afraid Kent would miss the ceremony. The rite of passage in front of his friends and family."

"Reese, too," Consuelo admitted.

"You're going to have to find a point of compromise. Talk to him. Find out what part of getting married is most important to him. I suspect it's not the ceremony as much as you think. I believe he wants you in his house and his bed on a permanent basis, that he wants to begin his life with you."

Taryn was impressed with Felicia's grasp of the complexities of human relationships. For all her freakish intelligence, she was starting to be intuitive, as well.

Another pitcher of margaritas was ordered

as they ate their way through the nachos. Taryn felt herself relaxing. These women were nice, she thought. Her friends. She could almost trust them.

She had the thought that she should do more than that. She should just emotionally put herself out there. These women were honest and caring. They wouldn't hurt her. Not on purpose.

Without wanting to, she remembered slipping off that ladder. Of reaching for her father so he could keep her from falling. She remembered the look in his eyes as he'd deliberately ignored her pleas and how she'd screamed the whole way to the ground. And she wondered if she would ever be able to let that go enough to reach out to another person. Figuratively or literally. Or if she would always hold herself back rather than risk the fall.

Taryn spread out several sheets of paper in front of Mayor Marsha. Each one had a different slogan on it.

"We did some preliminary work with the graphics," Taryn said, pointing at the different fonts and backgrounds. "That's just to show you what is possible. For now we need to focus on the actual phrase itself."

She'd arrived a few minutes early for her

meeting, just so she could go through her briefcase. She'd been worried Sam and Kenny would slip in a mock-up for Fool's Gold — Where Men Are Finally Coming. They'd been threatening it for days. Fortunately only the real slogans seemed to have made their way into her tote.

Taryn and the mayor read over the slogans together. All That Glitters. Town with a 24-K Heart. Go Gold Or Go Home. Join the Rush. Home of the Happily Ever After. A Destination for Romance.

"I like that one," the mayor said, pointing at the card that read Fool's Gold — A Destination for Romance.

"It's close to the old slogan," Taryn said. "But without the second meaning. We can work up some artwork if you'd like."

"Let me take it to the city council first," Mayor Marsha told her. "I'm hoping to get some kind of consensus before you put any more effort into this. Believe me, that may take a while."

"Not a problem. Just let me know when you're ready to move forward or if you need more suggestions." Although she wasn't looking forward to another session with Kenny and Sam. Lord knows what they would come up with if given the chance.

"I will. You were very thorough. Thank you."

Taryn started to reach for her tote, then drew back. "I have something else, if you have a minute."

"Of course."

Taryn sat at the large conference table, then wished she'd stayed standing. "I have a problem. . . ." She paused. "Not a problem, exactly. I want to do something and I'm not sure how to go about it."

The mayor's expression softened. "You'll need to give me a few more details if you want my help."

Sure. Because that made sense. Taryn twisted her hands together. Larissa would know exactly what to say, she thought glumly. Larissa would have already fixed the problem and found homes for kittens and a hedgehog by now.

"Do you know Bailey Voss and her daughter, Chloe?"

"Yes. It was very sad when Bailey's husband died. Things didn't turn out the way they'd planned."

"Bailey is looking to get back into the workforce. I made a comment about an interview suit. From the look on her face, I'm guessing she doesn't have one and maybe can't afford one. I want to give her one, but I don't know how."

The mayor looked at her for several seconds, then nodded. "Yes, I can see that is a dilemma." She stood. "Good luck with that."

Taryn blinked. "Excuse me? You don't have a suggestion? Isn't that what you do? Give directions and solve problems?"

Mayor Marsha smiled. "I'm not a traffic officer, my dear. And while I have been known to step in from time to time, in this case, I believe you will do better than I ever could. There must be some way you can get sweet Bailey a suit. I'm sure you'll figure it out."

When it was obvious the mayor was going to walk out of the room, Taryn rose. "That's it?"

"For now. I'm planning a trip. Did you hear? I'm off to New Zealand in a few weeks. Very exciting." The mayor started for the conference room doorway. "Good luck with your project."

CHAPTER SIXTEEN

"I don't get it," Taryn said as she poured soil into a large planter. There were already rocks at the bottom to help with drainage. "Mayor Marsha helps people. Everyone knows that. But she just blew me off. Do you think she's mad at me or something?"

Angel put down the two small trees he'd carried in from his SUV and walked over to her. He put his hands on her hips and turned her until she faced him. "She's not mad. She likes you a lot. She's being her normal meddling self."

Taryn felt her lower lip wanting to thrust out in something alarmingly close to a pout. "But she's *not* meddling. That's my point."

"Sure she is. You're right. She's usually in the middle of things and this time she's stepping back. Which has you in a tizzy. Catching people off guard is her style. She's manipulating the situation as much as if she told you what to do."

Taryn hadn't thought of it that way. She leaned into Angel. "Maybe you're right," she said, letting the warmth and strength of his body comfort her. "I've been running in mental circles since I left her office."

"She loves that." He moved his hands to her face and cupped her cheeks. "You'll figure out the best way to get Bailey a suit."

"I hope so. It just would have been easier if the mayor had offered a solid suggestion." She smiled at him. "Okay, I'm officially done with the topic."

"You don't have to be."

"We have trees to plant."

They'd spent the morning at Plants for the Planet where Taryn had chosen three different Japanese maple trees. They were all small enough to be happy in containers, which made them perfect for her small patio. Now they had to be moved into their new container homes.

After sliding the containers into place, Angel had put rocks in the bottom to help with drainage. Now she held the trees steady while he cut away the plastic. Once he'd tossed them aside, he freed the roots before lifting the trees into place.

"You're good at this," she told him. "I wouldn't have pegged you for a plant guy."

"I know things."

A casual enough answer, but she saw the tension in his shoulders and knew he was keeping his face deliberately away from her. She picked up the bag of soil and poured it in. As he smoothed it into place, she spoke.

"It's okay," she said quietly. "To talk about your life with Marie and Marcus."

Angel straightened and wiped his hands on his jeans. "It was a long time ago."

"But it's still a part of who you are. I understand. If Marie hadn't died, you wouldn't be here right now. We wouldn't have met. Your feelings about her have nothing to do with me."

His gray gaze settled on her face. "That sounds rational. But this isn't a rational subject."

"Why not? We're together because she's gone. You don't have to pretend you don't want it to be different. That you don't miss her."

Ignoring the fact that neither of them wanted a commitment, even if either of them was more traditional and wanted it all, she would still have to tend with a ghost in his past. A first love. It wasn't about being loved more or fighting memories. Loving Marie had made him who he was. She was a part of him, just as Taryn's past was a part of her.

If they were on a different course, she would still be okay with what had come before. Because the alternative was to fight what she could never change.

"I don't want you to pretend you don't love her," Taryn told him. "I like that you do. It makes you one of the good guys."

He pulled her close again. This time he hung on so tight she found it difficult to catch her breath. But that was okay — because when it came to Angel, she'd discovered she liked the feeling that he would never let go.

Taryn stared at the columns of numbers. She hated going over the books of a business. It was one of the reasons she was so fond of Sam. He protected her from that at Score. But he wasn't involved in her partnership at Paper Moon, and as he was still sulking because she insisted he plan the upcoming company party with Dellina, and he didn't want to, she had been pretty sure he would refuse any request for a favor.

Which was why she was stuck hunched over Isabel's desk, reviewing monthly statements and fighting a tension headache. She scanned the receipts for the construction, then checked the receivables and payables.

"You're coming in slightly under budget

on the remodeling," she said. "Is this all the receipts for fixtures?"

Isabel sat opposite her. "Yes. I got a great deal on some racks I wanted. Technically they were used but they never got out of the box. The people who bought them had a store that went under before it opened."

"A lesson to us all."

They'd decided to keep the two sides of the business distinctly different. Brides shopping for wedding gowns wanted the special experience of soft lighting, romantic music and gigantic dressing rooms. On the "regular" retail side, the design was more edgy, the music more rock and there was a whole lot less tulle.

Taryn straightened. "You're doing great." She opened her tote and pulled out a check that represented the final installment of her hundred-thousand-dollar investment. With it, Isabel would buy inventory and hire extra staff for both sides.

Isabel took the check and sighed. "We're really doing this."

"We are." Taryn smiled at her. "I thought a lot about what you said about Madeline. Bringing her into the business. I think that's a good idea. As you said, make her manager of the wedding gown side of things. Giving her skin in the game will make her even more motivated. Although you're going to have to warn her that initially there won't be any profits for her to share in."

Taryn opened a folder and handed Isabel a copy of the chart she'd made. It showed Madeline starting with an initial grant of 2 percent of the business, then over the next five years working her way to a 10 percent ownership. Taryn's hundred grand had given her a 40 percent stake. Her suggestion was that by the end of the five years the 10 percent would be divided according to the percentage of their stake. So Isabel would own 54 percent, Taryn would own 36 percent and Madeline would have the remaining 10 percent.

"At that point, we'll reevaluate," Taryn said. "You especially. In five years you'll want to start buying me out."

Isabel's eyes widened. "You'll leave the partnership?"

"I don't have to, but you'll be ready to be on your own. Trust me — having a partner looking over your shoulder is going to get old."

"Maybe, but right now I appreciate your business acumen."

Isabel wrote her a receipt for the check, then walked to a small refrigerator and pulled out a diet soda for each of them.

"Any aftereffects from our lunch a few days ago?" she asked.

Taryn grinned. "I was buzzed into the evening, that's for sure. But I'm fine today." She took the soda and popped the top. "Consuelo was surprising."

Isabel sat across from her. "Panicked, you mean? Their relationship is so unexpected. I mean Kent's a great guy, but the way Consuelo looks at him, you'd swear he has secret superpowers."

"Maybe for her, he does," Taryn murmured. "It's nice that she's so crazy in love. Or just crazy."

"He's a math teacher." Isabel shook her head. "I don't get it, but on the bright side, it does prove there is someone for everyone."

Taryn took a sip of her soda and refused to speculate on the obvious. Because it didn't matter if there was someone for her. She wasn't interested.

"It's fun that she's trying so hard to be conventional," she said instead. "I don't know a lot about her past, but I'm guessing this is the first time she's tried to be like everyone else."

"You're right," Isabel told her. "I swear, Ford is terrified of her."

"Angel won't admit to fear," Taryn said

with a grin, "but he gives her a wide berth. Which only makes me like her more. Yet it all comes down to pleasing Kent and wanting to fit in. I know guys will change when they get in a relationship, but it seems that women change more. Or are willing to. Maybe I'm generalizing."

"I don't think so." Isabel leaned toward her. "As a gender, we want to bond. The connection is important. Even for a woman like Consuelo. I don't know everything about her past, but I get the impression that she's always wanted to go her own way."

"Or maybe she's just had to," Taryn murmured, thinking people were often defined by what they'd been through.

She rose and walked over to the single rack of clothes Isabel had brought in. They were for her to try on. All beautiful, she thought, fingering the fabric. Custom-made by up-and-coming designers. They would go for anywhere from a few hundred dollars to a thousand.

Once the store was open, Isabel would carry a range of prices. While she would never be competing with a discount store, not every garment would be expensive. They were hoping to cash in on the tourists spending time and money in town. Her business plan also included selling to residents.

Still, could someone like Bailey afford to shop here?

"Fool's Gold needs a consignment store," she said absently.

Behind her, Isabel made a choking sound.

"Wh-what? Are you trying to put me out of business before I even get opened?"

Taryn glanced at Isabel and saw she was staring wide-eyed.

Taryn immediately held up both hands. "Sorry. I'm not trying to frighten you. I was just thinking there are people who can't afford a thousand-dollar handbag."

"So they don't need to buy one. A consignment store? Tell me you're not going to invest in one."

"I'm not." Taryn returned to the desk. "Seriously, it's okay. I was just thinking . . ." She sighed. "There's this woman I met. She's a single mom and she's about to enter the job market and from what I can tell she doesn't really have an interview suit. I'm not sure she can afford it. I don't know why that bugs me, but it does. And it's not like I can give her one. She's not going to take it. So I was thinking a consignment store would be the answer."

Isabel's breathing returned to normal.

"Why didn't you say so? You nearly gave me a heart attack."

"Which was not my goal for many reasons." She thought about Bailey. "I don't know what to do. I went to Mayor Marsha and she basically blew me off. She said she was sure I'd figure out a solution."

"Our mayor Marsha?"

Taryn nodded. "Shocking, right? That's what I thought, too. Doesn't she have a reputation for meddling? Which means I don't know how to help. Like I said, I can't really go up to her and hand her a suit. It's weird and she might be insulted."

Isabel picked up her soda. "So let's have an exchange party."

"A what?"

"A clothing exchange. We can hold it here. We invite a bunch of women to bring in clothes they no longer want and we exchange them with each other. We can ask for a small donation for a local charity if you want to make it seem like there's a cause involved. So your friend doesn't get suspicious."

"It's Bailey Voss. Do you know her?"

"No, I don't think so."

"She's great. If we wore the same size, I would give her one of my suits."

Isabel eyed her. "Is anyone your size?

Aside from supermodels?"

"Very funny. I like your idea of an exchange party. I could buy a couple of suits and pretend they're part of the exchange. How do I find out her size?"

"I'll take care of that," Isabel said, writing down the name. "After working in this place, I can judge a size at fifty yards." She looked back at Taryn. "Don't buy anything too fancy. She won't be comfortable in it."

Taryn nodded. "Should I let you take care of the suit purchasing?"

"No offense, but yes. I'll also have one of my tailors at the party to do instant alterations."

"I'll cover that cost," Taryn told her. She remembered Bailey's scuffed flats. "Let's do shoes and handbags. Why don't we say everyone has to put five dollars in the pot for every item they take? Can you judge shoe sizes?"

"Not as well," Isabel admitted. "How tall is she?"

"About five-seven."

"So nothing below a seven, most likely." Isabel grinned. "You have big feet. Bring some of your old shoes."

Taryn glared at her. "I do not have big feet. I'm tall. My feet are appropriately sized."

"You're a nine or a nine and a half. That's not petite."

"I'm ignoring you," Taryn told her. "Okay, we'll have an exchange party. Let's get the word out. Oh, wait. I know. I'll hire Dellina to organize the whole thing. We can have food and music." She thought about her ongoing tussle with Sam. "It's not like she's working on the company party."

"The what?"

"Nothing," Taryn said with a sigh. "Score business. Anyway, yes, let's do this. We'll have fun."

"Okay, this is a stretch, even for Fool's Gold," Taryn said as she and Angel walked through the center of town. "I'll accept celebrating the major holidays and summer and fall and harvest, but Rosie the Riveter Days? Seriously?"

"Haven't you been reading the posters?" Angel asked with a grin. "She might have come from around here."

"I don't think so."

"But you can't be sure. Besides, we're celebrating the contribution of women. You should support that."

"I'll support it more when there isn't any pay inequity left." She glanced at the tourists clogging the streets. "Not that I don't

336

love a good festival."

"You don't," he teased.

She smiled at him. "I'm getting used to them."

It was a sunny Saturday morning. Angel had called the previous night and suggested they spend the day together. They were going to cruise the festival through lunch, then maybe catch a movie. He would grill steaks for them that night and tomorrow they would work on her garden.

Implied in the invitation was him spending the night — a plan she could totally support. Lately she'd found herself sleeping better when Angel was in her bed. Of course that could be about the things they did *before* they fell asleep, but she was open to that, as well.

Now, as he took her hand, she laced her fingers with his and felt the swell of contentment in her body. Being around Angel made her feel good.

They moved slowly with the flow of the crowds. There were booths lining the streets. A schedule of events promised live music later.

"Angel, Taryn!"

Allison, a little blonde girl with glasses, ran up to them. She wore a pink T-shirt and white shorts. As she reached them, she pushed up her glasses.

"Hi. I saw you and wanted to introduce my uncle Ryder." She was dragging a good-looking guy behind her. He looked to be around thirty, with tanned skin and a crooked smile. He was tall, maybe six-three, so he towered over the little girl. "He's a really famous photographer." She paused to beam at them. "He's my favorite uncle."

Ryder shook hands with both of them. "Hi," he said. "Allison gets a little carried away. I'm not that famous."

Taryn liked how Ryder put his hands on Allison's shoulders in a gesture of love and support, rather than getting annoyed with her.

"You're her favorite uncle," Taryn said.

"I'm her only uncle."

Allison shook her head. "You'd be my favorite, no matter what. Angel is my Grove Keeper."

Ryder's mouth twitched. "That's right. You're an Acorn." He turned his attention to Angel. "How are you enjoying the FWM?"

"You know about it?" Angel asked.

"I lived in Fool's Gold until I was about ten. Then we moved to Denver." He glanced around. "Great place. I was sorry to go."

"He's visiting for the weekend," Allison

338

said, leaning against Ryder. "I showed him my beads."

They spoke a few more minutes, and then Allison dragged her uncle away to buy her an elephant ear. Taryn watched them go.

"You're good with the girls," she said. "They adore you."

"I'm their only Grove Keeper. They don't know any better."

"Which makes them easier to fool? I don't think so, big guy. They're crazy about you." She nudged his arm. "Besides, you can French-braid now. You're invaluable."

"I'd been looking for a skill to round out my résumé."

She was still laughing when they stopped in front of a display of hats. The hats themselves were cloth, with a brim that could be rolled up or left down. But what made them different were the silk flowers. Some of the arrangements were small, with only a few buds, while others were full-on bouquets.

Taryn tugged on Angel's hand, but he wasn't budging.

"No way," he told her. "I heard that this year it's all about accessories, so I'm buying you a hat."

A hat she would never wear, she thought as he selected, then rejected several options.

Then he picked up a soft black hat with dark red roses and plenty of green leaves and put it on her head. He adjusted the brim until it was how he wanted it, then turned her toward the mirror.

"What do you think?" he asked.

The hat wasn't anything she would ever wear, but that wasn't the point. She could see herself and part of him. He kept fussing with the way the hat sat on her head. As his fingers lightly stroked her cheek, she felt a tightness in her chest. A tightness unlike anything she'd experienced before.

Her breath caught and the world spun a little before settling. And then she knew. She was in love with Angel.

She who had vowed to never risk her heart, no matter what. She who defined her world by how much she controlled it. She who had always prided herself on her toughness, had fallen deeply and profoundly in love.

"Taryn?" Angel's voice was sharp. "What's wrong?" He turned her to face him. "You went pale." He touched her forehead, then reached for her wrist and felt for her pulse. "Your heart is racing. Are you sick?"

She was, she thought frantically. Sick with love. Oh God. How had this happened? Why hadn't she been paying attention?

But after the panic came certainty. This was right, she thought. Whatever happened, however this ended, she had fallen in love. And by giving her heart, she'd broken free of the last bond her father had on her. She'd overcome the fear.

She drew in a breath and smiled at him. "I'm okay. Just a little light-headed. I didn't eat this morning."

He tossed the hat lady the money for the hat, then put his arm around Taryn's waist and led her toward the food booths. "We'll get something into you right now."

His touch was sure, she thought. She knew he would take care of her. It wasn't love — he'd already given his heart and couldn't do it again. She understood that. Later, she would deal with that pain, but for now it was enough to know that she wasn't as freakish as she'd feared. She was almost like everyone else.

Angel got her a wrap and a soda for each of them, then made sure she ate all of hers. They were still discussing what to do that afternoon when Consuelo walked up and handed them each a piece of paper. There was an address on it.

"Five o'clock this afternoon," she said, glaring at them. "It's Kent's mother's house. There'll be food. Don't be late and don't tell me you can't make it. Do I make myself clear?"

"Yes, ma'am," Angel said.

Taryn smiled. "I'm not frightened by you, and yes, I'll be there, too. What's going on?"

"Nothing I want to talk about," Consuelo grumbled, and walked away.

Taryn hadn't been sure what to wear to Consuelo's undefined event. She figured it was something like a barbecue so chose a simple summer dress with a sweater to ward off any chill. As walking on grass might be required, she chose a platform sandal.

Angel picked her up at a quarter to five and they drove the few blocks to Denise's house. There were already a few cars parked in front and several people walking up the front walk.

"Big party," he said, then went around to the passenger side of his SUV and helped her out. As she slid to the ground, he leaned close. "Let's not stay too late."

The combination of his breath and his voice made her shiver. She looked into his eyes. "An early night sounds nice."

He brushed his lips against her cheek before they headed toward the front door.

Nevada Hendrix Janack, one of the Hendrix triplet sisters, met them in the foyer.

342

"Everyone's out back," she said. "Just go through the house. There's plenty of seating." She paused. "Angel, right?"

He nodded.

"My brother needs to speak to you." She pointed to a hallway. "Down there. Taryn, can you find your own way to the backyard?"

Ford appeared and grabbed Angel's arm. "You made it. Good. Hey, Taryn." With that, both of them were gone.

Taryn wondered what on earth was happening. She followed the directions to the rear of the house and entered a large kitchen. From there she could see out big windows. A huge tent had been set up outside. The sides were rolled up so she could see the twinkle lights decorating the poles. Chairs had been set up in rows, with a center aisle. There was a beautiful cake on a small table at the far end of the garden, a dance floor to the left and flowers everywhere. If she didn't know better, she would swear they'd been invited to a wedding.

Dellina came in from the backyard, saw Taryn and grinned. "Can't talk. Way too busy. Who plans a wedding with twenty-four hours' notice? It's not possible, but here we are."

Taryn didn't have to ask the name of the

bride. There was only one couple who would get married in Denise's yard like this.

She walked outside. The guests were talking and obviously excited about what was happening. Servers circulated with glasses of champagne and trays of appetizers.

"My lady."

She turned and saw Jack holding out a glass to her. She took it and smiled at him. "You're here."

"We were summoned," he said, motioning to where Sam and Kenny were talking to some people she didn't know.

"Larissa is going to be sorry to miss the wedding," Taryn said. Larissa had gone back to L.A. to visit one of her sisters for the weekend.

"I'll save her a piece of cake. Where's your date?"

"I don't know. He was whisked away. He might be part of the wedding party." Angel had known Consuelo a long time. She would guess the other woman wanted him involved.

"They pulled this together fast," Jack said. Despite the afternoon sun, he looked comfortable in his suit and tie. Of course Jack was comfortable everywhere.

"You have no idea." Taryn told him about her recent lunch with friends and Consuelo's meltdown. "Maybe this is how she could get it done."

Jack put his arm around her. "Marriage wasn't so bad."

"All six weeks of it?" she asked lightly.

He smiled at her.

Mayor Marsha moved to the front of the tent and asked everyone to find a seat. Taryn and Jack sat together. She saved a seat for Angel in case he joined them later. Music started. Kent, Reese and Ford appeared up by the mayor.

Felicia started up the aisle. The maid of honor, Taryn would guess. The wedding march began and the guests rose. She turned to see Consuelo in a full-on wedding gown, complete with veil, being escorted by Angel and Justice. She looked beautiful and fierce. Taryn had a feeling she was fighting serious nerves.

When she reached the end of the aisle, Justice and Angel lifted her veil and kissed her cheek. Then they stepped to the left, to stand by Felicia.

"Male and female attendants," Jack whispered. "Very modern."

She smiled, then turned her attention to the ceremony.

"We are delighted you could all attend this wonderful occasion," Mayor Marsha began.

"While I try to attend every wedding in town, I'm not always lucky enough to officiate at them. Thank you both for this joyous opportunity."

She glanced down at the book she held, then back at the guests. "Today we celebrate and witness the joining of Kent Hendrix and Consuelo Ly. Traditional vows will follow, but first our wonderful couple wants to say something to each other."

Consuelo handed her bouquet to Felicia, then faced Kent.

"I love you," she said, her voice trembling slightly. "Very much. I promise to always show up and to tell you when I'm afraid." She flashed a smile. "I can't say I'll always be normal."

Kent grinned. "I'll be normal enough for both of us." His mouth straightened. "I'll always take care of you, Consuelo. Be there for you." He glanced over his shoulder.

Reese stepped a little closer. "Me, too," he added. "We're going to be a family."

Taryn felt her eyes start to burn. She wondered if Angel would look at her, if he would communicate that while they didn't have that level of emotion between them, he cared. Only he didn't.

Instead Jack took her hand. "This is nice," he murmured.

"It is."

"There's something to be said for eloping."

Which they had done, she remembered. "Less money on catering."

He grinned. "Good point. I'm glad your friend there was the one who had to deal with the snake. It probably would have killed me."

She chuckled. "I'm sure of it."

"You've got a good man there."

She looked back at Angel. "Yes, I do."

As if he'd heard them, he turned toward her and gave her a slow wink. She smiled back and knew that her world had gotten just a little brighter.

CHAPTER SEVENTEEN

"You have children here to see you," Larissa said with a grin. "Two girls. They know you by name."

Taryn held in a smile. "Is that accusation I hear in your tone?"

"Children? It still surprises me to think about you hanging with them."

"You know I'm an assistant Grove Keeper."

"I've heard the words," Larissa said with a grin, and walked back out into the hall.

Taryn was still chuckling when Chloe and Layla, another Acorn, walked in. She stood and circled around her desk. "Hi, you two. What's up?"

Chloe set her backpack on a chair and pulled out a length of rope. "We're having trouble with our knots. Angel's busy and the campout is coming up soon. There's going to be a test after we set up our tents. We know there's a rabbit and a hole, but we can't remember about the tree."

Layla rolled her eyes. "I asked my dad, but he doesn't know."

She sounded desperately disappointed in the man.

Taryn kept her smile in place even as her stomach flipped over. Knot proficiency was required of Acorns. Angel had taught them at the last meeting. And while Taryn had been able to go through the motions with everyone else, she hadn't really been paying attention to the particulars. After all, Angel was the outdoor expert. She was simply faking it.

In the past few weeks they'd gone hiking twice and had repeated the kayaking without incident, but with sex, which made it even more fun. But knots? She knew next to nothing about knots.

But she couldn't say that to the girls, she thought. Nor could she fake her way through knot teaching. Before she could figure out a way to confess all and then look up knots on the internet, Kenny walked down the hall.

Taryn called to him. He stepped into her office, took one look at the girls and raised his eyebrows. "Something you want to admit to?" he asked.

She ignored the humor in his eyes.

"Kenny, these are two of my Acorns. Chloe and Layla. We were discussing the knots we have to learn and I was wondering if you knew anything about knots."

Kenny glanced from her to the girls and back. He leaned against the door frame as if he had all the time in the world . . . and he planned to use every second of it to torture her.

"Camping?" he asked.

Chloe nodded. "We're having an all-grove campout. Layla and I are Acorns, like Taryn said. We're the youngest. The other groves are Sprouts, Saplings, Sky-Reachers and Mighty Oaks. We're going to be Sprouts next year."

Layla nodded.

Kenny's mouth twitched and Taryn knew it had nothing to do with Chloe's innate cuteness. Instead he was storing information he would use against her when she was least expecting it.

She thought about pointing out that she hadn't been exactly *hiding* her position as assistant Grove Keeper from anyone. She just hadn't been talking about it much. Jack knew, but now that she thought about it, there was a good possibility the other two didn't.

"Sprouts, huh?" Kenny asked. "Which

means you belong to the . . ."

"Future Warriors of the Máa-zib," Chloe said helpfully. "FWM."

"Right. It sounds fun and I can see you're fierce warriors. I'm impressed."

Taryn was about to glare at Kenny when she realized how much Chloe had been talking. Usually she was the shy one but not, apparently, around Kenny. Interesting. He was a big guy. Tall and broad, with massive hands. People were often nervous around him. But not these two.

"Tell me about your knot experience," Taryn said. "Can you help?"

"Oh, I can," he said, grinning at her. "I used to be an Eagle Scout."

"I know what that is," Layla said. "My brother wants to be an Eagle Scout." She wrinkled her nose. "But he said he wouldn't help me with my knots." Her lips turned up at the corners. "He's mad because he snuck out to be with his friends last weekend and I told."

Taryn nodded at Kenny. "Still want to mock the FWM?"

"I wasn't mocking," he said as he walked to her desk and sat in one of the chairs. "But I'm impressed with your tracking skills," he told Layla.

"He goes out the window at the end of

the hall," Layla told him. "It's right by my room and the floor creaks really loud right there."

"Sounds like he deserved to get caught. Did he get in trouble?"

Layla nodded. "He's grounded."

"And pouting," Kenny said. "Otherwise, he would have helped you."

Both girls giggled.

Kenny held out his hand for the rope. Chloe passed it over. They told him what they were trying to do, and faster than Taryn would have thought possible, he'd twisted the rope into place and handed it back to them.

"Wow," Chloe breathed. "Can you teach us that?"

"I can."

Taryn sat back in her chair and watched as Kenny slowly went through the steps of the knot. The girls watched and nodded, and then each of them repeated his actions. She noticed that both of them crowded closer and closer until they were leaning against him. Chloe seemed especially smitten, watching his face when he talked and smiling up at him as if he were some kind of superhero.

When they'd mastered the knot, they thanked him and left. Taryn waited until they were gone to thank him.

He shrugged. "No big deal. Happy to help."

"You were good with them," she said. "They liked you."

Kenny's blue eyes gave nothing away.

"You're great around kids," she continued, watching him carefully as she spoke.

"Forget it," he said flatly.

"Kenny, you need to get over it."

"I have."

"No, you haven't. You're ignoring what happened. You don't talk about it."

"There's nothing to say."

He got up and left. Taryn sighed, not sure how hard to push him. Everyone had things from their past — she knew that better than most. But she hated to see Kenny avoiding getting involved because of what had happened before. It wasn't fair and it wasn't right. But it also wasn't her problem to solve.

Despite the quickie wedding Dellina had pulled together with what Taryn would guess was maybe fifteen minutes' notice, she still managed to get the clothing exchange organized in a matter of days.

The soon-to-be finished retail space at Paper Moon had been cleared of all construction equipment. The new carpeting was in place, as were most of the fixtures on the wall. Temporary racks held hanging clothes, while large tables were covered with sweaters, bags and shoes. There was even a display of costume jewelry. The dressing rooms were clearly marked and several mirrors had been set up around the room. Music played through hidden speakers.

All the clothes had, per the invitation, been delivered in advance. There were notes attached to most of them. Things like "I wore this once. Not sure why I bought it." Or "It shrank in my closet, which is weird because I never wore it."

Against the far wall was a mobile bar and buffet. Mostly finger foods easily eaten while shopping, along with a constant supply of girlie cocktails.

Taryn had been hoping to get ten or fifteen women to come to the exchange, but there were at least twice that many. Several were unfamiliar, but Isabel quickly made introductions. It didn't take long for the noise level to start climbing.

Madeline was in charge of the exchange. She suggested pieces to different people and offered to find matching shoes or bags.

"She knows about the outfits for Bailey, right?" Taryn asked in a low voice.

Isabel nodded. "I got her a suit but also bought her a dress."

Taryn stared at her. "Why?"

"I thought it would look good on her. It's navy, with a jacket. She can dress it up or down. Take off the jacket and it's a nice dress for dinner out. A suit is more limited. This is Fool's Gold. Where is she going to wear a suit every day? But a dress can be worn a lot of different places."

Taryn nodded. "You're right. I'm just so nervous."

She'd left the shopping to Isabel. The other woman already had her credit card number on file. What were a couple more purchases?

"Holy shit, Taryn, what size are you?"

Pia Moreno stepped out of one of the dressing rooms wearing one of Taryn's castoffs. The purple dress looked great until Pia turned and Taryn could see the zipper was about three inches from closing.

"You just had a baby," Montana said sympathetically.

"Yeah, but my waist will never be *this* small." Pia glared at Taryn. "Seriously, you're what? A four?"

Taryn nodded. "Mostly."

"They'll fit me," Noelle said, studying the dress Pia had on. "But your clothes are way too sophisticated. I am, however, having a serious love affair with some of your shoes."

Annabelle Stryker, a petite redhead, walked up. "Everyone here is too tall. The only one I could exchange with is Consuelo, and we don't share the same fashion sense."

Taryn thought about Consuelo's love of cargo pants and tank tops, then looked at Annabelle's floral-print dress. "I can see how that wouldn't work." Not that Consuelo was at the exchange. She was still off honeymooning with Kent.

Taryn saw Bailey stepping out of one of the dressing rooms. The other woman had on a navy dress that came to just above her knees. It fit well, skimming over her curves. The scoop neck flattered without being too low. When she slid into the cropped jacket, Taryn understood what Isabel meant about the outfit being versatile.

Taryn crossed to the accessory table and grabbed a couple of scarves, then picked up a necklace and earrings.

"Try these on," she said, offering the costume jewelry to Bailey. "Nothing says a woman is accomplished more than chunky jewelry."

Isabel grinned. "I hadn't heard that."

"It's a little-known truth in boardrooms across America."

Bailey laughed. "I'll try them, but I have to warn you, I've never owned a scarf — except to wear in the snow."

"Then this is a first," Taryn said as she put the scarf over Bailey's shoulders.

Five minutes later they'd all agreed the dress was a hit, that the navy, cream and gold scarf worked, but with the dress alone. With the jacket, it was too busy. And that, yes, chunky jewelry made a woman look as though she was in charge.

"You did good," Taryn whispered to Isabel when Bailey had returned to the dressing room. "That dress fits her perfectly."

"I do have an eye," Isabel said with a grin.

Nevada Janack, the triplet who'd greeted her and Angel at the wedding, came over with a deep purple Jimmy Choo tote in her hands. The leather was soft, with rows of buckles on the front.

"I don't understand this," Nevada said, lightly stroking the bag. "I don't even carry a purse. But I have to have this. I have to."

"Bag love is pure," Taryn told her. "Especially the first time. I hope the two of you will be very happy together."

Nevada nodded. "I'm putting in more than five dollars. It's so beautiful — how could I buy it for so little? It would be wrong."

As the money was going to a women's shelter, Taryn was happy to encourage people to put in as much as they could afford.

She looked around at the event, pleased to see so many women trying on clothes and shoes. The bowl they were using to collect money for the exchange had already been emptied once that night, and it was going to have to be emptied again.

Taryn thought about how Mayor Marsha had forced her to solve the Bailey problem on her own and had a feeling that once again the wily politician had been right.

The site of the FWM all-grove campout was about fifteen miles outside town. It was a public camping area that the groves had taken over for the weekend. Not only were there lots of trees, permanent restrooms and big fire pits for group bonfires, but the campsites themselves were separated into two levels. The lower level, by the stream, and the upper level, closer to the parking lot. The latter provided parents who wanted to stay close but not get in the way of the experience a place to hover out of sight. If one of the girls needed a parental hug in the middle of the night, Mom and Dad were there to provide it.

Angel had parked in the designated "Grove Keeper" section of the parking lot. His SUV was filled with all kinds of gear — most of which was new. He was the kind of guy who loaded up a backpack and took to the mountains. But this was different. He wanted his girls to enjoy everything about the experience. Which meant roughing it had to be done in a gentle way.

He loaded up with as much as he could carry and headed down the steep trail to the lower campsite. A couple of other Grove Keepers were already there.

Large trees provided shade and cover. The east side of the site was up against the mountains. The stream cut through on the west side, then flowed along the edge of the grounds. With the warmer days, the snow-pack was melting and the water moved at a fair clip. But it was shallow — eight inches or so. From what he could tell, the area wasn't prone to flooding.

He found the Acorn section and put down his pack and a couple of boxes. There were two picnic tables and a marked, paved path led to the restrooms. The area for the tents was big enough for them to be pitched in a circle, with the entrances facing each other.

Angel had brought along a mallet to help secure the stakes, and a rake to clear the site before they pitched the tents. Although there were eight Acorns, they would be sleeping two to a tent. Including his tent and one for Taryn, that was a total of six. The space was plenty big.

For a second, he thought about sharing a tent with Taryn. They could zip their sleeping bags together — something he would enjoy. He gave himself a minute to think of her naked, her long legs tangling with his, then shook off the image. He had a feeling somewhere in the Grove Keeper Handbook was a rule forbidding unmarried Grove Keepers to have members of the opposite sex in their tents.

He took the fresh food he'd brought over to the communal kitchen area. A small generator powered a portable refrigerator. The woman there picked up her clipboard when she saw him.

"You're with the Acorns?" she asked.

"That's me." He handed over the eggs and sausage he'd brought. The fresh fruit would keep in their site.

He made two more trips and brought down the rest of his gear. As he was locking up his SUV, Taryn pulled in next to him. When she stepped out of her car he saw she'd dressed in jeans and a T-shirt. She had her hair pulled back in a braid and even wore sensible hiking boots.

"Don't look so surprised," she said, slapping his arm. "I know how to dress for the occasion."

He peered at her. "You're not wearing any makeup."

She wrinkled her nose. "I know. Sunscreen only. I didn't think I could take it off tonight and reapply that easily so I'm going natural. Don't get used to it. Next time you see me, I'll be back in heels and mascara."

"If only that was all you were wearing," he murmured.

Her mouth curved up in a slow smile. "We might be able to negotiate that."

Which was one of the things he liked about her, he thought as she opened her trunk. She came to their relationship as his equal. She was willing to take him on and win. She was smart, sexy and unexpectedly charming. Just when he'd thought things couldn't get better, she'd taken care of him when he was haunted by missing his kid. She was a hell of a woman. Different from Marie, but amazing in her own way.

She hauled a huge backpack out of her trunk and slung it over her shoulders. Angel started to take it from her, but she shook her head.

"This is the stupid thing I have to wear

when we go out with Cole," she reminded him. "If I'm going to hike for a day in it, I should be able to trudge down to the campsite. But you can carry the rest of it."

"The rest of it" turned out to be supplies for the weekend, but not the kind Angel had brought. The shopping bags were filled with hair clips, ribbons and glitter nail polish, several kits for making sparkly jewelry and two small bouquets of flowers.

Angel stared at her purchases.

"Don't give me that 'what were you thinking?' look," she told him firmly. "We're here until four on Sunday. Do you know how long that is? Sure, there are grove activities, but there is still plenty of down-time. Do you really want eight bored girls on your hands? This stuff will keep them busy, and that's a good thing."

"Okay. What about the flowers?"

"I thought they'd look nice on the table."

"You've never been camping before, have you?"

"No, but that's not the point."

"I guess not."

He followed her down the trail to the lower-level campsite. At the bottom, Taryn waited for him to point out where their grove had been assigned. She let her back-pack slide off onto the ground.

"It's nice," she said, looking at the trees, then up at the sky. "It's been clouding up all day. I hope it doesn't rain."

"Your tent is waterproof."

She wrinkled her nose. "I don't care. Having it rain would really mess up the weekend. The outdoor activities wouldn't be as fun and my hair would frizz."

Angel laughed, then pulled her close and kissed the top of her head. "Dammit, Taryn, how do you do that?"

She looked up at him. "Do what?"

"Constantly surprise me."

She smiled. "It's a gift."

He stared into her eyes. He wanted her, but there was something else. An emotion that made him want to say . . .

He released her and stepped back. No getting involved, he reminded himself. He couldn't. Or maybe it was better to say he *wouldn't.*

"Angel! Taryn!"

They turned and saw Kate and Regan hurrying down the trail. Their parents were behind them and laden with camping gear. Over the next half hour the rest of the girls arrived. Allison's father hovered, as if he wanted to step in and help. Taryn walked over to him.

"She'll be fine," Taryn told him. "You're

just a few hundred feet away. If she needs you, she'll come get you."

The man nodded. "Yeah, I know. But this is her first campout. I don't want her getting scared."

Taryn murmured something Angel couldn't hear and Allison's dad reluctantly left.

"What'd you say to him?" he asked when she returned to his side.

"That she might be embarrassed by having him here. She wouldn't want her friends calling her a baby."

"Shame as parental control. Interesting."

She smiled. "Allison's a great kid. He should trust her to be okay." She glanced around at their camp area and then at all the tents piled up. "Do you have a plan for all this?"

Angel looked from the tents to the eight girls watching him. Taryn was right — he needed a plan. He stood and put his hands on his hips. "All right, Acorns. Line up."

The girls looked at each other, then at him. They slowly got in a semistraight line.

He frowned. "I said line up." He raised his voice slightly with the last two words.

Chloe started to giggle but straightened her part of the line. The other girls did the same and all of them grinned at him.

"Better," he told them. "We're going to pitch tents. We'll all work on every tent so you have a clear understanding of how they're the same and how they're different."

Chloe's eyes brightened. "For our camping bead."

"That's right, Acorn."

Chloe giggled. "You sound like you're in the army."

"I used to be. Now, which tent is first?"

They picked a tent and went to work. Ten people working on a tent that slept two was problematic, but they got through it. They rotated through jobs on the tents. Each of the girls got to practice sliding together poles and hammering in stakes. By the end of the exercise, they'd put up his tent without any help, then the eight of them crowded inside and collapsed in mock exhaustion.

By six they were all lined up for dinner. Taryn stood next to him.

"Our group is serving breakfast, right?" she asked.

"Sunday morning. I brought eggs and sausage. They're in the refrigerator." Each grove was responsible for a meal. The Acorns had the second breakfast. It was going to be easy work, he thought. The girls could cook the scrambled eggs and sausages while he and Taryn supervised.

"Good. I'm having Danish delivered," Taryn said.

Angel raised his eyebrows. "Isn't that cheating?"

"It's Danish. I don't think anyone is going to complain. To make sure, the delivery includes lattes for all the adults."

"Sneaky," he murmured in her ear.

"I try."

They waited while their girls served themselves from the buffet of burgers and salad, then joined the others in the communal dining area. After dinner, there was a quick cleanup, then Denise Hendrix started with announcements that included the schedule for tomorrow.

There would be a nature hike followed by the knot proficiency tests. After lunch there was an hour of free time before the group listened to a lecture by an ecologist from UC Fool's Gold. One of the fathers would then be demonstrating martial arts.

Chloe turned to Angel. "They should have asked you to do that."

Layla nodded. "You could so kick his butt."

Angel appreciated the support but knew it was important to have unit solidarity. "You haven't seen the other guy," he said.

"We don't have to," Chloe told him.

The other girls nodded.

"You're our hero," Taryn said, her voice teasing.

Angel cleared his throat and motioned for them to pay attention to the rest of the announcements. While he wouldn't admit it to anyone, he appreciated their faith in him. He was proud of his girls and pleased they were proud of him.

After the announcements, they went to sit by the big fire pit. Large logs surrounded the stone-ringed pit. Denise pulled a name from a box. The FWM girl called got to light the bonfire.

It didn't take long for the kindling to catch. The sun was setting as the flames reached up toward the sky. One of the Grove Keepers brought out her guitar and began to play. Taryn nudged Angel.

"Turn," she said, pointing to Regan, who sat next to him.

"What?"

"You and I are going to sit back-to-back."

He didn't know what she was talking about, but he did as she requested. Regan shifted so her back was to him, as did the girl in front of her and so on until four of the Acorns sat with their backs to him and four sat with their back to Taryn.

Taryn handed him four small rubber bands. "You're going to French-braid Regan's hair while she does Allison's and so on."

"Seriously?"

"It's our thing," she told him. "Go with it."

He dutifully finger-combed Regan's hair, then separated the strands on her crown into three sections. He worked easily now, not having to think about what he was doing.

Back when he'd first agreed to be a Grove Keeper, he'd been disconcerted to discover he would be working with girls. Now that he'd been with them nearly two months, he was pleased with the assignment. They brought something special to his life, and he hoped he did the same for them.

His initial plan had been to resign as their Grove Keeper at the end of the first year, but he was rethinking that. He wanted to see what would happen when they were Sprouts. It seemed that Mayor Marsha had known what she was doing.

CHAPTER EIGHTEEN

Taryn was enjoying the storytelling part of the evening right up until it started to rain. At first there was just a light mist, but that quickly turned into something steadier.

"Tell me again why we love camping?" she asked Angel as they led the girls back to their tents.

"This'll pass. Even if it doesn't, you'll be dry in your tent."

"Famous last words," she murmured before turning her attention to the girls. "Okay, let's get our toothbrushes and toothpaste and head to the bathroom. We'll get ready for bed, then all pile into Angel's tent until we're sleepy."

He looked at her. "Why my tent?"

"Because you're our Grove Keeper. Where else would we go?"

One corner of his mouth twitched. "You're paying me back because your hair is going to frizz, aren't you?"

"Something like that."

The girls dove into their tents and collected what they needed and then all trooped off to the bathroom. The other campers were there, so there was a line for the toilets and the sinks, but eventually they were all done with their evening ablutions.

Taryn went into her tent and zipped it closed. Angel had insisted they take the time to tuck the edges of their tarps under so that any rain would roll down to the ground rather than under the tent. At the time his concern had seemed silly, but now she appreciated his thoroughness. She wasn't all that interested in getting soaked in her sleep.

She hadn't brought a lot of clothes. Clean underwear and socks, a shirt for each day and a spare pair of jeans. For pajamas, she'd chosen yoga pants and a soft T-shirt. At home she favored sleep shirts but figured in a group camping situation she should make sure she was a little more covered up.

Undressing in the tent was harder than she would have thought. There wasn't a lot of headroom, so she was forced to sit on her sleeping bag, which was set on top of an air mattress. Concerned about providing some kind of shadow show on the side of the tent, she flicked off her flashlight and changed in the dark. Only it was really dark and she couldn't see what she was doing.

"Someone needs to explain to me what about this is fun," she muttered as she pulled on her yoga pants.

She decided that the T-shirt she was wearing would be fine for the night and that she would take off her bra later. She turned on her flashlight and unzipped her tent, then crawled out.

The rain had turned steadier and the temperature had dropped a few degrees. She shivered as she ran to Angel's tent.

The other girls were all there, except for Olivia, who came in a few seconds later. They huddled together, holding flashlights and looking expectantly at Angel. Taryn tried not to do the same, but it was difficult. He was the only one with camping experience.

"We're going to tell stories," he said when they were settled.

"Scary ones?" Taryn asked. She wasn't sure she wanted to deal with eight little girls who were too frightened to sleep.

"Can they be scary?" Charlotte's eyes widened. "Really scary?"

Some of the girls murmured in agreement, but a few of the others didn't look as excited at the prospect.

"Not scary," he told them. "I'll start. Once

upon a time there was a lonely bunny."

"I know this one," Regan told him. "My mom read me all the *Lonely Bunny* books when I was little. *Lonely Bunny Finds a Friend, Lonely Bunny Takes a Trip. Lonely Bunny and the Severed Hand.*"

Taryn tensed. "What? There's a children's book about a severed hand?"

Regan giggled. "No, I was kidding about that."

"Good to know," Taryn murmured, even as she wondered how Angel knew about the *Lonely Bunny* books at all. Had he read them to his son, years ago? A question she would wait to ask, she thought, then realized the rain had gotten a lot harder. It pounded on the tent like a drum. So far it wasn't seeping through the fabric, but wasn't that going to happen eventually?

Before she could ask Angel, one of the other Grove Keepers unzipped the front of the tent.

"We just checked the weather," the woman said. "It's going to be raining all night. The front that was supposed to go north of us has dropped south and parked overhead. Apparently it's been pouring up in the mountains for hours."

"Where in the mountains?" Angel asked,

careful to keep his voice calm. Because the stream in the campsite was fed from mountain runoff. Depending on where the rain was falling, the stream would start to rise. The question was how fast that would happen.

The other Grove Keeper shrugged. "I'm not sure. East of us. We're thinking we should pack up the girls and get them home."

Angel hesitated. Weather was a part of camping, and learning to deal with the elements would be good practice. On the other hand, his girls were young and for most of them, this was their first experience camping. He didn't want the rain to be the only thing they remembered.

He looked at Taryn, who shrugged. "I can argue both sides," she told him. "Yes, it would be nice if the weather were better, but that will never be a guarantee."

The girls listened but didn't offer an opinion.

The other Grove Keeper said, "I'll talk to the rest of the groves and see what they have to say. Then we'll make a group decision."

"Works for me," Angel said.

The woman stood and started to pull the zipper closed. As she did, there was a scream from another part of the camp.

Angel was through the opening and shifting the other Grove Keeper aside before the sound had finished echoing off the trees. He'd left on his boots, so he moved easily over the wet terrain. The rain soaked through his shirt and stung his eyes as he searched through the darkness to find the source of the problem.

"It's rising! It's rising fast."

He headed toward the woman yelling. Other Grove Keepers and a few of the older girls joined him. He found two women standing by the benches where they'd eaten dinner a few hours before. Only what had been an open area and a gentle slope down to a stream was now a rapidly flowing and quickly rising river.

"I don't understand," one of the women said.

"It's a flash flood," he said flatly, remembering the mention of rain in the mountains. "Combined with snowmelt. It's coming up fast. We have to get out of here." The other three stared at him. "Now!" he added in a loud voice. "Get your groves and get back to your cars. Keep a head count. Don't leave anyone behind."

Aware of his girls waiting for him, he went from campsite to campsite and got everyone else. Some of the girls grabbed gear; others simply started running for the trail. He circled back to his tent and found Taryn waiting in the rain. Water dripped down her face and she was shivering.

"The stream is rising," he told her. "There's a flash flood coming through. Get the girls and head for the trail. You'll be safe once you reach the cars."

"What are you going to do?"

"Check that everyone else got out, then join you by the cars." He grabbed her upper arms. "Do a head count when you get there."

She nodded.

He squatted down and opened the tent flap. Eight pairs of eyes stared at him.

"There's a flash flood," he told them. "We're getting out now. Taryn is going to lead you up the trail while I check to make sure all the other girls got out. Everybody pair up. You leave in pairs and you arrive in pairs. No one gets left behind."

He felt their fear. In his head, a voice kept reminding him that while he could save the world, he hadn't been able to protect his own. That these girls were just like Marcus, and Marcus was dead.

"You're ready for this," he told them gently. "I have faith in you. We'll meet at the top by the cars. Everybody ready?"

They nodded solemnly.

Angel waited until they were all out of the tent, then pulled the poles so it collapsed. He would do the same with the other tents, the easiest way to make sure no one snuck back inside to hide. He made sure Taryn knew the way up to the parking lot and then went back toward the swirling water.

He'd been gone less than ten minutes, but in that time, the water had risen at least six feet. Several of the tents were already half underwater by the time he reached the lowest campsites. The roar of the water echoed off the mountains.

He waded through icy runoff, ignoring the cold clutching at his midsection. He checked each of the tents, then hurried up to the next site.

At the third one he found a girl who was maybe eleven or twelve. She was crouched at the base of a tree, crying. Angel took her by the arm and pulled her to him. Rain poured over both of them.

"Let's get out of here," he told her.

The girl shook her head. "I can't swim."

"Then heading away from the water is the best plan."

She trembled but didn't move. Angel didn't bother to argue anymore. He picked her up in his arms and carried her to the main trail. At the base of it, he found Taryn waiting.

"What the hell are you doing here?" he demanded loudly.

"Making sure you get out, too," Taryn said. "Don't worry. The Acorns are all safe. I did a head count before I came back."

He swore under his breath, then thrust the girl at her. "She's in shock. Get her to the top and out of the cold."

"I will."

He wanted to say more, but he had three sites to check. The rain fell hard and he could hear the water even from here. It was rising fast.

"Go," Taryn told him. "I'll take care of her."

He nodded. In the distance came two sharp explosions. Trees, he though grimly as he hurried along the muddy path. The water had reached the tree line.

He couldn't see very far in front of him. Rain blinded him and he was cold to the bone. Still, he checked the last of the campsites. They were empty. He turned to the main trail only to find it was now covered in water that rose visibly every second.

As he watched, a couple of coolers floated by. There was a chair, then an air mattress.

He moved faster. He hoped to hell Taryn had gotten the girl off the trail, because it wouldn't be very long until there wasn't a trail.

He waded through the rising water. Something hard hit him and he nearly went down. He grabbed a nearby tree branch and managed to stay on his feet. But there was no way he could get back to the trail.

He did the only thing possible — he went straight up the mountain. Hand over hand, dragging himself under branches and around bushes. Mud and debris seeped into his clothing, but he kept moving. There was a rumble as part of the mountain started to give way. Then he was up over the side and pulling himself to his feet so he could get to the parking lot and do a head count.

He arrived there a couple of minutes later. There was chaos everywhere. Parents ran around frantically looking for their girls. Angel brushed the mud from his face and realized the rain had stopped. But the flood waters would keep rising.

"People! Please!" Denise Hendrix yelled, trying to get the group to pay attention.

Angel walked over to her, put two fingers in his mouth and whistled loud enough to wake the dead. Everyone turned toward him.

"Everyone get over here," he yelled. "Parents, line up in rows of ten. Stop crying and screaming and get over here — now! I went through the camps myself. The tents are empty."

By now they were all gone, but there was no point in mentioning that now.

"Line up," he repeated. "Only in groups of ten. Girls, stand with your grove. Grove Keepers, show them where you want them."

The number didn't matter, but he knew from experience that if people were busy figuring out how many were in their line, they would be less inclined to panic.

Everyone started to do what he said. Soon they were sorted and the head counts started.

He walked around, looking for his girls, only they weren't there. None of them. His chest tightened and breathing became impossible. Then he heard the second scream of the night.

Angel went running. He found several of his girls at the trailhead leading down to the lower campsite. But Taryn wasn't there. Neither were Chloe or Regan.

"Regan lost her bracelet," Allison told him, grabbing on to his hand. "She and Chloe went to look for it and when Taryn found out, she was really mad. She went

379

after them. They haven't come back yet."

Angel told her to get back. Other parents came and took charge of the girls. He started down the trail. The ground shifted under his feet and he was forced to retreat.

"Angel?"

He heard the small voice, so faint it nearly faded into the wind.

"Chloe?"

"Angel? We're here."

He followed the sound and moved to the right. He could hear the water but couldn't see anything. Several parents moved close and turned on their flashlights. Then Angel spotted movement. Regan and Chloe were clinging to a tree. Taryn was with them. Water lapped at their feet.

"We went to get my bracelet," Regan admitted when she saw him. "Taryn said to stay with the others, but we didn't. We're sorry."

Something Angel would deal with later, he thought as he started down the muddy side of the mountain. He braced himself against a still-standing tree and reached for Regan. She grabbed his hands and he pulled her to him.

Behind him several other Grove Keepers drew her up to safety.

"You're next," he told Chloe.

Nearby another tree snapped and the ground beneath them shifted. Chloe screamed.

"I'm here," Angel told her. "I'm not going anywhere. Just move up the tree and I'll grab you."

Chloe nodded and inched toward him. He leaned forward as far as he could, but it wasn't enough.

"Here!"

He felt something hit his back. A rope. He tied it around his waist, then felt it tighten as the others hung on to him. He leaned forward and reached for Chloe again. This time he grabbed her.

She clung to him like a monkey. He stepped back and felt them both being hauled up a few feet.

"Come on, Chloe," Denise Hendrix said firmly as she stuck out her hand. "I've got you."

Chloe reached for her, then scrambled to the top. Which left only Taryn.

Angel adjusted the rope at his waist, then moved toward her. The ground shifted and she screamed as the tree she was on cracked and bent. The night was dark and the flashlights didn't reach this far. He could only see shapes rather than details, but he knew she was watching him.

"Taryn," he said slowly. "Taryn, listen to me."

Because the tree she was on was going to be swallowed by the river any second. She was going to have to let go and grab on to him. She was going to have to trust him.

Defeat settled on his shoulders. There was no way he could convince her. Not so fast. Not with a lifetime of horror to recover from. Her father had reached out and had let her fall.

The water continued to rise. It was loud and he could see objects floating by. He felt the first waves lapping at his feet. Before long, the tree she clung to would be pulled into the current and she would go with it.

"Taryn, you have to trust me," he said, frustrated, scared and aware of the growing danger.

"You'll catch me, right?" she asked.

He nodded. As he wondered if he could simply lunge forward and hang on, she pushed against the tree and launched herself toward him. He caught her just as the tree cracked in half and fell into the swirling water.

"He's got her!" someone yelled. "Pull!"

Taryn had never been so cold her in her life. She couldn't stop shaking. It didn't help that her clothes were soaked and muddy. No matter how many blankets people piled on her shoulders, she knew she wasn't going to get warm until she could get home and step into a hot shower.

People kept coming up to her and asking if she was okay. She nodded, and kept counting heads of the grove. Eight heads, she told herself. All the girls were okay.

Angel stayed close. He, too, was being covered in blankets. He joined her in making sure their grove was all there, then kept his eye on her.

Regan's parents and Chloe's mother had already thanked them both about three times. While the adults looked shell-shocked, the girls couldn't stop talking about their adventure.

"The water rose really fast," Chloe was saying. "It was cold and we were scared, but Taryn kept us safe and Angel saved us."

They were all smiles, Taryn thought, knowing she would never forget the horror of turning around and finding the two girls had disappeared. In the second it had taken her to process the information, the stream had turned into a wild river and had risen what felt like twenty feet.

"I can't wait until next year," Regan told her folks.

Chloe grinned. "Me, too."

"I need a drink," Taryn murmured.

"Me, too."

Angel put his arm around her and led her to his truck. She started to mention that her car was here, then realized she had lost her bag in the flash flood. It was gone, along with her car keys, her house keys, her driver's license and credit cards.

She came to a stop. "I can't get in my house."

"I'll get you in."

"I lost my bag. My wallet."

"All replaceable."

He guided her to his SUV. He had his keys tucked in his jeans.

She hesitated before sliding onto the passenger seat. "I'm going to mess up the leather."

He grabbed her by her upper arms and gave her a slight shake. "You think I care about that?"

The intensity of his expression made her exhale. "Not really."

"Good. Now get in."

They drove to his house and collected clothes, then made the quick trip to her place. Angel used lock-pick tools to open her door. It took him about thirty-five seconds.

"I'm impressed and not the least bit surprised," she said as she dumped the blankets by the door and pulled off her wet and muddy boots. Her ruined socks followed.

Angel closed the front door, dropped his duffel on the floor, then removed his boots and socks. They walked down the hall to the master bath. She turned on the shower. As the water heated, she stripped off her clothes.

She was careful not to look in the mirror. She didn't want to know how bad it was. She was still shaking and felt a little light-headed. Shock, she thought. Not a huge surprise.

They went into her shower. Until that moment, she'd never appreciated the second showerhead. Now she turned it on so they were both under the hot, steamy spray. Angel reached for the shampoo and poured some in his hands.

He washed her hair, then his own. They rubbed soap on each other's bodies and cleaned off the mud. Somewhere in the rinsing process, she realized how slick his skin was and how his hands lingered on her breasts.

She turned to face him and saw desire in

his eyes. As she reached for him, he stepped close.

"I could have lost you," he said right before he kissed her.

His tongue tangled with hers. His hands roamed over her body, exciting her wherever he touched. She felt his erection against her belly.

She put her arms around his neck. He lifted her up against the wet, warm tile wall of the shower, then pushed into her. She wrapped her legs around his hips and hung on as he filled her over and over again.

He supported her by her butt, his fingers digging into her curves. The hot water flowed over them as heat grew inside her. With each stroke, she was more and more aroused and at the same time conscious of the mountain of emotions coursing through her. Relief, shock, gratitude and terror mixed with sexual need. The combination threatened to overwhelm her. She was close but not sure she could make it over the edge. Not sure she wanted to. Losing control now would be —

Her orgasm claimed her without warning. Pleasure poured through her and she cried out, her voice nearly a scream. Angel continued to fill her, drawing out her release, even as the emotional barriers fell and she began to sob.

He waited until she'd stopped shaking to finish, then lowered her to the floor and held her until the water started to cool.

One change of clothes, a quick hair blow-dry, a brandy and a bowl of soup later, Taryn was feeling more like herself. They sat on her sofa, watching HGTV. It was the most normal channel she could think of. It was after midnight, but she wasn't the least bit sleepy. She was still too wired.

Angel sat next to her, his arm around her, her head on his shoulder. She'd stopped shaking and was starting to feel as though the shock was wearing off.

"Better?" he asked.

"Yeah. I don't know how you did your military stuff. Going through this much stress, day after day."

"You get used to it."

She raised her head and looked at him. "Seriously?"

His gray eyes crinkled slightly as he smiled. "No. You never get used to it. You just get better at faking it."

"At least I didn't throw up."

He chuckled. "I've always admired your standards."

She laughed, then the humor faded. "I've never been so scared."

He took her hand in his. "You were brave and you kept yourself in the game."

"Now you sound like the boys."

"I'm serious. You could have freaked out and you didn't." His gaze locked with hers. "To be honest, I didn't think you'd let go of the tree."

She knew what he meant. "You didn't think I'd trust you enough."

"That, too."

Funny how in that moment she hadn't thought about her father. She'd understood what was happening and had known she had one chance at escape. So she'd jumped and Angel had caught her.

She knew he would have done the same for everyone, but she liked to think he'd been a little extra worried about her. She snuggled close again. "I want to call Bailey and Regan's parents in a bit. Check on the girls."

"Good idea. I can't believe they went down the trail instead of staying in the parking lot."

"I know. Regan wanted her bracelet." She touched her chest. "Just thinking about what happened terrifies me."

"They could have been killed," he said flatly.

She felt the tension in his body and had a feeling he was thinking they *all* could have been killed.

"You're not going to yell at me for going after them, are you?" she asked.

He kissed her. "No. You did the right thing."

"We are so going to have a talk about following instructions and being sensible at the next grove meeting."

"No kidding. We're also going to talk about how to handle an emergency." He squeezed her shoulders.

"I have to say, this doesn't make me want to go camping with the LL@R guy. I hope he wasn't expecting to use that campsite."

Angel chuckled. "You won't be going there. It's going to take a long time to get the campground usable again. Even after the water is gone, it's going to be a mess. Plus, once an area is known for having a flash flood, people are less inclined to want to spend the night."

"I'm sure Fool's Gold has other camp areas."

"You don't sound thrilled by that fact," he teased.

"Yeah, tell me about it."

"The groves will want to camp again next year."

"Goody," she murmured.

God knows there was plenty of wilderness all around the town. Not that it would matter to her, she thought. She'd helped Angel out with the grove because he was helping her learn to be outdoorsy for a client. Next year she wouldn't have that.

The realization was unsettling. She liked hanging out with the girls. The meetings were always fun and she enjoyed the various projects. She liked the idea of the grove being together for more than a couple of months. They could come up with a really cool community service project. Not that socializing the puppies wasn't fun — but next time they could find something that was more involved with life in the town.

Only there wasn't going to be a next year for her. Not with Angel and his grove. Because there wasn't going to be a next year for the two of them.

They had both been very clear about their relationship, she thought. Neither of them was looking for more than a temporary involvement. He'd been challenged and she'd been intrigued. They weren't young and foolish — they weren't looking to fall in love.

Except she had. Sometime when she hadn't been paying attention, she'd handed over her heart. Maybe that's why it had been so easy to trust him to catch her earlier today. She'd had nothing to lose.

"You okay?" he asked.

She nodded, then drew back enough to see his expression. "I love you. I'm not saying that because of the flood. I realized the truth before you played hero." She gave him a smile. "This wasn't part of the rules or what was supposed to happen, but it did. I love you, Angel. I wanted you to know."

She watched him closely, not sure what she would see on his face. She hoped he realized how significant this was for her. She'd never been in love before — had certainly never said the words. She didn't expect him to say it back to her in the moment, but maybe he could hint.

Only Angel didn't look happy at the news. For a second something dark and uncomfortable flashed in his eyes, and then his face went completely blank. It was like staring into a statue.

He shook his head finally. "No," he said. That was it. Just no.

Her body went cold — only this was so much worse than before. It came from the inside, not the outside, and she knew that she would never feel warm again. She willed herself not to react to his rejection, not to say anything. She wouldn't beg.

Not when he got up and not when he walked out of her house without saying another word.

She sat on the sofa, HGTV playing in the background. For the second time in less than a couple of hours, Taryn gave in to tears.

CHAPTER NINETEEN

Taryn walked out of the Fool's Gold branch of the California Department of Motor Vehicles office and had to admit, there were advantages to living in a small town. She had a temporary license to put in her new wallet until her permanent one was mailed. After she'd dealt with her credit card companies the day before, the DMV office had practically been easy. Except for her favorite Mally lip gloss and her Hello Kitty mirror compact — okay, and her heart — she'd replaced everything she'd lost in the flash flood.

It had been two days. Two days of having people ask if she was doing okay and praising her for her bravery. She'd tried pointing out she hadn't been brave, but no one wanted to hear that, so she'd stopped trying to explain. On the bright side, recent events meant no one was surprised if she was a little quiet or seemed upset. They assumed she was still dealing with the whole flood thing. Which meant she hadn't yet had to explain about Angel.

She hadn't seen him since he'd walked out. Hadn't heard a word. Not that she'd expected to, but it seemed that her heart was foolish and hopeful. Something of a surprise, she thought as she headed to Jo's Bar, where she was meeting her friends for lunch.

She smiled at people who greeted her on the street, then walked into Jo's and saw Dellina, Consuelo and Isabel already waiting. Noelle came in right behind her.

"How are you doing?" Noelle asked as they moved toward the table. "I can't believe what you went through. It must have been terrifying."

Her three friends rose and hugged her.

"Are you okay?" they asked together.

Taryn smiled at her friends. "I'm fine. We all made it out okay. I don't want to repeat the experience, but the Acorns I've talked to are all taking it well."

They sat down.

"Larissa can't make it to lunch," Taryn told them. "Jack sent her to a seminar on sports injuries. She's not a physical therapist, but she keeps up on the latest information in the field." She grinned.

Jo came and took their drink orders, explained the specials, then went back to the bar.

Isabel nudged Consuelo. "You're glowing. You know that, right?"

Taryn looked at the petite brunette. Consuelo seemed happy and tanned. Taryn had a feeling there was more going on here than a simple two-week vacation in a tropical paradise.

"Kent and I had a really good time on our honeymoon," she said with a shy smile. "We really talked about our lives and what we want."

"A baby?" Noelle asked, her eyebrows raised.

"We talked about it but we decided we're going to adopt instead. We're interested in older children. Siblings who don't want to be split up."

Taryn blinked. "That's a lot to take on."

"I know." Consuelo grinned. "I think we can handle it. We've talked to Reese about it and he's excited."

"Big news," Isabel said. "Congratulations."

"Thanks." Consuelo looked at Taryn. "I heard you had a party while I was gone. The clothing exchange."

"We did." Taryn turned to Dellina and

Isabel. "You two did a great job with it."

"Thanks," Dellina said. "It was a lot of fun. I think we should make it a semiannual event. People were really generous with the donations. We ended up with nearly a thousand dollars for the women's shelter."

Taryn was surprised. "That's great."

"It is," Noelle said. "I love what I took home. I think we could do a fall and spring party. You know — get ready for the season. I have a winter coat from last year that's still in great shape, but there's no way I want to wear it for another winter."

Isabel nodded. "One of the things I'm going to love about working on the boutique side rather than with the wedding dresses is being able to dress differently. For the designer clothes, I get to be trendy. On the bridal side, it's all about blending into the background."

Dellina grinned. "Tired of wearing your little black dress every day."

"Yeah. It's not like I got to wear something cute, either. Never outshine the bride. I dressed like I was constantly going to a funeral."

"Dress for comfort," Consuelo told her.

"Not everyone can get away with cargo pants and a tank top as work attire."

Taryn listened to their conversation. This

was nice, she thought. Relaxing and a distraction from the hole in her heart. She could go entire minutes without thinking about Angel, which was a welcome break.

"I'm going to check with the shelter," Noelle was saying. "I want to find out about volunteer opportunities."

"That's a good —" Dellina stopped in midsentence and turned to Taryn. "What? What is it?"

Taryn stared at her. "I have no idea what you're talking about."

Dellina shook her head. "No, it's something. Something big. What happened?" She touched Taryn's arm. "I have sisters and I know when a woman is holding back significant information." She bit her lower lip. "It's bad, isn't it? I can see it in your eyes."

Taryn wasn't sure which was more disconcerting. That she might be losing her steely exterior or that Dellina might be psychic.

Isabel stared at Taryn. "You're right." Her face softened as concern filled her eyes. "Tell us. Are you okay? Are you feeling sick or something?"

Noelle wrinkled her nose. "I'm so not in tune with what's going on," she said with a grumble. "Now you have to say or I'm going to feel like an idiot."

"Me, too," Consuelo grumbled.

397

Taryn thought about trying to lie her way out of the situation but wasn't sure she was capable. Not when she felt like emotional roadkill.

She cleared her throat. "It's Angel," she said quietly. "We, um, broke up."

"Why?"

"No way. You were great together."

Dellina continued to study her. "He hurt you."

Taryn shrugged. "I broke the rules. We were both clear. It was an affair, not a relationship. That's what we both wanted. Only I fell in love with him and when I told him . . ."

Tears filled her eyes, and her throat got tight. She had to breathe for a second before she could continue. "He left," she finished. "It's been a couple of days. I haven't seen him since."

All four of them reached for Taryn and hung on.

"Are you sleeping at all?" Noelle asked. "Can you eat? You have to keep up your strength or you'll get sick."

Isabel patted her hand sympathetically. "Want me to ask Ford to beat him up?"

Consuelo snorted. "He couldn't take Angel on his own. They know each other's fighting style too well. But Ford and me

working together could smack him down."
She looked at Taryn. "Want me to take care
of that? I will."

Taryn brushed away a tear and tried to
smile. "As strange as this is going to sound,
that's about the nicest offer anyone has
made to me. Thank you. I appreciate it.
You're all so great."

She bit her lower lip and did her best to
get control. "It's hard because it never occurred to me I could fall for him. I thought
I was stronger than that."

"Loving someone doesn't make you
weak," Consuelo told her. "It might seem
that way at first, but it's not true. Love is
complicated and messy but ultimately powerful."

"And in this case, a disaster," Taryn murmured.

She saw the other women exchanging
glances and had no idea what they were
thinking. The only thing that was clear was
that they were going to be there for her if
she needed them.

"I appreciate the support," she added. "I
need to work through this myself. Please
don't say anything to anyone. I'm not ready
to talk about it."

Isabel wrinkled her nose. "You sure about
that? There's kind of a Fool's Gold tradi-

tion when there's a breakup."

"What kind of tradition? I don't want to be a festival queen or anything like that."

"There's a girls' night," Dellina told her. "Everyone comes over with liquor and junk food. We get drunk and call the guy names."

Taryn held in a shudder. That meant talking about what had happened. She would rather not have that conversation ever.

"I'm not ready for that," she said firmly. "Seriously, please don't tell anyone." She was too humiliated to have the information go public just yet.

"Let us know if you change your mind," Noelle told her. "We have ways of making you forget."

Taryn did her best to smile at the joke.

Losing Angel had been horrible, but finding friends was one of the good things that had happened to her since moving to town. Eventually she would heal and move forward.

She'd been reminded that love was a disaster and trusting men led to pain. It was a lesson that she was never going to allow herself to forget, ever again.

After lunch, Taryn left Jo's. She was feeling a little better. At least she wasn't crying anymore and the gnawing pain in her chest had faded to something she was going to be able to stand.

It was being around her friends, she thought. They were good women and she appreciated them and their support. As she headed to her car she wondered how different her life would have been if she'd had friends like this earlier. Like in high school. Not that she would have trusted anyone enough to let them know what was going on. Or maybe it wasn't all about trust. Maybe shame was a component, too.

She drove back to Score and parked in the lot. A battered Subaru pulled in next to her and Bailey got out.

Taryn smiled at the other woman. "How's Chloe? Is she doing okay?"

Bailey circled her car and nodded. "She's great. I was afraid the whole flash flood experience would give her nightmares, but it didn't. She's not afraid or anything bad." Bailey wore a T-shirt over jeans. She shifted her car keys from hand to hand.

"Taryn, I want to thank you for all you and Angel did with her. Being in the Acorns has really allowed Chloe to find her way back to the wonderful girl she was before. I've been worried about her. Losing her dad was horrible. She got so quiet. I talked to her pediatrician and she suggested I give it time, but that if she wasn't making strides in a few months, we should try therapy. I kept putting that off. I guess I didn't want there to be anything wrong with her."

Taryn could understand that concern. Especially when it came to a child.

"Once she joined the Acorns, everything changed. She has friends again. She's talking all the time."

"Too much?" Taryn asked, her voice teasing.

Bailey smiled. "Maybe a little, but I keep telling myself I'm not going to complain." Her smile faded. "When we lost Will, we were both devastated. It was one thing when he was away on deployment, but knowing he was never coming back . . ."

Taryn nodded. "I'm sorry," she whispered, knowing her pain was nothing when compared to losing a husband. She was tough. She would get over this and no one would ever know she'd been broken in the first place.

"I appreciate the sympathy, I do, but it's okay. It was worth it. Will was a good, good man. He loved me and he loved Chloe. We were his world and we both knew that."

Bailey paused. "Watching Chloe blossom again has helped me so much." She shrugged. "Sorry. I'm talking too much."

"You're not. I'm so happy we could help. Chloe is a wonderful girl. You have every right to be proud of her."

"I am." Her mouth twisted. "After the campout, Chloe's mentioned I should find her another daddy."

"Angel?" Taryn asked before she could stop herself.

"What? No. Oh, is that what you thought?" The smile returned. "He's amazing, but there's no way I could handle a man like him. He's much more your style. You're strong and powerful and he needs that."

The assessment of them as a couple and of her individually was both kind and unexpected.

"I'm not feeling especially powerful today," Taryn admitted.

"It'll come back."

Taryn leaned against her car. "So if not Angel, is there someone else?"

"I don't think so. I'm not ready to date." She ducked her head. "And I'd have to lose thirty pounds. I think I'd rather eat cookies."

Taryn watched Bailey and for a second thought she saw a blush on the other woman's cheeks. Was it possible Bailey had someone in mind? She'd made it clear that she wasn't interested in Angel, which was good. Taryn didn't need another kick in the gut right now.

"You don't need to lose any weight," Taryn told her. "You're gorgeous."

"Thanks, but we both know that's not true." Bailey shrugged. "Right now I don't care enough to deal with my weight. I have enough stress in my life what with job hunting." She tilted her head. "I never thanked you for the dress."

Taryn cleared her throat. "You mean the party? I didn't do any of the work. Trust me, Dellina took care of most of it and Isabel handled the rest. My skill is delegating."

Bailey's green gaze settled on Taryn's face. "You bought me the dress, Taryn. I know you did. If I had a bigger ego I'd say you arranged the whole clothing exchange party so you could give it to me without me thinking it was charity."

"Uh, I have no idea what you're talking about."

"Yes, you do, but you can pretend if it makes you feel better. You're a really good person. Thank you. I know you'd never accept money for what you did, so I'm going to repay you by doing something like that for another person, when I get the chance."

Taryn felt her eyes burning again. There

was no way she was going to cry out in the Score parking lot, but Bailey's words touched her.

"It wasn't me," she said firmly. "But I'm glad you have the dress for your interviews."

"I do, and shoes." Bailey smiled. "I signed up for a computer refresher course at the community college. It's three Saturdays and by the end, I'll be familiar with the new versions of the popular spreadsheet and calendar programs. Then I'll be getting résumés and starting the job hunt."

"Getting on with your life."

"I am." Bailey paused. "I know you hear this all the time, but I have to say it. You're an inspiration, Taryn. I admire all you've accomplished. You're successful and tough, but you do it with your own style. I mean, seriously — look at how you dress. It's fantastic."

Taryn glanced down at her Dolce & Gabbana silk brocade dress. It was sleeveless and bright with a floral print. "This old thing?" she said with a grin.

Bailey flung her arms around her. "You know what you like and you go after it." Bailey released her. "We could all learn from you."

"I don't understand why my clothes are such a big deal."

"They signify who you are. You don't care if it's Fool's Gold or Los Angeles. You're going to wear what you want and do what you want and live how you want. You have style and you're good at your job and you're a great friend. I guess I'm saying I want to be like you when I grow up."

The tears were back. Taryn didn't try to stop them. Instead she sniffed. "That's the nicest thing anyone has ever said about me. But I have to tell you, I'm a complete mess. Just so you know."

"We're all a mess, Taryn. But you always look good."

Taryn laughed. "Style over substance." She wiped away her tears. "I'm glad about Chloe. She's wonderful."

"Thanks. I can't take all the credit, but I think she's pretty amazing, too."

The women hugged. For a second Taryn thought about creating a position for Bailey at Score. Only they didn't need anyone and she knew Bailey would prefer to find a real job on her own. There was a difference between getting a little help — like a dress — and living the life of a fake job.

"Let me know if I can help in any way with the job search," Taryn told her.

"I will. In fact, I'd appreciate you looking over my résumé."

"Happy to."

Bailey waved and headed back to her car. Taryn walked into the office. There was still a giant hole where her heart had been, but she thought maybe, just maybe, she'd taken the first step in what would be a long journey to healing.

"I never thought anything like that could happen here."

"I've never heard about anything like that!"

"The water came up so fast."

"I couldn't stop screaming, which wasn't helpful."

Angel had already endured far too many hugs and pats since showing up at the Grove Keeper meeting. Everyone wanted to know if Taryn and the Acorns were okay. Then it seemed there was going to be a real-time recounting of the night's events.

Denise finally got them all to sit down.

"We have a lot of end-of-year business to discuss," she said. "Next Saturday is the parade. All the groves will be marching together. Once again Plants for the Planet is kind enough to donate the wreaths for everyone to wear. So if you need a new plant or want to take someone flowers, please give them your business and tell them how much we all appreciate their support."

"Wreaths?" Angel asked the Grove Keeper sitting next to him.

"Like little crowns," the woman told him. "They have ribbons flowing down the back. They're completely adorable. Each grove has its own color. The girls love being in the parade. At the end, they get their family bead and then move up to the next level of FWM. Later, there's a graduation ceremony for the girls who are now leaving the organization."

"Thanks," Angel said, thinking he really had to read the entire Grove Keeper Handbook. But every time he went past the Acorn pages, he found something that made him uncomfortable. Like lessons on the feminine cycle.

Thinking about that reminded him of how Taryn had laughed when he'd first mentioned it. She'd pointed out he wouldn't have to deal with any cycles for a while and that if it came up, she would handle it. Only that wasn't going to happen now. She wouldn't be around. Not in the FWM. He'd made sure of that.

It had been over a week, he thought grimly. He'd caught sight of her twice but was pretty sure she hadn't seen him. Which was how he wanted things. Fool's Gold was small enough that eventually they would run into each other, but he would prefer that to be later rather than sooner.

Thinking about her made him wonder how she was. If she was doing okay. He hoped so. He wanted her to be happy. There was a part of him that wanted her to be happy with him. Only he knew . . .

His gut twisted as longing washed over him. He missed her more than he would have thought possible. He missed her laugh, her humor, her shrewd intelligence. He missed how she loved her "boys" and terrorized them at the same time. Probably because that reminded him of Consuelo, who was like family to him. He missed her sassy walk, her ridiculous shoes and the way she smelled. He wanted her in his arms and his bed and he wanted to be able to tell her that, yes, he loved her, too.

Only he couldn't. He got it — the irony. That he could save her from a flood only to dump her because she'd been stupid enough to fall for him. Talk about a hero. He'd gotten her to trust him, then punished her for doing just that.

He wanted to tell her that he'd done it for her own good. That he wasn't anyone she should count on. He hadn't been able to protect Marie and Marcus and he sure as hell couldn't protect her.

Only this was Taryn and he knew that she would tell him she was more than capable of taking care of herself. She didn't want a knight in shining armor; she wanted a partner. Someone she could count on. She would say she believed in him.

The problem was, he couldn't believe in himself. Not enough to risk her.

Mayor Marsha walked into the meeting. She spoke to Denise before addressing the Grove Keepers.

"I've talked to all the parents," the mayor said. "Everyone appreciates how well the unexpected flash flood was handled. You especially, Angel."

All the Grove Keepers turned to look at him. Denise smiled as if he'd just done something brilliant.

"You went back into danger," the mayor continued. "Risking your own life to save our girls." Her expression shifted to stern. "I hope you'll be talking to Chloe and Regan about following instructions."

"I already have," he assured her. "We're also discussing it at the grove meeting."

"Good." Mayor Marsha shook her head. "The flash flood surprised everyone. The storm wasn't supposed to park over the mountains. We were very fortunate. The situation could have been much worse." She sighed wearily. "I don't like to think about how bad it could have been. We really need to get serious about a search-and-rescue group in town." She smiled at them. "But that is not for you to worry about. Thank you, everyone. You handled our emergency extremely well."

With that, she nodded and left.

The meeting continued. Angel took notes because he wasn't listening and he would need to know what to do later. He kept thinking about Taryn and how he'd failed her. He wanted what she offered, but at the same time, he knew the danger of going there. Better for both of them if he didn't mess up her life, too. If he didn't let her think he would take care of her.

In his head he knew that the storm and single-car accident that had claimed his wife and son weren't anything he could have prevented, but his gut told him otherwise. His gut warned him that giving in, leading with his heart would end with the destruction of the one person he most wanted to keep safe.

CHAPTER TWENTY

Taryn nodded and the head designer clicked on the next slide. "Market projections make it clear that the trend is going to continue for at least the next five years. While consumers can be fickle, the market research firm we used has a ninety percent accuracy rate. By staging the campaign, we'll be able to judge success at predetermined points and make any adjustments necessary."

The presentation for Living Life at a Run had started early. Or maybe the problem was she still wasn't sleeping, she thought as she smiled at Cole, then took her seat at the conference table. Jude turned on the overhead lights.

Jack rose. "You can see why we keep Taryn around," he said with a wink. "She could easily moonlight as a field general."

Cole, a short guy with broad shoulders and a stocky build, nodded. "I see where you're going and I like it."

That was something, Taryn thought, careful to keep her expression pleasant. Cole was one of those people who rubbed her the wrong way. She hadn't liked him from the second he'd walked into Score that morning. But she had worked with clients she didn't like before. She and Cole didn't have to be friends.

The thought of an "outdoor weekend" with him in a couple of weeks made her skin crawl, but she'd survived worse. The boys would be there as a buffer. And thanks to Angel, she would be able to hold her own whether kayaking or hiking. As long as there wasn't another flash flood, she would be fine.

As soon as those thoughts formed, she pushed them away. Thinking about Angel was a mistake. She could get lost in the memories for hours at a time, and right now LL@R was her primary focus.

Cole looked at her, then back at Jack. "Okay, great. You've shown me you're all about equal opportunity and all that nonsense. Now can we lose the eye candy and get on with the presentation?"

The words were delivered so casually, at first Taryn was sure she'd misunderstood what he'd said. Kenny, Jack and Sam seemed equally stunned. But when Cole flicked his finger from her to the door, she knew she'd heard exactly what he'd said.

She started to stand. Before she could do much more than get the thought formed, Sam, Jack and Kenny rose as one. Each of them leaned toward Cole.

"You didn't just say that," Kenny told him.

Cole leaned back in his chair. "Come on, guys, seriously?"

Sam smiled. But it was the smile of a wolf about to take down a rabbit. "Over her, over any woman, anywhere." He looked at Kenny and Jack. "I know you had high hopes for this campaign, but we don't work with assholes."

"Damn straight," Jack said. "Cole, you're going to apologize to Taryn and then you're leaving."

Cole sat up straight. "What? Are you kidding me? Do you know what my account is worth? We had an afternoon planned. What about playing golf with Josh Golden and Raoul Moreno?"

"Not happening," Kenny told him. "Now apologize to the lady."

Cole bristled. "I was just calling a spade a spade. A woman dressed like that, who *looks* like that, what could she be here for?"

"She's here because she's smart and capable and because she wears the pants around here, figuratively speaking," Jack said without missing a beat.

Cole seemed to realize he was seriously outgunned. He swallowed, then turned to Taryn. "No offense, ma'am."

"Yeah, I don't think so," she told him. "You did mean to offend because you're a misogynistic jerk." She stood. "You have five seconds to leave this building or I turn them loose on you."

Cole blinked, then scrambled to his feet and literally ran from the room. A second or two later, they heard him yelling, "Where the hell is the exit in this place?"

And then he was gone and she was alone with her boys.

"Well, that sucks," she said. "Do you know how much time and effort we put into that presentation? Face it, gentlemen. We're not meant to have retail clients. We'll make do with our niche markets. Frankly, I can't go through this again."

Sam walked over to her and kissed her lightly on the cheek. Then he put his arms around her and squeezed. She hung on until he released her. Kenny followed. He, too, kissed her, then hugged her. Jack was last. Only he didn't let her go.

"He was a jerk," Jack told her. "You okay?"

She stared into his brown eyes. "I will be."

Because the pain in her heart had nothing to do with the jerk who had just scurried out of the building and everything to do with the dark-haired man who had stolen her heart.

She leaned against Jack and thought for the millionth time how much easier everything would have been if she'd been able to fall in love with him. But no. Her heart was nothing if not difficult.

"Thank you," she said as she stepped back. "You were all great."

"Anytime," Kenny said.

Taryn got home, changed clothes and contemplated the long hours until she could realistically go to bed. The fact that she hadn't been sleeping didn't help things. She was exhausted and yet every time she closed her eyes, all she saw was Angel.

The killer of it was, she got why he'd freaked. He'd told her about what had happened with Marie and Marcus. She knew he blamed himself for their deaths. She knew his emotions ranged from feeling that he hadn't been able to protect them when he should have to the sense that loving anyone else was a betrayal of what he'd had before.

She wanted to tell him that she knew he

would always love Marie. That loving Marie was part of what *she* loved most about him. That she respected his past and his devotion. But he wouldn't listen and if he did, he wouldn't believe her.

Someone knocked on her door. For a second she allowed herself to hope. It fluttered like a trapped butterfly in her chest until she opened the door and saw Kenny standing on her porch. He had a stack of DVDs in his large hand.

"Hey," he said. "Am I the first one here?"

"First one?" She groaned, realizing she was about to have an invasion. "What's going on?"

"We played basketball this morning," he said. "Angel wasn't there. Jack asked why. Ford told him the two of you weren't seeing each other anymore." Kenny's blue eyes were sympathetic. "If you dump a guy, you're all about calling him scum. You haven't said a word."

"We broke up. It's no big deal."

Kenny stepped into the house and closed the door behind him. "No. He left you? Want me to kill him?"

Kenny was taller and had more muscle, but Angel knew things. "You've seen the scar on his neck," she said.

Kenny nodded.

"You don't want to be the other guy."

Kenny put down the DVDs, then rested his hands on her shoulders. "What do you need? Are you pregnant?"

She swore and drew back. "Don't you dare propose." That had already happened once in her life and she wasn't going to repeat it. "I'm not pregnant."

"Want some revenge sex?"

She held in a sigh. While it was a nice suggestion, he didn't mean it. They were family. It would be like sleeping with his sister. "You're sweet to offer."

"We could do it. You're hot."

She raised her eyebrows.

He took a step back. "Okay, yeah. Not gonna happen." His face brightened. "You could sleep with Jack. You two had sex before, right?"

"I don't need help getting laid, but thank you."

There was another knock on the door. She opened it to find Sam and Jack. Sam held bags of takeout and Jack had a couple of six-packs and a bottle of tequila.

Five minutes later they were all in her living room. Jack had put in the first DVD. It was all highlights from his career. Next would be Sam's DVD and then Kenny's.

The DVD began and an announcer's

voice filled the room.

"The Stallions are down by three with the clock ticking. McGarry's playing with a bad shoulder, but everyone knows if the Stallions are going to make it out of the playoffs, it's up to him. We're watching the clock. There's the snap. McGarry steps back and finds . . ."

"Rib?" Jack asked, passing her an open container.

She was about to refuse when she realized she was kind of hungry. She took one and a napkin.

Sam and Kenny had each taken one of the oversize club chairs, while Jack sat next to her on the sofa. She'd already had two shots of tequila, so it was just a matter of time until the ache inside faded just a little.

She'd specifically asked her female friends not to give her one of those "he's such a bastard, you need to feel better" parties. Looked as though she was going to have one anyway. In a kind of twisted way. With her family. Maybe that was the way it was supposed to be.

"They're so pretty," Olivia said as she opened the box from Plants for the Planet.

Angel stood behind her and glanced down. Yup, there they were. Wreaths done in tiny pink flowers. With matching ribbons. Nine of them. The girls would be —

"There's nine," he said. "Who gets the ninth one?"

Even as he asked the question, a voice in his head screeched the answer. He held up both hands. "No way."

Char grinned at him. "You have to. You're our Grove Keeper."

"It's not for him," Chloe said. "It's for Taryn."

"Where is Taryn?" Sarah asked.

Angel knew fighting about the wreath would be easier. "Taryn's, ah, not coming to the meeting."

Kate frowned. "But this is our last one. We have to be in the parade."

Layla shook her head. "She's not coming. I heard my mom talking on the phone. I wasn't supposed to be listening." She bit her lower lip. "Taryn and Angel are getting a divorce."

Eight pairs of eyes stared at him accusingly.

"We're not getting a divorce," Angel muttered. "We weren't married." That wasn't making it better, he thought grimly. "I mean we were going out and now we're not."

Regan's eyes filled with tears. "What happened?"

"Sometimes relationships don't work out." He felt small and crappy. Worse, he knew that Taryn would know what to say way better than him. "We're still friends," he added lamely, although that was a lie. They weren't friends. They weren't anything.

He waited for Chloe to yell at him, but she only turned away. He put his hand on her shoulder. "What is it?" he asked gently.

She looked at him. Her skin was pale and her freckles stood out. Gone was the happy, outgoing girl she'd become.

"We're getting our family beads today," Chloe reminded him. "After the parade. You can't be part of a family if you don't have Taryn."

There were a lot of different ways to answer, he thought. Telling her that his relationship with Taryn was a grown-up thing and she wouldn't understand. Explaining that he'd had a family once and lost it. That he hadn't been able to keep them safe.

As he stared at Chloe, he saw the flash flood again. Her fear and how she'd reached for him. He'd saved her. He would have died to save her — to save any of them.

He hadn't had the chance to try to save Marie and Marcus because he hadn't been there. He couldn't be there every second of every day. It was an impossible task. Even if he could make it happen, Marie wouldn't have wanted that for either of them. She had wanted to live her life and have him live his. They had stayed together out of love, but she wasn't looking for a bodyguard. She'd wanted a partner. He'd been that. He'd been a father and a husband.

"We miss Taryn," Olivia said.

"Me, too," he admitted.

There were no guarantees, he thought suddenly. No promises. There was only this moment and what he had accomplished so far in his life. If he were to die right now, he would regret not telling Taryn that she mattered to him. He would regret that he didn't admit what had been so obvious all along.

"We need to get to the parade," he told the girls. "Now."

He passed out wreaths. When Chloe handed him the ninth one, he sighed once, then stuck it on his head.

They went to the start of the parade and got in their place. The music began. Angel walked with his girls but searched the crowds on the side. Whatever had happened, Taryn wouldn't miss this. He was sure of it. She would be here and he would get his chance to talk to her.

He wondered how much he'd hurt her. Why couldn't he have figured this out sooner? That she was so important to him. That somewhere, when he hadn't been paying attention, he'd fallen in love with her, too.

He heard a loud whistle and saw Ford and Isabel. Ford gave him a thumbs-up. "Looking good, big guy."

Angel smiled. He would get Ford back tomorrow — in the gym.

He saw a lot of people he knew. Parents of his Acorns, families from town. Montana with a couple of service dogs in training. The lady from —

The back of his neck tingled. He swung around, searching. Taryn was here. He couldn't see her yet, but she was here. He studied the crowd lining both sides of the street, then spotted Kenny, Jack and Sam and knew he'd found her.

"Come on, girls," he said, breaking from the rest of the groves and heading to the sidewalk. All eight Acorns scampered along with him.

As he approached, the three large football players formed a protective flank. Angel knew that together, they could do a lot of damage, but he wasn't concerned. Taryn might have three football players watching her back, but he had eight Acorns and he would bet that heart beat brawn anytime.

He stopped in front of the guys. They all stood with their arms folded across their wide chests. Their expressions were menacing. At least until Chloe smiled and gave a little wave.

"Hi, Kenny."

The tallest of the three smiled back, tentatively. "Hey, munchkin."

Taryn pushed her way through the phalanx. "It's okay," she told the guys, then looked at him. "Angel."

He hadn't seen her in nearly two weeks. She was pale and there were dark circles under her eyes. She'd always been thin, but he would guess she'd lost weight she couldn't afford to lose. Her eyes were wary; her mouth trembled at the corner.

In that moment, he saw what he'd done to her and he was ashamed. Taryn had been nothing but an unexpected gift and he'd emotionally brought her to her knees. What had he been thinking?

"I'm sorry," he told her. "Taryn, I'm sorry. I was wrong. Incredibly wrong. When I lost Marie and Marcus, I kept telling myself that if I'd been there, I could have saved them. What I didn't realize was that while that was true, it wasn't real. I could never be there every second."

A muscle tightened in her cheek. Otherwise, there were no changes and he didn't know what she was thinking. Around them the parade went on. Music blared from speakers, and friends and family called out to their FWM girls as they walked by. Except in their little corner.

"I felt guilty and lost," Angel continued. "I loved them. They were my family and then they were gone. I didn't think I could go on. But I did. I made my way here and I started to heal."

He took a chance and reached for her hand. She let him, but he continued to wonder what was going on behind those blue-violet eyes of hers.

"Then I met you." He smiled. "You're amazing. Smart and determined. Strong as . . ." He stopped as he remembered the Acorns listening intently. "Really strong. I was intrigued and impressed. I thought we would be good together. But I never thought I'd fall in love again. You see, I learned the wrong lesson from loving Marie and Marcus. Instead of learning that love is a gift to be treasured for as long as we have it, I learned that I hadn't kept them safe. So I could never keep anyone safe."

He heard a sniffle from behind him. Before he could turn and figure out who was upset, Kenny pushed past him and dropped to his knees.

"Munchkin, what's wrong?"

"I'm okay," Chloe said, sniffing again. "Sometimes I miss my dad. But Angel's right. I loved him and he loved me and that's like a gift."

Kenny pulled the little girl to him. His hands were huge on her narrow back, but she clung to him fiercely. Kenny shot Taryn a "for God's sake, help me" look, but she turned back to Angel.

"You kept me safe," she told him. "You saved Regan and Chloe and me."

"I know, and it scared me. That I could have lost you. That I was there. When you said . . ." He paused, aware of their audience. "You know what you said."

"Did you tell him you love him?" Olivia asked. "My mom says men have trouble with that sometimes because they're emotionally immature."

"Gee, thanks," Sam told the girl.

Taryn's mouth twitched. She looked back at Angel. "When I said I loved you, you freaked out."

"I did," he admitted. "I felt guilty and confused. I wanted to be with you, but what if I couldn't keep you safe, either? What if we had kids and something bad happened?"

The girls started whispering.

426

Taryn's mouth curved up into a smile. "Stop," she said. "No one is pregnant. Are we clear?"

Chloe stepped away from Kenny. "I'd like a little brother or sister. I've told Mom, but she says that isn't going to happen." She turned to Regan. "She would have to get married first."

Angel swore under his breath. When had he lost control of the situation? This was not how he'd planned on telling Taryn how he felt.

He looked at her and realized control was nothing but an illusion. All any of them had was this moment. He'd been blessed with two amazing women in his life. It was about time he recognized that.

He pulled the wreath off his head and put it on Taryn's, then reached for her other hand.

"I'm sorry I hurt you," he told her, staring into her eyes. "I'm sorry I didn't recognize how lucky I was to have you love me. I'm sorry I disappeared without an explanation. It won't happen again."

"Okay," she said slowly.

"I love you, Taryn. I think I have from the first time I saw you."

Her lower lip began to tremble, but she didn't speak. Tears filled her eyes.

He pulled her into his arms. She went easily, fitting in as if she'd always belonged with him. Her arms came around his body and pulled him close.

"I love you," he whispered, so only she could hear. "For always. Later, I want to do it right. On one knee. But just so you know, I mean to marry you and grow old with you."

"Naked?" she asked softly.

He pulled back a little and stared at her. "You want me naked when I'm old?"

She giggled. "No. During the proposal."

He gave her a slow smile. "I can make that happen."

"What are they saying?" Allison asked. "I can't hear them."

"Probably for the best," Jack said. "All right, you two. That's enough emotion for any afternoon. Break it up. These girls have to be in a parade."

Angel held out his hand to Taryn. "Come with us."

Taryn felt the hole in her heart finally heal. She hadn't been looking for love, but somehow it had found her. Found them. She took Angel's hand and knew, no matter what, she was never letting go.

They stepped into the street and the girls walked with them.

When they reached the end of the parade, Denise Hendrix was waiting. As each girl walked by, she handed her a small wooden bead.

"The family bead," Angel said.

Taryn pulled her leather bracelet out of her pocket. "I'm ready for mine."

Denise saw them and smiled. They each took a bead. Before Taryn could put hers on her bracelet, he drew her close and kissed her.

"You know I agreed to continue with the grove," he told her.

"I hadn't heard."

"I'm going to need an assistant."

"Yes, you are."

He touched her cheek. "I'd like it to be you."

She sighed happily. "I'm pretty sure that can be arranged."

ABOUT THE AUTHOR

New York Times bestselling author **Susan Mallery** has entertained millions of readers with her witty and emotional stories about women and the relationships that move them. *Publishers Weekly* calls Susan's prose "luscious and provocative," and *Booklist* says, "Novels don't get much better than Mallery's expert blend of emotional nuance, humor and superb storytelling." While Susan appreciates the critical praise, she is most honored by the enthusiastic readers who write to tell her that her books made them laugh, made them cry, and made the world a happier place to live. Susan lives in Seattle with her husband and her tiny but intrepid toy poodle. She's there for the coffee, not the weather.